P9-CQQ-220

POWER OF THREE

WARRIORS

DARK RIVER

POWER OF THREE

WARRIORS
DARK RIVER

ERIN
HUNTER

HARPERCOLLINS*PUBLISHERS*

Dark River

Copyright © 2008 by Working Partners Limited

Series created by Working Partners Limited

Library of Congress Cataloging-in-Publication Data

Hunter, Erin.

    Dark river / Erin Hunter. — 1st ed.

        p.   cm. — (Warriors, power of three ; [bk. 2])

    Summary: As Hollypaw, Lionpaw, and Jaypaw, grandchildren of the
legendary Firestar, continue their training to be warrior cats, each is
haunted by a different internal struggle that could lead to trouble for all
Clans.

    ISBN 978-0-06-089205-0 (trade bdg.)

    ISBN 978-0-06-089206-7 (lib. bdg.)

    [1. Cats—Fiction. 2. Brothers and sisters—Fiction. 3. Adventure and
adventurers—Fiction. 4. Fantasy.] I. Title.

PZ7.H916625Daq 2008   2007029609

[Fic]—dc22   CIP

                                                                    AC

Typography by Ray Shappell

1 2 3 4 5 6 7 8 9 10

First Edition

For Geof

Special thanks to Kate Cary

ALLEGIANCES

THUNDERCLAN

LEADER
    FIRESTAR—ginger tom with a flame-colored pelt

DEPUTY
    BRAMBLECLAW—dark brown tabby tom with amber eyes
    APPRENTICE, BERRYPAW

MEDICINE CAT
    LEAFPOOL—light brown tabby she-cat with amber eyes
    APPRENTICE, JAYPAW

WARRIORS
    (toms, and she-cats without kits)

    SQUIRRELFLIGHT—dark ginger she-cat with green eyes

    DUSTPELT—dark brown tabby tom
    APPRENTICE, HAZELPAW

    SANDSTORM—pale ginger she-cat
    APPRENTICE, HONEYPAW

    CLOUDTAIL—long-haired white tom
    APPRENTICE, CINDERPAW

    BRACKENFUR—golden brown tabby tom
    APPRENTICE, HOLLYPAW

    SORRELTAIL—tortoiseshell-and-white she-cat with amber eyes

    THORNCLAW—golden brown tabby tom
    APPRENTICE, POPPYPAW

    BRIGHTHEART—white she-cat with ginger patches

    ASHFUR—pale gray (with darker flecks) tom, dark blue eyes
    APPRENTICE, LIONPAW

SPIDERLEG—long-limbed black tom with brown underbelly and amber eyes

APPRENTICE, MOUSEPAW

BROOK WHERE SMALL FISH SWIM (BROOK)—brown tabby she-cat, formerly of the Tribe of Rushing Water

STORMFUR—dark gray tom with amber eyes, formerly of RiverClan

WHITEWING—white she-cat with green eyes

BIRCHFALL—light brown tabby tom

GRAYSTRIPE—long-haired gray tom

MILLIE—silver tabby she-cat, former kittypet, blue eyes

APPRENTICES

(more than six moons old, in training to become warriors)

BERRYPAW—cream-colored tom

HAZELPAW—small gray-and-white she-cat

MOUSEPAW—gray-and-white tom

CINDERPAW—gray tabby she-cat

HONEYPAW—light brown tabby she-cat

POPPYPAW—tortoiseshell she-cat

LIONPAW—golden tabby tom with amber eyes

HOLLYPAW—black she-cat with green eyes

JAYPAW—gray tabby tom with blue eyes

QUEENS

(she-cats expecting or nursing kits)

FERNCLOUD—pale gray (with darker flecks) she-cat, green eyes, mother of Dustpelt's kits: Icekit (white she-cat) and Foxkit (reddish tabby tom)

DAISY—cream long-furred cat from the horseplace

ELDERS   (former warriors and queens, now retired)

LONGTAIL—pale tabby tom with dark black stripes, retired early due to failing sight

MOUSEFUR—small dusky brown she-cat

SHADOWCLAN

LEADER   **BLACKSTAR**—large white tom with huge jet-black paws

DEPUTY   **RUSSETFUR**—dark ginger she-cat

MEDICINE CAT   **LITTLECLOUD**—very small tabby tom

WARRIORS   **OAKFUR**—small brown tom

ROWANCLAW—ginger tom
APPRENTICE, IVYPAW

SMOKEFOOT—black tom
APPRENTICE, OWLPAW

SNOWBIRD—pure-white she-cat

QUEENS   **TAWNYPELT**—tortoiseshell she-cat with green eyes, mother of Tigerkit, Flamekit, and Dawnkit

ELDERS   **CEDARHEART**—dark gray tom

TALLPOPPY—long-legged light brown tabby she-cat

WINDCLAN

LEADER   **ONESTAR**—brown tabby tom

DEPUTY   **ASHFOOT**—gray she-cat

MEDICINE CAT **BARKFACE**—short-tailed brown tom
  APPRENTICE, KESTRELPAW

WARRIORS **TORNEAR**—tabby tom
  APPRENTICE, HAREPAW

  CROWFEATHER—dark gray tom
  APPRENTICE, HEATHERPAW

  OWLWHISKER—light brown tabby tom

  WHITETAIL—small white she-cat
  APPRENTICE, BREEZEPAW

  NIGHTCLOUD—black she-cat

  WEASELFUR—ginger tom with white paws

QUEENS **GORSETAIL**—very pale gray-and-white cat
  with blue eyes, mother of Thistlekit, Sedgekit,
  and Swallowkit

ELDERS **MORNINGFLOWER**—very old tortoiseshell
  queen

  WEBFOOT—dark gray tabby tom

RIVERCLAN

LEADER **LEOPARDSTAR**—unusually spotted golden
  tabby she-cat

DEPUTY **MISTYFOOT**—gray she-cat with blue eyes
  APPRENTICE, DAPPLEPAW

MEDICINE CAT **MOTHWING**—dappled golden she-cat
  APPRENTICE, WILLOWPAW

WARRIORS **BLACKCLAW**—smoky black tom

  VOLETOOTH—small brown tabby tom
  APPRENTICE, MINNOWPAW

  REEDWHISKER—black tom
  APPRENTICE, POUNCEPAW

MOSSPELT—tortoiseshell she-cat with blue eyes

APPRENTICE, PEBBLEPAW

BEECHFUR—light brown tom

RIPPLETAIL—dark gray tabby tom

QUEENS   **DAWNFLOWER**—pale gray she-cat

GRAYMIST—pale gray tabby, mother of Sneezekit and Mallowkit

ICEWING—heavily pregnant white cat with blue eyes

ELDERS   **HEAVYSTEP**—thickset tabby tom

SWALLOWTAIL—dark tabby she-cat

STONESTREAM—gray tom

OTHER ANIMALS

PIP—black-and-white terrier who lives with Twolegs near the horseplace

POWER OF THREE
WARRIORS
DARK RIVER

© 2008 Gary Chalke

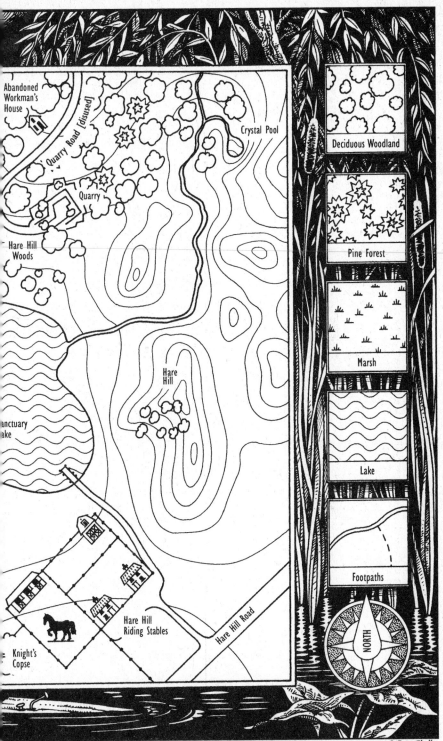

Abandoned
Workman's
House

Quarry Road [disused]

Crystal Pool

Quarry

Hare Hill
Woods

Sanctuary
Lake

Hare
Hill

Hare Hill
Riding Stables

Hare Hill Road

Knight's
Copse

Deciduous Woodland

Pine Forest

Marsh

Lake

Footpaths

NORTH

© 2008 Gary Chalke

PROLOGUE

❧

The indigo sky stretched over the moorland, holding in the night's chill.

Wind stirred the heather and set the hillside rippling. Between the low bushes, feline shapes, their fur slicked flat by the breeze, streamed down the slope.

Among them, a tabby queen kept pace with a young tom. "Are you sure you are ready for this?"

"I'm ready," the tom answered, his green eyes flashing in the moonlight.

"You're my eldest, Fallen Leaves," the queen whispered. "The first of mine to face the ordeal."

"I'll be fine."

"He was trained well!" a low voice called from behind.

"Even trainin' can't prepare a softpaw for rain!" growled another.

Fallen Leaves glanced up. "But the sky's clear."

"I smell rain on the wind, I tell you."

Murmurs of alarm spread among the other cats.

"The sky's clear!" Fallen Leaves insisted as he stepped out from the swath of heather and halted. The moon lit his ginger-and-white pelt. His Clanmates crowded at his heels, their tails flicking. Beneath his forepaws, the slope fell away steeply. Here, moons of wind and rain had flayed the moorland, peeling away the earth until the stone beneath lay bare, a wall of jagged rock amid the rolling heather.

"Good luck, softpaw!"

Fallen Leaves bounded down the cliff and landed lightly on the sandy earth at its base. His mother scrambled after him. "Take care!"

Fallen Leaves brushed muzzles with the queen. "I will see you at dawn," he promised.

Ahead of him, a black gash opened like a wound in the cliff face. The fur along his spine lifted. He had never been inside. Only chosen cats entered the Cave.

He padded forward, feeling the darkness swallow him. There must be some light to show the way! He struggled to crush the fear thrashing in his chest like a landed fish.

The tunnel will take you to the cave, his tutor's voice echoed in his mind. *Let your whiskers guide you.*

His whiskers shivered, alert to the slightest touch, steering him along the narrow passage.

Suddenly, pale light glowed ahead. The tunnel opened into a cave. Its arching walls glowed in the weak moonlight that filtered through a gap in the roof. The sound of rushing water echoed around the rocks.

A river? Underground?

Fallen Leaves stared at the wide stream that split the sandy floor in two. Its black water glimmered dimly in the half-light.

"Fallen Leaves?"

A croaking mew made the young tom jump. He jerked his white muzzle up to see who had spoken and his eyes narrowed as he saw a creature crouched on a high ledge, lit by moonlight pooled on the cave wall.

Was this Rock?

The creature's pelt was like moleskin, the fur gone except for a few tufts along his spine, and his sightless eyes bulged like eggs. His long, twisted claws flexed on the smooth branch that lay at his paws. The branch was stripped of its bark and, even in this light, Fallen Leaves could see claw marks etched along it, a crowded series of straight lines scarring the pale wood.

This *must* be Rock.

"I can feel your surprise," the blind creature croaked. "It pricks my pelt like gorse."

"I—I'm sorry," Fallen Leaves apologized. "It's just I did not expect—"

"You did not expect a cat could grow so ugly."

Fallen Leaves froze with embarrassment. Had Rock read his mind?

"A cat needs wind and sun to shine his fur and good hunting to trim his claws," Rock went on, his mew rasping like stones on stone. "But I must stay close to our warrior ancestors; those who have taken their place beneath the earth."

"And for that we thank you," Fallen Leaves murmured respectfully.

"Don't thank me," Rock growled. "It was a destiny I was

bound to follow. Besides, you may not feel so grateful to me once your initiation has begun." As he spoke he ran a long claw over the lines scratched into the smooth branch. A second scratch crossed some lines, but not all. "The uncrossed lines mark the cats who went into the tunnels but did not come out."

Fallen Leaves stared at the dark holes lurking like mouths at the edge of the cave. If they did not lead to air and safety, where did they end up? "Which tunnels did they go into?"

Rock shook his head. "I cannot help you. To become a sharpclaw, you must find your own way out. I can only send you on your way with the blessing of our ancestors."

"Can't you give me *any* advice?"

"Without light, you will have only your instincts. Follow them and if they are true, you will be safe."

"What if they are not true?"

"Then you will die in darkness."

Fallen Leaves squared his shoulders. "I'm not going to die."

"I hope not," Rock mewed. "You know you are not allowed to return to this cave? You must find a tunnel that leads straight back to the moor. Is it raining?" he asked suddenly.

Fallen Leaves stiffened. Should he mention the tingling in the air that hinted rain *might* come? *No.* Rock might tell him to go back the way he had come and wait until another day. He couldn't put off becoming a sharpclaw any longer. He wanted to do this now. "The sky is clear," he promised.

Rock ran his paw once more over the lines etched in the branch. "Then begin."

Fallen Leaves eyed the tunnel beneath Rock's ledge. It seemed larger than the rest, and appeared to slope upward. Up to the moorland, high above? This was the way he would choose.

Heart pounding, he leaped across the river and headed into the bone-chilling darkness.

By dawn I will be a sharpclaw. His pelt bristled. *I hope.*

CHAPTER 1

❧

"Look out!" Lionpaw lashed his tail. "ShadowClan warriors behind us!"

Hollypaw whipped around, her black pelt standing on end. "I'll take them!"

Lionpaw glanced at his brother. "Scent anything, Jaypaw?"

"More warriors coming!" the gray tabby warned. His blind, blue eyes were round with alarm. "Prepare for attack!"

"We'll ambush them as they come through the camp wall!" Lionpaw ordered. He jerked his head toward Hollypaw. "Can you handle those three?"

"Easy!" Hollypaw rolled onto her back then sprung to her paws, claws glinting in the afternoon sun.

Lionpaw darted forward and crouched behind the prickly wall of thorns. "Quick, Jaypaw! Beside me!"

Jaypaw scooted over and dropped into an attack crouch. "They're coming!"

A tabby warrior trotted through the entrance.

"Now!" Lionpaw screeched. He hurled himself at the warrior. Jaypaw scrambled between the enemy's paws. With a grunt of surprise, the invader tripped and tumbled onto his side. Lionpaw was on him in an instant.

"Enough!" Squirrelflight's sharp mew rang around the small clearing.

Lionpaw stopped pummeling Brambleclaw's back with his hind legs and stared at his mother as she hurried through the gap in the bramble wall. "But we're pretending ShadowClan are attacking!"

Jaypaw skidded to a halt. "We'd almost won!"

Brambleclaw got to his paws, shaking Lionpaw off. "Good ambush," he purred. "But you know you're not meant to be playing here."

Lionpaw slid to the ground. "It's the only good place to practice a surprise attack," he mewed sulkily. He looked around the half-finished den; its bramble walls jutted out from the side of the warriors' den. Once branches had been pushed over the top to form the roof, an opening would be made to join the old den with the new one.

Hollypaw padded toward them, leaving her imaginary foes behind. "We're not getting in anyone's way," she pointed out. She fluffed out her fur against the wind. Newleaf sunshine had taken the chill from the hollow, but the afternoon had brought with it a breeze from the mountains that reminded Lionpaw that leaf-bare was less than a quarter moon behind them.

"What if every apprentice decided to practice their battle moves here?" Squirrelflight demanded. "The walls would be broken in no time and all Birchfall's and Graystripe's hard work would be wasted."

"We need to expand the warriors' den before you and the other apprentices become warriors," Brambleclaw added. "It's already too crowded."

"Okay, we get the point!" Jaypaw lifted his chin. His fur was ruffled and bits of leaves were sticking out of his pelt.

"Look at you!" Squirrelflight licked Jaypaw roughly between the ears. "You've made yourselves filthy," she scolded, "and we'll be leaving for the Gathering soon."

Lionpaw began to wash the dried leaf-dust from his chest before his mother started on him.

Jaypaw ducked away from Squirrelflight's tongue. "I can wash myself, you know," he complained.

"Leave them be," Brambleclaw meowed to his mate. "I'm sure they'll smarten themselves up before we leave."

"Of course we will," Lionpaw promised. There was no way he was going to let the other Clans see him looking like a hedgehog. This would be the first Gathering the three of them had attended together. "We've been looking forward to this for *ages*. Haven't we, Jaypaw?"

Jaypaw flicked his tail. "Yeah, right."

Lionpaw flexed his claws. Why did Jaypaw have to be grumpy all the time? This would be his first Gathering ever. He *must* be looking forward to it. He had missed the last two, once as a punishment and once because his medicine duties had kept him in camp. Lionpaw knew his littermate well enough to know how important it was to be able to do what the other cats did, despite his blindness—and that included going to Gatherings.

"Hurry up! Out of here, before Firestar notices!" Squirrel-flight ordered, herding her kits toward the gap in the wall. "Go and find something on the fresh-kill pile. You've a long night ahead."

Lionpaw's tail pricked with excitement at the thought of the Gathering. He could almost smell the pine scents of the island.

But Hollypaw's eyes glittered with worry. "I hope the other Clans don't pick on us again. Do you know if Millie's coming? Perhaps she should stay behind this time."

When Graystripe had returned to the Clan two moons ago, he had brought with him his new mate, Millie, a kittypet whom he had met while the Twolegs held him captive. He had trained her as a warrior and in return she had helped him make the long, perilous journey to the lake in search of his lost Clan. Her kittypet roots made her an easy target for the other Clan's jibes, and she wasn't the only ThunderClan cat who was taunted for not being Clanborn.

"Millie can take care of herself," Squirrelflight pointed out.

"Besides, the contest seemed to have smoothed things over a bit," Brambleclaw added.

"But for how long?" Hollypaw mewed. Lionpaw knew his sister had never been entirely convinced that the daylight Gathering would heal the rifts between the Clans. The four Clans had competed in friendly contests to test their skills, pitting their apprentices against one another in an effort to put aside growing distrust and border tensions. Lionpaw remembered the day for a different reason, though: He and the WindClan apprentice Breezepaw had fallen into an old badger set and nearly suffocated in choking sand before Jaypaw had found them.

"You're always fretting about something," Jaypaw snorted at Hollypaw. "It's like living with an anxious owl."

"Newleaf is here now," Squirrelflight pointed out. "There's more prey running around, so the Clans should be less prickly."

Hollypaw glanced at Jaypaw. "Some cats are still prickly even with a full belly!"

"Hush." Squirrelflight nudged her with her nose. "Go and eat."

"I was only telling the truth!" Hollypaw started forward, but Jaypaw barged past her. She let out a yelp, glaring after Jaypaw, who was already halfway to the medicine den. "He nipped me!"

Lionpaw's whiskers twitched. "You can fight off three ShadowClan warriors single-pawed," he teased. "But one nip from your brother and you squeal like a kit."

Her soft tail flicked his nose. "You'd have squealed, too!"

"I haven't squealed since I left the nursery!"

Hollypaw narrowed her eyes mischievously. "How about I nip you and see how brave you really are?"

"You'll have to catch me first!"

Lionpaw darted away, Hollypaw pounding after him. "Here!" He skidded to a halt beside the fresh-kill pile and tossed a mouse at Hollypaw as she caught up. "Nip this instead."

* * *

The full moon floated in a clear blue-black sky. Ahead, the island rose from the lake, its trees lifting brittle branches to the stars.

Lionpaw walked beside Hollypaw, following his Clanmates along the pebbly shore. He glanced at Jaypaw again. His brother was padding beside Leafpool, nose twitching as he scented the unfamiliar ground. Occasionally, Leafpool's flank would graze Jaypaw's, steering him around sharp stones or protruding roots.

Should he warn Jaypaw about the tree-bridge? It was surprisingly slippery; Lionpaw had almost fallen off on his first crossing.

Hollypaw mewed beside him. "It'll be good to see Willowpaw."

"Willowpaw?" he echoed distractedly. There was only one apprentice Lionpaw was hoping to see at the Gathering: Heatherpaw, the pretty WindClan apprentice with smoky blue eyes. He let out a small sigh.

"What are you thinking about?" Hollypaw nudged him. "You're moons away."

"Er, Jaypaw," he mewed quickly. "I was wondering if he could make it over the tree-bridge."

"Don't let him hear you say that," Hollypaw warned.

Lionpaw suddenly felt cold water seep over his claws. Firestar had led them onto the marshy shore at the edge of RiverClan's territory. Sandstorm picked her way after him. Brambleclaw and Squirrelflight padded beside Millie and

Graystripe while Birchfall and Dustpelt followed, talking quietly. Hazelpaw was listening to her mentor while Berrypaw dodged from side to side, sniffing among the clumps of grass as though any moment he might flush out prey.

"This is *RiverClan* territory," Hollypaw hissed, reminding him that hunting on another Clan's territory was forbidden.

"I know," Berrypaw retorted. "But there's no harm in looking."

"So long as you just *look*."

Graystripe let out a loud purr. "Firestar?" he called. "It sounds like Hollypaw's preparing to challenge you for leadership."

Lionpaw glanced at his sister. Was this the gray warrior's gentle way of telling her not to be so bossy?

"She can challenge all she wants," Firestar purred back. "I don't think I have to worry until she gets a bit bigger."

"Hey!" Hollypaw fluffed out her fur indignantly. "I was just telling him!"

Firestar halted among the snaking roots of the fallen tree that crossed the water between the shore and the island. The scents of WindClan and ShadowClan were fresh on the bark; they must be here already. Lionpaw pricked his ears. Faint mews drifted from the island. Sandstorm jumped up nimbly and wove her way between the stumps and knots until she reached the other side. One by one, the others followed. Lionpaw stood back as Hollypaw leaped after Hazelpaw.

"Aren't you coming, Lionpaw?" she mewed, steadying herself.

"Of course," Lionpaw hissed back at her.

"He's waiting to make sure I don't fall in," Jaypaw mewed from behind him.

"Only because I nearly fell in the first time," Lionpaw explained quickly. "It's tricky if you don't know where to put your paws."

Jaypaw reached up into the tangle of roots, feeling his way with his forepaws.

"Here," Leafpool meowed, jumping up past him onto the trunk. "It's not too high."

Jaypaw lifted his nose and sniffed, judging how far away his mentor was. Then he pushed up with his hind legs and clawed his way onto the trunk beside her. Instantly, his forepaws slid from under him.

Lionpaw's heart lurched as Jaypaw shot sideways. Leafpool darted toward him but Jaypaw had already dug his claws into the rotting bark and steadied himself, his tail lashing as he fought to regain his balance. Beneath him the dark water lapped at the shore. Lionpaw fought the urge to jump up and help as Jaypaw began to pad past his mentor and along the trunk. Leafpool crouched, tense and silent, ready to spring if Jaypaw slipped again. One slow paw step at a time, the blind apprentice felt his way along the bridge.

"Jump this way, Jaypaw!" Hollypaw called from the shore on the far side. "The sand's a bit soft, but it's clear."

Jaypaw leaped down, landing a little clumsily, but straightened up at once.

Lionpaw felt a wave of relief.

"Hurry up, Lionpaw!"

Berrypaw was trying to push past him. Lionpaw leaped onto the trunk to block his way, but the tree trembled as Berrypaw leaped straight up after him.

"Come on!" Berrypaw urged.

Lionpaw felt his denmate's breath on his heels, hurrying him forward. Clutching tightly with his claws, he scrambled along the tree.

"There's no need to rush." Brackenfur's warning mew sounded a tail-length behind them. But Berrypaw kept pressing up behind Lionpaw.

"Stop hanging arou—"

The apprentice's mew suddenly turned to a yelp. Lionpaw glanced back to see him sliding off the trunk, his cream pelt plummeting toward the black water.

Brackenfur lunged forward and grasped Berrypaw by the scruff. Berrypaw jerked and dangled, his paws churning the air, the tip of his thick, cream tail rippling the surface of the lake.

"Hold still," Brackenfur grunted through clenched teeth. Muscles straining beneath his pelt, the golden warrior heaved Berrypaw up onto the trunk. "I told you not to rush!"

Lionpaw blinked. *Thank StarClan it wasn't me!* He turned and padded the rest of the way, glad that Berrypaw wasn't still trying to shove past him. The fresh scent of RiverClan drifted from the shore; their patrol must have been heading down to the lake. Lionpaw scanned the edge of the water but saw no sign of them.

"Is everyone ready?" Firestar called as he, Berrypaw, Brackenfur, and finally Ashfur jumped down onto the beach.

The cats nodded. Firestar signaled with his tail, and the party began to head into the trees.

Lionpaw watched Hollypaw's black pelt disappear into the bracken. His paws tingled with excitement as he prepared to spring after her. But Jaypaw wasn't moving. He was just staring into the trees. *Is he nervous?*

"It's only bracken," Lionpaw reassured him. "Just push through. The clearing's not far." He rested his tail on Jaypaw's flank and felt his brother's muscles, strong and lean, beneath his pelt.

"Come on, you two!" Hollypaw came crashing back through the bracken. "Why are you dawdling?"

"Just planning our entrance." Jaypaw flicked his tail and padded forward.

The brittle fronds of bracken scratched Lionpaw's nose as he followed his littermates toward the clearing, but he could feel soft baby fern leaves curled under his paws. *New leaves for newleaf.*

"ShadowClan and WindClan are waiting in the clearing," Hollypaw called over her shoulder. "But RiverClan haven't arrived yet."

"They're on their way," Lionpaw mewed. "I smelled them from the tree-bridge."

Jaypaw lifted his nose. "You're right." His whiskers twitched. "But there's something odd . . ."

Lionpaw opened his mouth and tasted the fresh scent of

RiverClan again. It seemed the same as usual to him. "Probably just been eating too much fish," he guessed.

"Let's make sure we beat them." Hollypaw urged them through the bracken and out onto the edge of the clearing.

As they emerged into the open, Jaypaw stiffened. "Are there always so many cats?" he whispered.

Lionpaw gazed at the warriors, apprentices, and medicine cat who crowded the clearing. It looked like an ordinary Gathering to him. *Was Heatherpaw here?*

"Hey! Kittypet!"

Whitetail, a WindClan she-cat, was rushing toward Millie. Whitetail's apprentice, Breezepaw, hurried after her, ears flattened. Lionpaw unsheathed his claws, ready to defend his Clanmate.

"Hi, Millie!" Whitetail rubbed muzzles with Millie and twined her tail with hers as if they were old friends.

Lionpaw let his claws slide back in.

"Do they know each other?" Hollypaw gasped.

Lionpaw shrugged.

Breezepaw stared wide-eyed as his mentor stepped away from Millie and blinked warmly at her. "Thanks for the rabbit you gave us at the contest," she purred. "You share like a Clan cat."

Millie dipped her head. "It was a day for sharing," she meowed.

"It looks like the contest did some good after all," Hollypaw whispered to Lionpaw.

But another WindClan warrior, Tornear, was staring at

Millie through narrowed eyes. He clearly didn't like the sight of his denmate talking with a kittypet. Russetfur was watching, too, pelt bristling as she leaned forward to whisper something into a Clanmate's ear.

Breezepaw didn't say anything, just padded away from his mentor and pushed his way through the busy clearing. Berrypaw and Hazelpaw were chatting with a crowd of ShadowClan and WindClan apprentices. As Breezepaw joined them, Lionpaw's pelt bristled with expectation. Was Heatherpaw's pale tabby fur anywhere among the jumble of pelts?

He couldn't see her.

"What are you so disappointed about?" Jaypaw asked.

Lionpaw stared at him. "D-disappointed?" Jaypaw always had an uncanny way of guessing what he was feeling. "I'm not disappointed!"

"A mouse on the moor could have heard your tail hit the ground," Jaypaw mewed.

"I was hoping to see someone," Lionpaw admitted.

Hollypaw flicked her ears anxiously. "Heatherpaw?"

"Well, *you* want to see Willowpaw!" he retorted, his fur bristling at her accusing tone.

"It's not the same."

"Yes, it is!" Lionpaw protested. "We're just friends." As he spoke, he smelled a warmly familiar scent. Heatherpaw was racing across the clearing toward him.

"Lionpaw! You're here!"

He felt his heart skip, then glanced nervously at Jaypaw. Was he listening to his heartbeat, too? As though burying prey ready to taste later, Lionpaw pushed his excitement away. "Hello, Heatherpaw," he mewed coolly.

"You don't sound very pleased to see me." The WindClan cat's ears twitched. "I've been on my best behavior all moon so that Crowfeather couldn't possibly leave me behind."

Lionpaw felt a flash of guilt about his lack of enthusiasm. Then anger pricked his paws. Why should he feel guilty? She was *just a friend*. "I'm glad you made it," he mewed.

Hollypaw stepped in front of him and lightly brushed muzzles with Heatherpaw. "StarClan have given us fine weather again," she mewed politely.

"You brought your brother!" Heatherpaw's eyes shone as she noticed Jaypaw. Jealousy ran like cold water along Lionpaw's spine. He wished she hadn't been around to watch Jaypaw rescue him from the collapsed badger set.

He was almost grateful when Jaypaw snapped at her hotly, "Nobody *brought* me! I came with my Clan!"

"Of course," Heatherpaw mewed at once. "I'm sorry. I know you can travel by yourself. It's just—"

"Jaypaw!" Leafpool's call rescued Heatherpaw from her flustered apology. "Come and join us!" She was sitting with Barkface and Mothwing.

Lionpaw watched Jaypaw weave his way over to the other medicine cats. "Take no notice of Jaypaw," he mewed to Heatherpaw. "He's as grumpy as a badger."

"Who's grumpy?"

Lionpaw jerked around to see who had spoken. His heart plummeted when he saw Breezepaw padding toward them.

"You're not going to waste your time chatting to these two, are you?" The black-pelted WindClan apprentice sat down beside Heatherpaw. "Ivypaw and Owlpaw have just challenged Berrypaw to a competition to see who can jump the highest." He licked a forepaw and drew it over his ear.

"Why don't you go and watch it, then?" Heatherpaw replied.

"Why don't you come with me?" A challenging glint sparked in Breezepaw's eye.

Lionpaw heard the ferns rustling and smelled a familiar tang. "RiverClan is here," he mewed.

Hollypaw stretched up on tiptoe beside him to watch RiverClan file into the clearing.

Something seemed wrong. Their tails were down and their ears were flat back. Jaypaw's words buzzed in Lionpaw's ears. *There's something odd. . . .*

Hollypaw narrowed her eyes. "Leopardstar doesn't look very happy."

The golden tabby she-cat was touching muzzles with Firestar, but her tail flicked impatiently, her gaze flitting around the clearing.

"Hollypaw!" Willowpaw broke away from her Clanmates and hurried to greet Hollypaw. "I can't stay." The RiverClan medicine cat apprentice was out of breath. "I have to join Mothwing. But I just wanted to say hello."

"Is everything okay?" Hollypaw asked. "With your Clan, I mean. It's just that you all seem a bit—"

At that moment, Crowfeather padded over to join them. Lionpaw's whiskers twitched with frustration. Would he never get a moment alone with Heatherpaw?

"Heatherpaw," the WindClan warrior greeted his apprentice briskly. "Why don't you go and talk to some of the apprentices from the other Clans? This is a good chance to get to know different cats." His gaze flickered over Lionpaw and Hollypaw.

"Come on," Breezepaw urged. "Let's see if Ivypaw out-jumped Berrypaw."

Heatherpaw glanced at Lionpaw, then shrugged. "Okay, then."

Lionpaw's tail stirred the needle-strewn earth behind him as he watched Crowfeather and Breezepaw guide her away.

"Let all the Clans gather beneath StarClan!"

Blackstar's loud meow sounded from the Great Oak. The four leaders were lined along the lowest branch, silhouettes in the moonlight, their eyes shining in the dark. Lionpaw hurried after Hollypaw as she pushed her way in among her Clanmates and sat down beside Brackenfur. Lionpaw squeezed in front of her and sat beside Ashfur.

"Hey!" Hollypaw hissed. "Keep your head down. I want to see."

Lionpaw ducked, suddenly realizing that he was larger than his sister now, outpacing her in size if nothing else as they grew with the passing moons.

"ShadowClan brings happy news," Blackstar announced. "We have three new kits born to Tawnypelt."

Meows of congratulations rose from the crowd, the loudest from Squirrelflight. "Well done, Tawnypelt!"

Blackstar went on. "They are named Flamekit, Dawnkit, and Tigerkit!"

The meows died in the throats of the older warriors at the name Tigerkit. Lionpaw blinked. How could Tigerstar still frighten them when he was nothing but a memory from long ago and far away? They were as superstitious as owls!

"If they're Tawnypelt's kits," he whispered over his shoulder to Hollypaw, "they'll be our kin!" It felt odd to have kin in another Clan. For the first time he tried to imagine how his father must feel about Tawnypelt. She was Brambleclaw's sister, yet she had found her destiny with another Clan. Had he ever had to face her in a fight?

"Anything else to report?" Firestar's voice jolted Lionpaw from his daydreaming.

"Did I miss anything?" Lionpaw glanced back at his sister. She shook her head, but her eyes were shaded with worry.

Blackstar had tucked his tail over his paws and was looking satisfied. Onestar turned his head from the ThunderClan leader, signaling he had nothing to say.

Firestar nodded. "All has been well with ThunderClan, too." He turned to the RiverClan leader. "Leopardstar? You've shared no news."

"There's no news to share," she meowed curtly. "The fish are returning to the edge of the lake. Hunting is good. My Clan is well."

"I'm pleased to hear it," Firestar replied.

"Then the Gathering is over," Leopardstar declared.

The Clans began to pad away from the Great Oak as their

leaders bounded down from the low branch. Lionpaw stretched, feeling cold from sitting still.

Hazelpaw nudged him with her muzzle. "Three new ShadowClan cats!" she mewed. "We're going to have to train harder than ever!" She began to follow her Clanmates across the clearing.

Lionpaw hurried after her. "But they're only kits."

"Kits become warriors!" Hazelpaw reminded him.

Lionpaw felt Hollypaw pressing beside him. Her pelt was bristling. "Do you think we'll ever have to fight them?" she whispered anxiously.

"Let's not talk about fighting now." Squirrelflight had joined them and overheard. "Three kits are a blessing to any Clan." She was clearly pleased at Tawnypelt's news.

Leafpool caught up, Jaypaw at her side. "I noticed Tawnypelt was expecting last time I saw her."

Squirrelflight looked surprised. "You never mentioned it."

"It was not for me to say when it still lay in the paws of StarClan," Leafpool answered.

"Besides, it was none of your business!" A gruff mew startled the cats.

Lionpaw turned to see Rowanclaw, a ginger ShadowClan warrior, staring at them with narrowed eyes. *He must be the father.*

Squirrelflight returned his gaze. "Congratulations, Rowanclaw. You are blessed to have three healthy kits."

Rowanclaw curled his lip. "Three healthy *Clanborn* kits," he growled.

"That is only a blessing if they remain loyal to the Clan they were born to," Squirrelflight pointed out sharply, letting her temper flare.

Rowanclaw let out a low growl.

Leafpool stepped between the two warriors. "There's no need to argue."

"He was only speaking the truth."

Who said that? Lionpaw snapped his head around. *Breezepaw!*

The WindClan apprentice was standing beside his father.

Crowfeather was staring at Leafpool, his eyes glittering. "Don't forget, Breezepaw, ThunderClan actually *celebrates* mixed blood."

Leafpool jerked her head backward as though Crowfeather had raked his claws across her muzzle. She turned quickly and hurried away.

"He's acting like there's something wrong with Thunder-Clan!" Lionpaw unsheathed his claws, then felt his mother's tail run along his flank.

"Come along, Lionpaw. Don't forget the truce." She pressed against Lionpaw and padded toward the edge of the clearing, steering him away from Crowfeather, Breezepaw, and Rowanclaw.

Lionpaw glared over his shoulder at the three cats, wishing he could ignore the stupid truce and rip a piece of fur from each of them.

"Lionpaw!" Heatherpaw was bounding toward him.

"What?" Lionpaw stopped and faced Heatherpaw. Squirrelflight paused beside him.

Heatherpaw gazed up at her. "Can I speak to Lionpaw, please?"

Squirrelflight's ears twitched, but she nodded. "Don't be long." She padded into the bracken after Leafpool, Hollypaw, and Jaypaw.

"Please don't be angry," Heatherpaw begged. "Crow-feather's always bad-tempered. It's just his way. And Breezepaw thinks he's a warrior already."

"But you heard what they said about mixed blood in ThunderClan! They just can't let it go, can they?"

"Maybe they can't, but can we forget it?" Heatherpaw's eyes were shining. "I've got a plan."

"To get back at them?"

Heatherpaw's eyes widened. "Of course not! They're my Clanmates!" She flicked her tail. "My plan is something else entirely."

Lionpaw tipped his head to one side. "What, then?"

"Instead of waiting till the next Gathering, why don't we meet up before?"

"Before?" Lionpaw echoed in surprise. Wasn't it against the warrior code to meet with cats from another Clan without permission?

"Tomorrow night," she whispered.

"But how? Where?"

"At the boundary in the woods. Near the yew tree. We can slip away while our Clanmates are sleeping."

"But—"

Heatherpaw's whiskers twitched. "Come on! It'll be exciting. And it's not like we'd be hurting anyone."

Lionpaw felt guilt and worry tug at his belly, but Heatherpaw's blue eyes were sparkling at him hopefully. It did sound like fun. He could always say he'd been practicing his night hunting. And Heatherpaw was right. They wouldn't be doing any harm, like stealing prey or spying. No cat would even know if they were careful about it. *I'll still be loyal to my Clan and I won't fall behind in my duties.*

He blinked at Heatherpaw. "Okay."

CHAPTER 2

Hollypaw was dreaming. She was charging through the forest as rain pounded the leaf-strewn earth. She could glimpse Willowpaw's striped pelt through the trees. The RiverClan medicine cat apprentice was running fast, always a few steps ahead.

"Wait for me!" Hollypaw called. "There's something I want to ask you."

"I'll tell you if you catch up!" Willowpaw called back.

Hollypaw pushed harder, her paws skidding on the mud, but Willowpaw stayed a tail-length out of reach.

"There's something wrong with RiverClan, isn't there?" Hollypaw yowled.

"I can't hear you. The rain's too loud."

"Tell me what's wrong!"

The rain pelted down more fiercely, rattling against the leaves and bouncing off the ground.

"Willowpaw!"

"I can't tell you unless you catch me!"

"Slow down!" Hollypaw narrowed her eyes against the downpour. "Willowpaw?"

Willowpaw had disappeared.

Hollypaw was alone in the drenched forest.

She blinked open her eyes. Rain was battering the den roof, finding its way through the thick foliage of the yew branches and dripping into the nests. Hollypaw shivered and snuggled deeper into the moss but something wet was pressing against her.

Lionpaw's pelt.

Hollypaw shoved him away. "Move over. Your fur is soaking."

Lionpaw rolled back against her.

"Lionpaw!" She scrambled to her paws and stared at her brother. Dawn light was filtering through the branches, just enough to give color to the pelts of the sleeping cats. Lionpaw's fur was drenched, as though he had spent the night out in the rain, though he was fast asleep now. Hollypaw sniffed him suspiciously. Perhaps he had just gone out to make dirt and slipped back into the den for more sleep.

She yawned and stretched, her tail shivering with the effort. She felt cold to the bone. Mousepaw, Berrypaw, and Honeypaw were asleep despite the rain. Poppypaw's and Hazelpaw's nests were empty but their scent was fresh; they must have gone out with the dawn patrol.

"Hollypaw?" Cinderpaw lifted her head and blinked open her eyes. "Did the rain wake you?"

Hollypaw shook her head. "Lionpaw did," she mewed. "He's soaking wet."

"He's been out in this?" Cinderpaw rubbed her eyes with a paw.

"It looks like it." Hollypaw's fur was starting to itch with curiosity. This wasn't the first time Lionpaw had done something weird. He had woken her before dawn only a few days ago, slinking back into the den. He said he'd been out to make dirt, but his fur smelled of leaves, as though he'd been farther into the forest than just the dirtplace. *And* he'd snapped the answer back as though she was prying. She was sure he was up to something.

Cinderpaw's belly began to rumble. "I wonder if there's any fresh-kill on the pile yet?"

"There may be some left over from last night," Hollypaw suggested. "Let's go and see."

She picked her way among the warm bodies of her sleeping Clanmates and peered out of the entrance. She could hardly see the fresh-kill pile. The dawn sky was dark with clouds and the rain was so heavy that mud danced over the clearing.

Cinderpaw squeezed up beside her. "Let's make a dash for it."

"Okay." Hollypaw screwed up her eyes and darted out of the den.

Stormfur and Brook crouched beneath Highledge, sharing a soggy robin beneath the sheltering overhang.

"This weather's too wet even for RiverClan!" Stormfur called in greeting.

Hollypaw paused, blinking the rain from her eyes. "Now I know how fish feel!"

Cinderpaw scooted past her.

"Don't sit there like a startled rabbit, Hollypaw," Brook urged. "Find shelter!"

Hollypaw hurried after Cinderpaw and sent up a spray of mucky water as she skidded to a halt by the fresh-kill pile. A few sodden pieces of prey lay plastered in mud. She picked up a sorry-looking mouse and carried it to the shelter of the brambles that crowded one side of the medicine den.

"Yuck!" Cinderpaw dropped a dripping wren on the ground and shook herself. Hollypaw flattened her ears as the spray showered her.

"Sorry." Cinderpaw crouched and took a bite of her wren. "This tastes like mud!" she mewed with her mouth full.

At the entrance to the medicine den, the dripping brambles shivered and Leafpool hurried out, her jaws clutching a bundle of herbs. She dashed across the clearing and disappeared into the nursery.

"I hope Icekit and Foxkit are okay," Hollypaw mewed.

"Daisy was sneezing last night," Cinderpaw told her. "I think she has a cold."

Hollypaw peered up through the brambles at the gray sky. "We'll all have colds if this rain doesn't stop soon. That, or webbed feet." It had been nearly a half-moon since the Gathering, and it seemed to have rained every day.

The rest of the camp was beginning to stir. Thornclaw yawned as he padded around the clearing followed by Dustpelt. As Hollypaw swallowed the last mouthfuls of cold mouse, Firestar emerged from his cave on Highledge and surveyed the camp. Brambleclaw darted from the warriors' den and bounded up the rockfall to meet him. The two warriors vanished into Firestar's cave, their tails low against the rain that hurled against the cliff.

Mousefur peered out from the honeysuckle-draped bush that formed the elders' den, before disappearing back inside with a snort of disgust. Graystripe padded from behind the warriors' den, where he shared a makeshift den with Millie. His thick gray pelt was plastered against his body. He picked two birds from the fresh-kill pile and hurried back to his nest.

Brackenfur emerged from the warriors' den and stretched, arching his tail and reaching out with his forepaws until his chest touched the ground. Then he straightened and shook himself, fluffing out his golden fur. "Hollypaw?" He peered toward her through narrowed eyes, rain streaming from his whiskers. "Is that you?"

Hollypaw padded out from the shelter of the brambles. "I was just eating with Cinderpaw," she greeted him.

"Well, if you've got a full belly, you can come hunting with me."

Hollypaw felt a surge of delight. Hunting would warm her up. "Can Cinderpaw come too?" she asked.

Cinderpaw shook her head. "Cloudtail asked me to clean out the elders' bedding this morning."

"I'll bring you back a warm mouse if I can," Hollypaw promised.

"One without mud, please," Cinderpaw purred.

"Come on, Hollypaw." Brackenfur was already racing for the camp entrance.

Outside, the forest floor was soaked, the dead leaves slimy and rotten underpaw, but Hollypaw soon began to feel warm as she chased Brackenfur up the steep slope and they headed into the forest. The rain was beginning to ease and for the first time that morning she opened her eyes wide. The trees ahead were thickening and the forest darkened where pines began to grow among the leafless trees. ShadowClan territory lay this way. Hollypaw thought of the new kittens—her kin—in the camp beyond the border. If they shared her blood, would they share her scent as well? Was it blood or Clan that decided scent? How would they tell whose marker was whose?

"Brackenfur?"

Brackenfur skidded on the wet leaves and turned to face her, his eyes bright. "Do you smell prey?" he asked hopefully.

Hollypaw shook her head. "I was just wondering . . ." She searched for the words to explain the unease that was nagging her.

"Yes?"

"Well, I was wondering . . ."

Brackenfur shook the rain from his whiskers. "What is it, for StarClan's sake?"

"If the new kits in ShadowClan are my kin, do I still have to fight them in battle?"

"Of course, if they threaten your Clan." Brackenfur turned away and started padding through the forest once more, his nose twitching as he hunted for scent among the wet undergrowth.

Hollypaw hurried to keep up with him. "But what if my Clan threatens them and I don't think it's fair?"

"Why should we do that?" Brackenfur's ears pricked and he dropped into a hunting crouch.

"But just say we did? Shouldn't I feel some loyalty to kin?"

"A true warrior is loyal to her Clan above everything." Brackenfur began to knead the ground with his hind paws; he had spotted something ahead and was preparing to pounce. But Hollypaw's mind was hungrier than her belly.

"You can't hurt cats that share your blood," she argued. "Does that mean there are more important things than the warrior code?" She blinked in alarm. "If that's true, then how do we know what's right—"

"Hush!" Brackenfur's hiss silenced her as a leaf trembled a fox-length away and a small brown shape shot away into the safety of its burrow.

Brackenfur sat up and stared crossly at his apprentice. "Why don't you stop thinking about the warrior code and start following it? Your Clan is hungry and wet. You should be concentrating on feeding them, not on deciding what's wrong and what's right!"

Hollypaw's tail drooped. He was right. She had scared off prey that could have fed her Clanmates. "I'm sorry," she murmured.

"Now stop asking questions and find something to take back to camp!"

Hollypaw hunted even harder than usual and returned to the camp carrying three mice. Brackenfur led her through the thorn tunnel, a crow in his jaws. He dropped it on a fresh-kill pile that had already been restocked by another hunting patrol.

"You did well," he congratulated her. She felt relieved that she had made up for losing him the mouse. "Now go and get dry in your den," he advised. "I'll take food to Mousefur and Longtail."

The rain had stopped but the forest was still dripping. Hollypaw padded to the apprentices' den. Inside, the nests were empty except for Lionpaw's. Hollypaw could see his golden pelt rising and falling gently as he slept. How could he sleep the morning away while everyone else was busy looking after the Clan?

"Doesn't Ashfur have any jobs for you?" she called irritably.

"Huh? What?" Lionpaw's head shot up and he stared, blinking, at her. "Is it dawn already?"

"It's halfway to sunhigh!"

Lionpaw leaped to his paws. His eyes were round with guilt. "Has Ashfur been looking for me?"

"I don't know. *I've* been out hunting," Hollypaw answered pointedly. She began tugging at the damp bedding closest to her, pulling at it with her teeth and shaking it to let moisture out and fresh air in. "Why are you so tired anyway?" she asked, her mew muffled by the moss.

"I didn't sleep well," Lionpaw replied.

Hollypaw glanced at him, but he was staring at the ground, as if avoiding her gaze. "Is there something wrong, Lionpaw?"

"No," he mewed quickly.

"Are you sure?"

"Of course!" His mew was tetchy.

Hollypaw felt a wave of sadness. They used to share every-thing, but now getting details out of her brother was like try-ing to pick fleas off a hedgehog. Unless they jumped out by themselves, there was no way she could reach them.

"Okay, okay! There's no need to bite my head off!" She started plucking at the moss again.

Lionpaw padded past her. "I wasn't biting your head off," he muttered. "But sometimes it's nice to be able to do stuff without being asked so many questions!" He stalked out of the den, leaving Hollypaw alone.

She sighed and let the moss she was working on drop to the ground. Perhaps Jaypaw knew what was up with Lionpaw. He always seemed to guess what *she* was thinking. Perhaps he could do the same with Lionpaw. She headed for the medi-cine den and pushed her way through the brambles.

Jaypaw was sorting through herbs at the back of the cleft in the rock wall. "I'm busy," he mewed without looking up. "Leafpool wants me to see what herbs we need before she gets back from the nursery."

"Are the kits sick?" Hollypaw asked anxiously.

"Daisy has a cold," Jaypaw replied. "Nothing serious, but with all this rain, Leafpool wants to treat it before it gets worse."

"I wanted to talk to you about Lionpaw," she ventured.

"Is he ill?"

"No." Hollypaw sat down, wishing Jaypaw would stop

messing around with the herbs and talk to her properly. "He's just been so tired lately, and grumpy. Every time I talk to him he practically nips my whiskers off."

"How should I know what's wrong with him?" Jaypaw pushed a pile of dark green leaves together. Hollypaw tried to remember their name—she had, after all, trained as a medicine cat for a while—but she hadn't a clue.

"It's just that you usually know."

"*You* share a den with him," Jaypaw pointed out. "I'm stuck over here with Leafpool most of the time." His voice prickled with resentment.

Hollypaw sat in silence for a moment. On top of worrying about Lionpaw, her dream about Willowpaw was still nagging at the back of her mind. But if Jaypaw wasn't going to help her work out what was up with Lionpaw, there wasn't much hope he would care what was bothering her RiverClan friend. And yet . . .

She decided to try coming at it sideways. Always a good hunting move when stalking tricky prey.

"Did you speak to Willowpaw at the Gathering?" she asked casually.

"Not much."

"I think she's worried you don't like her."

"Why do I have to like every cat I meet?" Jaypaw grumbled.

"Why do you have to *dis*like every cat you meet?" she shot back. "Willowpaw's really nice. You don't have to go out of your way to make her feel uncomfortable."

"I don't *make* her feel anything." Jaypaw turned back to his herbs. "She feels what she wants to feel."

"Didn't you think she was feeling anxious at the Gathering?" Hollypaw decided to press on. "Didn't you think the whole of RiverClan was acting oddly?"

Jaypaw turned from his herbs. "Perhaps." His ears were pricked as if Hollypaw had finally said something that interested him.

"So I didn't just imagine it?"

"Imagine what?"

"That something's troubling RiverClan?"

"Do *you* think there is?" Jaypaw was leaning toward her now.

"I don't know." Hollypaw didn't want to start a rumor that would make RiverClan look weak. It felt disloyal to her friend. And besides, it might not be true. "Do you?"

"I couldn't tell."

Hollypaw felt a wave of frustration. This conversation was going in circles!

"But I might be able to find out something when we go to the Moonpool," Jaypaw went on.

Of course! The medicine cats would be traveling together to the Moonpool at half-moon. That was only a few days away. "If there is something worrying Willowpaw, will you tell me?" Hollypaw asked.

Jaypaw narrowed his eyes. "Sure. I know how I'll be able to find out."

Hollypaw's pelt began to prick with unease. "I'm not ask-

ing you to *spy* or anything," she mewed. "Just let me know if
I'm right to worry. . . ."

"Okay." Jaypaw shrugged and began pawing at another pile
of herbs.

"Hollypaw!" Brackenfur was calling her from the clearing.

Feeling slightly relieved, she hurried out of the medicine
den. A small patch of blue had opened in the clouds above the
hollow.

"We may as well do some training in the forest while the
rain holds off," Brackenfur meowed. "Cloudtail's taking
Cinderpaw out to explore and I thought we could join them.
Get to know the territory a bit better."

Cinderpaw came bouncing toward them, followed by
Cloudtail and Birchfall.

"Firestar wants us to check out the old fox den," Birchfall
called. "Make sure those fox cubs haven't returned."

Hollypaw shivered. She still remembered the awful day
when she and Jaypaw and Lionpaw had set out to chase the
fox cubs from the den and had ended up being chased themselves. In his terror, Jaypaw had fallen over the side of the
hollow and nearly died.

"Don't worry, Hollypaw," Cinderpaw whispered. "I'll
watch your tail."

Hollypaw brushed gratefully against her friend as they
padded out of the camp after the three warriors. "And I'll
watch yours."

As they neared the narrow glade that sloped down to the
den, Hollypaw sniffed the air. Her paws tingled. Fox!

"Young, female, but it's stale," Cinderpaw interpreted, nose twitching.

"How can you be sure?" Hollypaw asked in surprise. As far as she knew, Cinderpaw had never met a fox, and couldn't know their scent well enough to distinguish all that.

Cinderpaw shrugged. "I just know," she mewed.

"She's right about it being stale," Cloudtail meowed. "There's been no fox here since leaf-fall."

Hollypaw glanced at her friend. Cinderpaw sometimes said or did things that suggested she knew more than she let on. But holding back secrets was not like Cinderpaw. The gray apprentice was usually three paw steps ahead of herself and would rather leap in, whiskers first, than stop and think. Perhaps she had been here before and just forgotten.

Cloudtail was obviously wondering the same. "Have you been here with another patrol?"

Cinderpaw shook her head. "This is definitely the first time," she mewed.

Cloudtail and Brackenfur exchanged glances, and Hollypaw guessed that they were as puzzled as she was.

An owl screeched far above the hollow, and Hollypaw rolled over in her nest, half-woken by the noise. She stretched her forepaws, feeling for the reassuring warmth of Lionpaw, and found emptiness.

She blinked open her eyes.

"Lionpaw?" she hissed under her breath.

No reply.

She reached farther into his nest, wondering if he had rolled to the far side but no, he was definitely gone.

"Are you looking for Lionpaw?" Poppypaw yawned from the other side of his nest. "He left the den a while ago."

Hollypaw sat up, her heart racing. Lionpaw had gone missing once too often.

"Is something wrong?" Poppypaw's eyes gleamed in the darkness.

"N-no." Hollypaw didn't want to arouse the suspicions of the other apprentices.

"Has Lionpaw gone to make dirt *again*?" Cinderpaw's mew sounded behind her. "It must be that stale old thrush he ate."

Hollypaw felt a wave of gratitude toward her friend. She was clearly covering for Lionpaw, stopping Poppypaw from answering any more awkward questions. The thrush had been perfectly healthy, caught fresh that day.

"I'll go and check if he's okay," Hollypaw mewed.

She crept from the den and hurried as silently as she could around the edge of the slumbering camp, keeping to the shadows. Lionpaw's scent led to the entrance, following the same furtive route. *Let me find him making dirt,* Hollypaw prayed.

Paw steps sounded behind her.

Hollypaw froze and glanced over her shoulder.

"It's just me." Cinderpaw's mew sounded from the darkness, and the gray tabby stepped out of the shadows. "I thought you might want company."

"Thanks." If Lionpaw was really making dirt, there was no harm in Cinderpaw's knowing, but if he wasn't and, as

Hollypaw feared, he was out in the forest, she would be pleased to have a friend with her.

One after the other, they squeezed through the small tunnel to the dirtplace.

"He's not here," Cinderpaw whispered.

Hollypaw sighed, her heart heavy. "No."

"What do you think he's up to?"

Hollypaw didn't dare reply. She could guess why he might have left the camp under cover of night, but she didn't want to believe it.

"His trail leads this way," Cinderpaw announced, pointing with her nose up the lakeward slope.

Hollypaw's belly tightened. The trail led up over the ridge and then around onto the moorland: WindClan territory. *Perhaps he's just exploring.* Hope stirred in her chest, but beneath it, like a rock, lay the dark suspicion that he was meeting Heatherpaw.

"We're going to follow him, aren't we?" Cinderpaw was staring at Hollypaw, her eyes clouded with worry. Had she guessed, too? Surely not. How could she know?

"Perhaps it's none of our business," Hollypaw suggested feebly.

"Of course it's our business! Our denmate is out there alone. What if something happened to him?"

"Is that the only reason you want to follow him—because he might be in danger?"

"No." Cinderpaw sat down. "I think he may be doing something he will live to regret."

Hollypaw was taken aback by her friend's serious tone. "Do you know something I don't?" she asked.

Cinderpaw shook her head. "It's just a feeling I have. I can't explain it. A feeling that Lionpaw is making a mistake that's been made before, that should never be made, that only leads to trouble. . . . " Her mew died away but her eyes were shining with emotion.

"Okay." Hollypaw could not ignore the strength of her friend's feeling. Nor could she ignore her own. All her instincts told her that Lionpaw was breaking the warrior code, and it was her duty as a Clan cat to stop him. She charged up the slope, sniffing the twigs and brambles for Lionpaw's scent, following the path he had taken to the top of the ridge. Cinderpaw bounded after her and they quickly reached the edge of the trees. The ground sloped away in front of them, down to the shore where the lake sparkled in the moonlight. Hollypaw scanned the distant moorland, half hoping to see Lionpaw, half hoping she wouldn't. If Lionpaw was roaming around at night, she wanted it to be on ThunderClan territory.

There was no sign of movement in the shadowy heather. Hollypaw plunged down the slope, following an old rabbit track through the coarsening grass. Underpaw the ground grew more peaty as they neared the WindClan border. Heather bushes sprouted on either side of the track as the slope flattened and the sound of water lapping the shore grew louder.

"Did you hear that?" Cinderpaw's hiss startled Hollypaw.

She pricked her ears. A small hollow, ringed by heather, lay in shadow ahead of them. From it came the sound of voices. Hollypaw's tail bristled as she recognized Lionpaw's mew. He sounded happy; happier than she had heard him in days. She crept forward, keeping low, and ducked into the swath of heather that shielded the hollow. Setting the bushes rustling, she wriggled between the bare stems and peered over the top of the slope.

Her brother was charging after a ball of moss like an excited kit. He dived at it as it landed and, with a tremendous swipe, sent it flying back in the other direction. A lithe shape leaped up from the grass to catch it. Its tabby pelt glowed in the moonlight. Hollypaw's heart sank like a rock. Heatherpaw!

"You don't seem surprised." Cinderpaw had slid in beside her and was peering down into the grassy dip.

Hollypaw shook her head. "I'm not." Reluctantly she wriggled out from the heather. "Lionpaw!" she called.

Lionpaw and Heatherpaw froze, staring at each other in alarm. The moss ball fell to the ground.

"What are you doing here?" Hollypaw demanded.

Slowly Lionpaw tore his gaze from Heatherpaw's and turned to face his sister. His eyes sparked with defiance. "What are *you* doing here?"

"Looking for you!"

"*Spying* on me!"

Hollypaw flinched. "You shouldn't be here, playing with her!" She glared at Heatherpaw.

"Why not? She's just a friend."

"A friend from another Clan!"

"*You're* friends with Willowpaw!"

"I don't sneak off every night to see her."

Lionpaw opened his mouth to object, but no words came out. Hollypaw knew she had won the argument. But her brother's eyes did not concede anything. They shone with rage. He turned to Heatherpaw. "I'd better go."

Heatherpaw dipped her head. "I know," she sighed.

Hollypaw clenched her teeth as Lionpaw brushed muzzles with the WindClan apprentice. Did he really believe it was just friendship that brought him here?

Lionpaw padded up the slope and glared at Cinderpaw. "Did you have to tell the whole Clan?" he hissed at Hollypaw.

Cinderpaw flicked her tail. "I just came to make sure Hollypaw was safe," she explained. "No one else knows."

"And they won't know," Hollypaw added, "so long as you stay away from Heatherpaw."

Lionpaw glared at her. "Is that a threat?"

Hollypaw backed away. She had never seen Lionpaw this angry. Even when they had quarreled as kits, there had always been a lighthearted twinkle in his eyes. But not now. His eyes were cold as stars.

"If you continue meeting Heatherpaw, I will have to tell Brambleclaw," she insisted, trying not to let her voice tremble.

Lionpaw bristled.

"There's a good reason why the warrior code forbids mixing with cats from other Clans," Hollypaw went on. "How can you be loyal to your own Clan when your heart lies in another?"

"Are you accusing me of disloyalty?" Lionpaw flattened his ears.

"I know you'd never be disloyal," Hollypaw mewed. "But you're making it difficult for yourself. That's why you must stop this." It was hard enough having kin in another Clan without deliberately making friends outside the forest. Weren't Lionpaw's Clanmates enough for him?

A low growl sounded in Lionpaw's throat. He barged past Hollypaw and padded toward the trees. Hollypaw felt Cinderpaw's tail run along her flank, smoothing her ruffled fur.

"He'll get over it," Cinderpaw promised.

"I hope so," Hollypaw sighed. She knew she'd done the right thing, but she hadn't expected Lionpaw to react so angrily, as if he believed that he'd done nothing wrong. Would he ever forgive her?

CHAPTER 3

Jaypaw winced as grit from the trail dug into his pads. At least they did not ache with cold. The stony path to the Moonpool was warming up as newleaf took hold.

Ahead of him, Leafpool chatted with Mothwing. Their mews were only just audible over the rush of water, because the stream that flowed beside their path was swollen by snowmelt from the distant mountains. It carried the scent of frost and rock, and below them, the level of the lake would be rising with the extra water.

Littlecloud and Barkface had taken the lead while Willowpaw trailed behind with Kestrelpaw. Jaypaw slowed occasionally in case the two apprentices wanted to catch up to him, but Willowpaw adjusted her soft step, and Kestrelpaw quickly matched it so that they were always a little behind.

It was a silent challenge but Jaypaw was content to walk alone. At least he could listen to snatches of the medicine cats' conversation—who had recovered from greencough, who had sprained a paw, which herb best treated the mange that was currently running rife in the ShadowClan apprentice den. As he listened, he let his mind wander, feeling for what emotion lurked behind the words.

"I've tried comfrey for the itching," Littlecloud sighed.

He blames the apprentices for not keeping their pelts clean in the first place.

"We didn't think Morningflower would recover from greencough, but she has lived to see another newleaf," Barkface confided.

But your anxiety tells me that you think it will be her last.

"Is Mousefur completely recovered?" Mothwing asked Leafpool.

Jaypaw searched Mothwing's mind, but only found the blankness that always seemed to shield her emotions. He flicked his attention to Willowpaw. If Hollypaw was right and RiverClan were in trouble, Willowpaw would be the one to betray it. Her mind was usually as open as the moorland. He concentrated on the RiverClan apprentice, sniffing out her emotions as though they were scent. Sure enough, unease enfolded her. Jaypaw tried to delve farther into her thoughts but it was as though she had wrapped herself in brambles. Thorny barbs drove him back. Frustrated, he gave up.

I'll find out more when she dreams.

The path had reached the steep rocks that walled the ridge. Conversation died as the medicine cats climbed, their words turning to breathless gasps as they bounded up rock after rock. Jaypaw scrambled ahead of Leafpool. He felt his mentor's watchful gaze warm his pelt as he leaped onto a tricky ledge. Thankfully, she said nothing. He had been this way often enough to make it to the ridge without help.

As he hauled himself over the edge he was caught by the fresh scent of the Moonpool. Frost and rock and sky.

"Look how big it is," Willowpaw breathed as she climbed up beside him.

"Meltwater," Leafpool meowed.

"It's wide enough to hold every star in the sky," Kestrelpaw mewed.

There is room for all tonight, a whispering breeze sang into Jaypaw's ears. The voices had come to welcome him. He wondered if they welcomed the others, too.

"Did you hear that?" he asked casually.

Leafpool's gaze scorched his ears. "Hear what?"

"That'd be the wind," Littlecloud explained.

"It sounds different up here because it's echoed by the rock," Barkface added.

Their matter-of-fact tone answered Jaypaw's question. These cats heard only the wind. The voices spoke to him alone.

Jaypaw thought again of the prophecy he had heard in Firestar's dream: *There will be three, kin of your kin, who hold the power of the stars in their paws.* His pelt prickled with excitement. This must be part of his power, the ability to hear things no other cat could.

Willowpaw shifted her weight from one paw to another. "Where shall we lie? The water has covered our usual places."

Jaypaw heard Mothwing's tail swish the air. "The rocks are flat over there."

He followed Leafpool down toward the pool. The breeze stirred his fur, and the voices whispered in his ear again. *Welcome, Jaypaw.* The stone beneath his paws was dimpled, worn into a pathway by countless paw steps.

Water suddenly lapped his paws. They were only halfway down the slope! Tingling with surprise, he followed Leafpool around the water's far-reaching edge and settled on the rock beside her. He heard Leafpool's breath stir the pool and then deepen as she fell into dream-sleep.

The other cats lay down, their fur brushing the rock, and soon the hollow echoed only with the sound of breath and wind upon water. Willowpaw was the last to settle. Jaypaw waited while she slid into sleep. Focusing on her mind, he leaned forward and touched the Moonpool with his muzzle.

Instantly, he was swept away in a torrent of seething water.

He struggled and flailed with his paws, his heart bursting with terror as he gasped for air. He looked up and saw a stormy sky clouding above him and all around, churning water that stretched to endless horizons. Then he saw Willowpaw's head bobbing above the waves. She was swimming, her eyes filled with determination, her jaws clutching a mouthful of herbs as her paws churned. Jaypaw clutched at the water, struggling to keep his head above the surface. The water sucked at his hind paws, dragging him down. Water filled his mouth and nose. Splashing, coughing, he tried to claw his way back into the safety of consciousness.

He opened his eyes. He was lying on damp grass. Trees leaned over him, their leaves blocking out the sun, and ferns crowded around him. Jaypaw struggled to his paws and looked around. Was this Willowpaw's dream or his own?

"You must hurry!" A husky mew hissed beyond the ferns. Jaypaw stretched warily onto his hind legs and peered over the ferns. A brown tom, stiff with age, was nudging Willowpaw forward. "You must leave," he meowed.

"What about my herbs?" Willowpaw dug her claws into the grass. "You know I can't leave them behind, Mudfur."

"Take what you can, find the rest when you get there."

"Get where?" Willowpaw's voice sounded close to panic.

"There is no time for questions," Mudfur mewed. "If you stay, the Clan will be destroyed."

"But there's nowhere to go!"

Jaypaw dropped back onto four paws. There *was* something wrong in RiverClan. Something very wrong.

"Spying again!"

Jaypaw spun around. He had heard this voice before, and it had lost none of its mocking sharpness.

"I don't see how you can accuse *me* of spying," he objected, "when you keep turning up in all my dreams!"

"But they're not your dreams, are they?" Yellowfang stared at him, her amber eyes cloudy, her thick coat as unkempt as ever.

Jaypaw felt a rush of anger. "*I'm* dreaming, so it's *my* dream!"

"Clever," croaked Yellowfang, "but not honest. You intended to trespass on Willowpaw's dream the moment you closed your eyes."

"If you knew what I was going to do, why did you let me do it?" he demanded.

Yellowfang turned her face away.

"You can't stop me, can you?" Jaypaw felt a rush of delight, like a bird escaping grasping claws. "I have the power of the stars in my paws!"

Yellowfang swung her head around and glared at him. "Do you really believe that?"

"Are you telling me it's not true?"

"Just tell me this—what exactly do you have the power to *do*?"

Jaypaw stared at her.

"You have no idea, do you?" she pressed.

Jaypaw's whiskers twitched. "Do *you*?"

Yellowfang blinked slowly but did not reply.

"I have this power for a reason!" Jaypaw insisted.

"Then find out what that reason is before you use it!" Yellowfang turned away. As she disappeared into the ferns, Jaypaw woke up.

Blackness pressed in on him. He was blind once more.

Beside him, Leafpool was stretching. "Did you dream?" she yawned.

"Yes." Jaypaw scrambled to his paws and whispered in her ear, "About RiverClan."

"Tell me once we have left the others." She jerked away from him. "Mothwing! Is everything okay?"

What, in her dreams about hunting squirrels and chasing butterflies? Jaypaw had long since guessed that there was something wrong with Mothwing's connection with StarClan, some secret that Leafpool shared but would not betray.

He heard grit skidding across the rock. Willowpaw had leaped to her paws. "Mothwing!" Jaypaw could tell the young cat was trying to stop her voice from trembling. "We have to go home at once!"

"What did you see in your dream?" Anxiety was pricking from Leafpool's pelt; Jaypaw could feel it like lightning in the air.

They had left the others at the WindClan border and were heading up the slope toward the forest. The wind was chilly and carried the freshness of unfurling leaves. Jaypaw guessed that dawn was close.

"RiverClan is in trouble," he announced. "I saw Willow-paw swimming in a huge lake, bigger than this one. She said RiverClan have to find a new home and she was talking to some old cat called Mudfur—"

"He was RiverClan's medicine cat before Mothwing!" Leaf-pool gasped. "What was he doing in your dream? What was either of them doing . . . " Her voice trailed away and Jaypaw felt anger flare from her. "You went into Willowpaw's dream, didn't you?"

"Hollypaw told me to find out if RiverClan were in trouble."

"Did she tell you to trespass on her friend's dreams?"

"Of course not. Hollypaw doesn't understand that stuff. She just wanted to know what was wrong, so I tried to find out."

"As a favor to your littermate." Leafpool's mew was scathing. And yet beneath her anger Jaypaw could sense fear, which puzzled him. What was there to be scared of?

"StarClan *let* me do it," he told her. "Why are you making such a fuss? The most important thing is that we know RiverClan is in trouble."

"You shouldn't be able to find things like that out so easily," Leafpool murmured, half to herself.

"Just because you can't do it, doesn't mean it's wrong," Jaypaw snorted impatiently.

"That's got nothing to do with it!" Leafpool snapped. "I'm worried it'll be like last time."

"When I dreamed about the dogs attacking WindClan?"

"When *Barkface* dreamed about the dogs attacking Wind-Clan!" Leafpool was fighting not to raise her voice. "StarClan shared with him so he could protect his Clan. You wanted to take advantage of their vulnerability."

"Well, this time I'm just doing Hollypaw a favor," Jaypaw mewed.

"Don't tell anyone else what you're doing," Leafpool begged.

"Why not?" Jaypaw flexed his claws. "Why should I keep secrets about a gift StarClan has given me?"

Why was Leafpool so fond of secrets? Secrets about his gift, secrets about Mothwing and StarClan. He suspected there were even more secrets buried in his mentor's heart, secrets that she guarded so closely he had never been able to glimpse them.

"Knowledge can be dangerous," Leafpool warned.

Frustration clawed at Jaypaw's belly. He lived his life in darkness; he longed for light and clarity, not shadows. He forced away his anger. Leafpool had lived too long with secrets. He couldn't change her mind in a single night. But why did she have to drag him into her complicated world?

"We will tell Firestar about RiverClan, though, won't we?" he prompted.

"We might as well." Leafpool paused. "But please don't mention how you found out."

Jaypaw didn't reply. It was just like the WindClan dream. He hadn't cared then whether the other cats knew what he could do or not. He didn't care now. But he didn't like Leafpool making the decision for him. He hurried ahead, familiar now with the ground beneath his paws. They were almost back at camp. He broke into a run and heard Leafpool's paws pattering on the fallen leaves behind him. She was right on his tail as he burst into the camp.

"Leafpool?" Firestar's mew sounded from the Highledge. "Is something wrong?"

"I need to talk to you," Leafpool called. She whisked past Jaypaw, heading toward the tumble of fallen rocks.

We *need to talk to you!* He followed her up to Highledge.

"Come inside." Firestar led the two cats into his cave. Jaypaw could scent Sandstorm and hear the steady lapping of her tongue.

"Good morning, Leafpool." Sandstorm paused from her washing. Her voice softened as she addressed him. "Good morning, Jaypaw." A twinge of resentment stabbed his belly. *She still thinks I'm a kit.*

"I had a dream—" he began.

"—about RiverClan." Leafpool quickly finished his sentence. "Jaypaw dreamed they were in trouble. There seemed to be a problem with their home."

Firestar's tail swished over the ground. "Was there any message about ThunderClan?"

"ThunderClan wasn't involved," Leafpool meowed carefully.

"And there was no clear sign about what their problem is?" Firestar queried.

"Not exactly," Jaypaw admitted.

"Then I don't see what we can do," Firestar concluded.

"Shouldn't we try to help them?" Leafpool's mew was brittle with surprise.

"If they need help, they'll ask for it." Firestar shifted his paws. "It's none of our business."

"Why not?" Jaypaw bristled with frustration.

"I haven't forgotten the last time you came to me with a dream," Firestar growled. "It's not part of the warrior code to attack every Clan that seems weak!"

Jaypaw's ears burned. "I never said anything about attacking them! We could help them." If ThunderClan helped now, RiverClan would be in their debt.

"Perhaps we could pay them a friendly visit," Leafpool suggested.

"No." Firestar was firm. "We have our own Clan to worry

about. I don't know why StarClan can't send you dreams about *us* instead of announcing every other Clan's problems!"

Leafpool took a step forward. "You could send a patrol though, just to see. If they stayed near the shore, it wouldn't break the—"

"They live on the other side of the lake!" Firestar cut her off. "I think Onestar has had enough of our meddling. And Blackstar is always looking for an excuse to get even with ThunderClan. StarClan knows why! I'm tired of acting for the best and then finding I've only made ThunderClan the focus of every resentment and jealousy in the other Clans."

Jaypaw felt disappointment pulse from his mentor. Her paws scuffed the earthen floor of the cave as she padded out. He followed her, scrabbling down the rockfall.

"Aren't you going to argue with him?"

"I tried," Leafpool sighed.

"But he has to listen to you! You're the medicine cat."

"He's the leader." Leafpool started to pad away. "I want to check on Daisy," she meowed. "You go and sleep."

Jaypaw flicked his tail. He wished his dream had been clearer. Then Firestar might have acted. Warm sunshine dappled his pelt as he padded toward the medicine den. He was tired after the long trek to the Moonpool. He needed rest before he could think of doing anything.

"Jaypaw, wait!" Hollypaw's voice rang from the apprentice den. She skidded to a halt beside him. "Was Willowpaw there? Did you talk to her?"

"No." Jaypaw wanted to sleep, not chat.

"She wasn't there?" Panic edged Hollypaw's mew.

"She was there. I just didn't talk to her."

"Did you find *anything* out? Perhaps Mothwing told Leafpool something."

"RiverClan is definitely in trouble," Jaypaw mewed.

"What's wrong? How can you be sure?" Hollypaw paced around him.

"I saw Willowpaw in a dream. She's worried that she has to find a new home."

"A new *home*!" Hollypaw froze. "That's dreadful! What's Firestar going to do?"

"Nothing," Jaypaw reported. "He doesn't want to interfere."

"But he must!" Hollypaw gasped. "RiverClan is in trouble."

"Firestar says it's their problem." Jaypaw's pelt itched with annoyance as he remembered the way the Clan leader had dismissed him. *Again.*

"So we have to stand by and watch?"

"Look, I'm tired." Jaypaw began to pad toward the medicine den. "Go and argue with Firestar. He's the one that makes the decisions."

He left Hollypaw, feeling her gaze follow him across the clearing, sensing the indignation prickle from her pelt, hearing her shift her paws as she wondered whether to confront Firestar or not.

It wasn't like Hollypaw to be so indecisive. Would she be more certain if he shared what he knew about the three cats who held the power of the stars in their paws? *Not yet.*

Something held him back, some pleasure in saving the knowledge for himself, some fear that speaking his destiny out loud might change it.

Right now all he wanted to do was rest his aching paws and sleep.

CHAPTER 4

"I'm still really tired," Jaypaw complained.

Leafpool was leading him down to the lake. "But sunhigh's the best time to collect mallow, when the leaves are dry."

Jaypaw yawned. His paws were still sore and he felt as if he'd hardly closed his eyes before Leafpool nudged him awake. At least the day was warm. There was no chance of newleaf being driven back by the long claws of leaf-bare now. The sunshine striking through the new foliage was hot enough to make his pelt itch as they padded through the trees. Birds called to one another, and far off he could hear the shrieks and splashes of Twolegs playing in the water. Jaypaw shivered, remembering his fall into the lake when Crowfeather had rescued him. He wasn't going to get his paws wet again if he could help it.

Water babbled nearby. He had only been this way once before. A brook ran down out of the forest and into the lake. Like the stream that led up to the Moonpool, it carried the scent of the mountains. Leafpool led him along the edge, weaving around the trees that lined its path. The grass felt soft and cool on his pads and he was sorry when Leafpool veered off the grassy bank and down onto the pebbly shore.

"The lake's higher than I'd hoped," she meowed, stopping. "We won't be able to collect all the herbs I wanted, but I can see a clump over there." She darted away toward a sweet scent, and Jaypaw began to pad after her.

Suddenly, in the forest behind him, leaves fluttered and paw steps beat quick and light on the forest floor.

A squirrel!

Tiny paws skittered along the bank of the stream behind him and scrabbled up a tree, rustling its leaves. Then splashing. A hunting patrol was plunging toward him, down the shallow stream.

"Did you hear where it went?" Birchfall's excited mew sounded from the trees.

Jaypaw flicked his nose toward where the squirrel was leaping along a low branch.

"I'll get it!" Pebbles rattled and water splashed as Mousepaw scooted from the stream and up the tree trunk. Jaypaw ducked and blinked as shards of bark sprayed him, gouged out by Mousepaw's eager claws. The branch overhead creaked, and Jaypaw heard a surprised squeal.

But it wasn't the squirrel. It was Mousepaw.

The apprentice tumbled off the branch and crashed onto the pebbles beside Jaypaw.

"Fox dung!" Mousepaw scrambled to his paws, embarrassment flashing from his ruffled pelt.

"Catch it?" Jaypaw inquired.

Leaves rustled above them as the squirrel made its getaway.

"Nice try!" Spiderleg called from the stream.

"Next time, I'll get it!" Mousepaw called back to his mentor.

The scent of the stream had confused Jaypaw, but as the ThunderClan patrol clambered out, shaking water from their paws, he recognized their distinctive smells. Ashfur and Lionpaw were with Birchfall, Spiderleg, and Mousepaw.

Lionpaw bounded down onto the shore. "Hi, Jaypaw."

"Good morning for hunting," Jaypaw replied, flicking his brother's pelt with his tail.

"Mmm."

Jaypaw stiffened, curious. Lionpaw was distracted, his mind not entirely on the hunt.

"What are you doing down there, Jaypaw?" Birchfall called from the bank.

"I'm helping Leafpool collect herbs," Jaypaw told him, nodding toward Leafpool, who was farther down the shore scuffling among the mallow stems.

"What's she doing?" Lionpaw asked.

"Digging up mallow," Jaypaw told him. "Can you see any more of it about?"

"There's a clump of it by an old stick over there." Lionpaw nudged his brother in the right direction. "Look out though, there are lots of twigs and lumps of wood washed up on the shore. Don't trip."

"Come on," Ashfur called impatiently. "Let's get back to the hunt!"

"Can you manage?" Lionpaw wound around Jaypaw.

"Of course!"

"Okay. See you later." Lionpaw bounded away, making the pebbles clatter.

Jaypaw listened to the patrol disappear back into the trees, envying his brother a little. In this weather, hunting would be way more fun than gathering leaves. He turned with a sigh toward the patch of mallow Lionpaw had spotted. He could smell it now, its sweet rose scent warmed by the sun. Carefully, he picked his way over the shore, avoiding the rubbish left washed up by the floodwater. He stretched out his nose, touching a mallow leaf and sniffing deeply.

His front paw bumped into something hard. Was this the stick Lionpaw had mentioned? He leaned down to sniff it and felt it smooth on his nose. The bark had been stripped away, the wood beneath it bone-dry. It could not have been in the water long, or it still would be sodden despite the newleaf sunshine. Jaypaw ran his paw over it. The exposed wood felt sleek beneath his pad.

He could feel something odd, too: scars scratched across the branch, too neat and regular to be natural. Some of them were crossed by other lines, like two paths going in different directions.

"What's that?" Leafpool's voice close behind him made him jump. He had been so absorbed that he hadn't heard her approach.

"A stick." With an effort, he rolled it from beneath the mallow plant where it had lodged. "Look at the lines."

She sniffed it. "No scent," she commented. "From by the lake, I expect."

"But the lines feel strange," Jaypaw prompted. "They're too even."

"You're right," Leafpool agreed. "I wonder what made them? A fox, maybe a badger?"

"They're too fine to be badger or fox marks."

"Perhaps it's some Twoleg thing," Leafpool suggested. She flicked her tail. "Come on. I'll dig up some roots from this plant to add to the others I've collected."

Jaypaw could smell the fishy stench of lake mud on her paws.

"You start stripping off some leaves," Leafpool went on. "If we're lucky, they'll dry before the next rain."

Why wasn't she more interested in the stick? They had never come across anything like this before. Reluctantly, Jaypaw slid his paws from the branch. His pads felt warm where they had been touching it. He stripped a pawful of leaves from the mallow plant while Leafpool dug around a root and plucked it from the waterlogged earth with her teeth.

"Let's get this stuff back to camp," she meowed. "I left the other roots over there." She bounded away and Jaypaw picked the leaves up with his teeth and began to head up the beach.

He paused. *What about the stick?* He couldn't leave it lying where it was. It might get washed away. He dropped the mallow leaves, turned back, and began to roll the stick up away from the waterline with his paws.

"We can't carry that home as well," Leafpool meowed,

returning to his side. The roots she was holding in her teeth muffled her mew.

"But we can leave it somewhere safe." *I want to come back and look at it again.*

"Okay, but hurry. I want to lay the leaves out while the sun's still warm."

Jaypaw tugged at the stick, rolling it over the pebbles and heaving it past the lumps of wood and rubbish that cluttered the shore. At last, panting, he felt grass brush his pelt. He had reached the bank that edged the stream. He felt around until he found a gap behind a twisted root and shoved the stick into it, hoping it would hold fast if the water rose more. A spark of anxiety flickered in his chest at the thought of losing the stick to the lake.

"Come on." Leafpool sounded impatient.

Jaypaw darted back to pick up the leaves he had dropped and followed her into the trees. His paws felt heavy and unease fluttered in his chest. Leaving the stick felt wrong. He wanted to understand why.

I'll be back, he promised.

CHAPTER 5

♣

Lionpaw stiffened when he saw Hollypaw's eyes flash in the darkness, even though they had closed by the time he reached his nest. Hollypaw had been watching for him to slip back into the apprentices' den.

"It's okay," he hissed into her ear. "I only went to make dirt." He flexed his claws. Why did he have to explain every movement to her? She rolled over without replying. He curled down into his nest, his back to Hollypaw.

Outside the moon was high, the sky clear, the wind warm. He longed to sneak out of camp and meet Heatherpaw. *She* didn't watch him with that narrowed gaze like she was waiting to prove he was a traitor to his Clan. *She* knew they were just playing, not swapping Clan secrets. Lionpaw closed his eyes, anger like a hard knot in his belly, and buried himself in sleep. He began to dream.

Hollypaw blinked at him. Her eyes shone from the darkness of a burrow. They were full of warmth and excitement as they had been when they played as kits. Lionpaw crept closer to the entrance. What was she doing in there?

"Hollypaw?"

"I'm going to get you," she mewed teasingly.

So that was it.

A game.

Lionpaw crouched and crept closer. Hollypaw twitched her whiskers mischievously, her amber eyes glittering in the darkness.

Lionpaw's blood turned to ice.

Amber? Hollypaw's eyes were green!

Lionpaw stepped backward. The eyes had lost their playful glint. They fixed him with a vicious stare. This wasn't Hollypaw. A growl sounded from the burrow. Fox! Lionpaw tried to run but his paws seemed to have turned to stone. Snarling, the creature shot out at him, teeth bared and red with blood.

Lionpaw woke and leaped to his feet. Pale light filtered through the branches of the den, speckling the sleeping cats.

Hollypaw's head shot up. "Are you okay?"

"Just a nightmare," Lionpaw panted.

Hollypaw leaned toward him. "What about?"

"A fox," Lionpaw breathed.

"There are no foxes in here." Cinderpaw padded from her nest and blinked encouragingly at him.

Lionpaw bristled. Wasn't anywhere safe from this prying pair? He barged past them. "I'm going to get some food," he mewed, stalking out of the den.

Brambleclaw was watching the camp from Highledge. Firestar must be on patrol, Lionpaw guessed. Jaypaw was washing himself beside the halfrock that jutted from the earth on the farside of the clearing. He paused as Lionpaw crossed the camp.

"Are you okay?" Jaypaw tipped his head to one side.

"I had a nightmare, that's all," Lionpaw grumbled. He padded to the fresh-kill pile, picked up a small, stiff mouse and carried it back to Jaypaw.

They shared it in silence. At least Jaypaw didn't seem to want to poke his nose into everything Lionpaw had done in the last moon.

"Lionpaw!" Ashfur padded out of the warriors' den. "We're training with Brackenfur and Hollypaw in the hollow this morning."

Oh, great! Can't I ever get away from her?

The thorn barrier trembled as an early hunting patrol raced into camp. Firestar and Sandstorm were both holding prey in their jaws. Spiderleg and Mousepaw each carried a mouse, and Whitewing gripped a plump thrush between her teeth.

"Is everything all right?" Brambleclaw called down.

Firestar dropped his prey on the fresh-kill pile. "All quiet and as you can see, the prey is running."

Berrypaw was already at the fresh-kill pile, sniffing the thrush Whitewing had dropped. He picked it up and carried it to the nursery.

"Hi, Jaypaw." Hollypaw was bounding across the clearing with Cinderpaw. "Any food left?"

"You can eat later, Hollypaw!" Brackenfur was pacing up and down in front of the camp entrance. "Training first."

Lionpaw gulped down the last of his mouse, feeling a twinge of satisfaction. Hollypaw had probably been gossiping about him. *Serves her right if it means she goes hungry.* He got to his paws and hurried toward Brackenfur. Ashfur bounded across the clearing to join them.

"I'm starving!" Hollypaw complained, catching up.

"We'll hunt after battle training," Brackenfur promised.

The golden warrior darted through the tunnel. Lionpaw fell in beside Ashfur, leaving Hollypaw to hurry after them. They padded to the training hollow in silence. Sun was slanting through the bright green leaves, and the air trembled with birdsong. Lionpaw saw Hollypaw lick her lips.

Ashfur sat down in the center of the hollow, his tail whisking over the mossy ground. "Today, we're going to be thinking about how other Clans fight—their strengths and weaknesses, and the best way to exploit them."

"So, what strengths do the other Clans have?" Brackenfur prompted.

"RiverClan can swim," Hollypaw mewed, "which means they can approach from water."

"WindClan is well camouflaged and small, so they are hardest to detect," Lionpaw offered.

"Unless they're upwind," Hollypaw pointed out, "in which case their rabbity scent gives them away."

Lionpaw bristled with indignation. Heatherpaw didn't smell rabbity.

"What about ShadowClan?" Ashfur asked.

"Well, they are just evil," Hollypaw growled, "so you never

know how low they'll stoop in any attack. That makes them unpredictable."

"And weaknesses?" Brackenfur pressed.

"ShadowClan is weak because they think they are braver than they actually are," Hollypaw mewed. "And RiverClan is so well fed that they're slower than us."

Lionpaw shifted on his paws, searching for something to say. Hollypaw was answering everything first.

Ashfur glanced at him. "What about WindClan?"

Lionpaw's mouth turned dry. Ashfur's gaze seemed to be boring into him. Had Hollypaw told her mentor about his meetings with Heatherpaw? Lionpaw started to panic as he realized that all three cats were staring at him, waiting for his answer. His paws began to itch. *Come on! I know this!*

Hollypaw rolled her eyes. "Lionpaw thinks WindClan has no weaknesses." Her accusation made his ears burn with embarrassment. Why was she being so obvious? Was she reminding him she had the power to get him into big trouble?

Anger rose in his throat. "That's not true!" he hissed.

"What's not true?" Brambleclaw came padding down the slope toward them, Berrypaw at his side.

Lionpaw lifted his chin. "Hollypaw's accusing me of favoring WindClan!"

"Why would she do that?"

"I was just teasing," Hollypaw mewed. "Lionpaw's being touchy. He had a nightmare."

Lionpaw lashed his tail. Was Hollypaw determined to make him look like an idiot? He'd show her! "WindClan is fast, but not as strong as us because they don't have any trees to climb on the moorland," he growled, glaring at her.

"Good." Brackenfur nodded. "You seem to know the basics. Let's practice some moves. First, let's try one that will work on a RiverClan cat."

Brackenfur darted under Ashfur's belly and nipped him on his hind leg. Ashfur rounded on him ready for the counter-attack, but Brackenfur had already shot out of reach. Ashfur leaped toward him but Brackenfur rolled out of the way, sprang to his paws and launched himself onto Ashfur's back, unbalancing the gray warrior and sending him rolling onto his side. The two warriors jumped to their paws, shook the earth from their pelts, and turned to face their apprentices.

"Now you two try it," Ashfur meowed.

"Lionpaw." Brackenfur touched Lionpaw's flank with his tail. "You be the RiverClan cat because you're bigger and more powerful. Hollypaw, you try and unbalance him like I did with Ashfur."

Hollypaw nodded. "Don't make it easy for me!" Her eyes were shining with determination.

"Don't worry, I won't," Lionpaw hissed through gritted teeth. Didn't she know how much she was annoying him?

He felt her dart underneath him, felt her teeth graze his hind leg. But he wasn't going to let her get away as easily as Ashfur had done. He dropped his whole weight onto her before she could scamper free, then grasped her with his paws and tugged her over onto her side.

"Hey!" she squealed. "That's not how you're meant to do it!"

"You should have been faster!" Lionpaw spat, and began raking her spine with his hind claws while he gripped her shoulders with his forepaws.

"You're hurting me!" Hollypaw shrieked, struggling to free herself.

"Lionpaw, stop!" Brambleclaw's sharp command made Lionpaw freeze. Hollypaw slid from his grip and scrambled to her paws. Brambleclaw was staring down at Lionpaw, his eyes blazing. "This is training! We don't want any cat hurt!"

Lionpaw got to his paws. "Sorry," he mewed. "I got carried away."

Hollypaw was lapping at the scratches Lionpaw had given her. He felt a wave of guilt for letting his temper get away from him. He hung his head. "Sorry, Hollypaw," he murmured. The rage that had been seething in his belly all morning faded away. "I'm really sorry." He glanced nervously at his father, expecting anger, but Brambleclaw's eyes were filled with concern.

"Will you two train Berrypaw and Hollypaw this morning?" The ThunderClan deputy directed his request at Ashfur and Brackenfur. "I'm going to take Lionpaw hunting."

His pelt burning with shame, Lionpaw followed his father out of the training hollow. He braced himself for a lecture, but Brambleclaw only padded silently through the trees.

"I shouldn't have let my temper get the better of me," Lionpaw blurted out, deciding to get straight to the point. "But she's been bugging me all morning."

Still Brambleclaw said nothing.

"I know that's no excuse," Lionpaw went on. "It won't ever happen again."

"I know," Brambleclaw meowed. He stopped and gazed at Lionpaw. "It's so unlike you." The tabby warrior sighed. "I've always relied on you to take care of your littermates."

Lionpaw hung his head. He had let his father down.

"Is something worrying you?" Brambleclaw asked. "Something . . . " The tabby warrior paused. " . . . *troubling* you?" he meowed at last.

Lionpaw knew he couldn't tell his father about Heatherpaw and how Hollypaw had stopped him from meeting her. "It's just . . . " He trailed off. How could he explain his anger? "It feels like Hollypaw doesn't trust me to be a loyal warrior."

Brambleclaw nodded. "I know what that's like." He began padding through the trees again. Puzzled, Lionpaw hurried after him.

"Being Tigerstar's son has meant I've had to win the trust of every ThunderClan cat over and over," Brambleclaw went on quietly. "So I know how frustrating it is when you have to prove something that shouldn't need proving."

The leafy forest floor sloped upward before them and they sank their claws into the sweet-smelling earth to help them climb.

"The trouble is that everyone only saw evil in Tigerstar. They forgot what a bold and brilliant warrior he was."

Lionpaw pricked his ears. Was Brambleclaw *defending* Tigerstar?

"I haven't forgotten how Tigerstar betrayed his Clan,"

Brambleclaw meowed, as if he had noticed Lionpaw's surprise. "But we all have strengths and weaknesses. It must be sad to be remembered only for your weaknesses. I hope I'll be remembered for my strengths instead."

"Of course you will be," Lionpaw mewed. His fur prickled at the thought of his father being nothing but a memory. "Every cat in the Clan respects you."

"I wish that were true."

"What do you mean?"

"I think there may be one Clanmate who wishes me harm." The words came in a whisper.

Lionpaw's heart lurched. "Who?"

Brambleclaw shook his head. "It's not important. Forget I said anything."

"But if there's some cat you don't trust—"

Brambleclaw cut him off. "If you want to be remembered for your strengths, you must work on them. And if that means proving yourself to those who doubt you, then do it. You can't force Hollypaw to believe in you. You have to show her that you are worth believing in."

Lionpaw felt weariness weighting his paws. Why should he have to prove himself to Hollypaw? *I haven't done anything wrong!*

Crack!

A stone clattered against the wall of the camp and thumped onto the ground outside the apprentices' den.

Lionpaw lifted his head and blinked in the darkness. Was

a rabbit foraging near the top of the hollow?

Crack!

Couldn't be a rabbit. The first clatter would have sent it fleeing into the forest.

Curious, Lionpaw got quietly to his paws. He glanced at Hollypaw. She was sound asleep. *Thank you, Brackenfur!* Hollypaw's mentor had taken her hunting deep into the forest. She had come back exhausted, her paws sore, but happily carrying three mice.

Lionpaw slipped past her nest and ducked out of the den.

Crack!

Thump!

A pebble landed near his paws. He skittered backward and looked up cautiously. Two round eyes shone at him from the top of the cliff, then blinked.

Someone was spying on the camp! Should he tell someone? He glanced around the empty moonlit clearing. No cat stirred. He didn't want to wake anyone until he was sure there was danger. He would look foolish if he called the alarm because some inquisitive fawn had discovered the hollow. He would investigate first and call the alarm if there really was any danger.

Whitewing's pelt glowed at the camp entrance. She must be on guard. If there was trouble he could call to her.

Lionpaw slipped around the edge of the clearing and pushed his way among the brambles beside the medicine den. He knew he could climb the cliff behind them. Reaching up through the prickly branches he felt the first ledge with his paws and hauled himself up. Then, moving carefully so as not to send grit showering down, he scrabbled up from ledge to ledge until finally he pulled himself onto the grass at the top. Panting a little, he began to creep around the edge of the hollow.

"Lionpaw!" A soft mew hissed from beneath the ferns ahead. He froze as Heatherpaw slipped out from beneath the arching fronds. "Thank StarClan it's you."

"Did you drop those pebbles?" Lionpaw stared at her in alarm. What if she were caught here? "Is everything okay?"

"I had to see you!"

He felt a glow inside his chest. She was even braver than he thought. But he had to get her away from the camp. "Follow me," he hissed. He hared off lakeward down the slope. But Heatherpaw didn't follow.

"Come *on*!" Lionpaw begged, skidding around and looking back.

Her eyes were shining. "Don't go that way! I've got something to show you!" She turned and ducked away under the ferns.

Lionpaw hurried after her. "Where are we going?"

"Wait and see!"

She seemed to be heading toward the old fox den. Lionpaw slowed down. "Be careful!" he warned.

"It's okay," she told him. "There aren't any foxes." She paused in front of the thick brambles that crowded the bottom of a steep slope. "Wait here."

She dived beneath them, and Lionpaw watched her tail

disappear into the dense foliage, making the bushes tremble. Where was she going? An owl called in the branches above his head. Lionpaw fluffed out his fur and glanced around nervously.

"Here!"

Lionpaw looked up the steep slope and saw Heatherpaw blinking at him from the entrance to a small tunnel. "What are you doing in there?" It looked like a rabbit burrow.

"You'll never believe what's inside! Come on!" Heatherpaw scooted backward into the darkness.

Paws pricking, Lionpaw squirmed under the brambles, wincing as their barbs tugged his fur. He heaved himself up the slope, out of the thorny tangle, and paused at the burrow entrance. "Heatherpaw?" he called, his heart pounding.

"Come inside!" Her mew echoed strangely from the shadows.

Lionpaw squeezed in after her.

The tunnel was pitch-black. Crouching, he wriggled forward, damp earth pressing against his pelt. What was Heatherpaw up to? This place was hardly big enough for a rabbit, let alone a cat. Suddenly, he felt space around him, cold air washing over his fur. The tunnel had widened. Relieved, he straightened up and padded forward until he felt Heatherpaw's breath on his cheek.

"It leads to a cave!" she mewed. "There are loads of tunnels under this part of the hill, and one of them leads right to WindClan territory."

"How in StarClan's name did you find it?"

"Breezepaw sent me to catch mice between the rocks just over the top of the moor, not far from camp. I chased one down into a crack and realized that the crack opened into a tunnel. When I went inside I found that there were tunnels leading everywhere."

"Weren't you frightened of getting lost?"

"I explored slowly at first, making sure I got to know each route really well before trying another. And then I found one that led to a cave. It's amazing. There's a hole in the roof where the light comes in. Then I found a way into your territory!" Her mew was triumphant. "Isn't it wonderful?"

Lionpaw could hardly believe his ears. "A tunnel from our territory to yours!" he gasped. "That's fantastic! If there was an attack or a fire, ThunderClan could use it to escape—"

"No!" Heatherpaw's mew was sharp with frustration. "We mustn't tell anyone else. Don't you see? This can be *our* place!"

"Our place?"

"We can meet here without anyone ever finding us! Even Hollypaw won't guess where you're going."

Lionpaw's whiskers twitched. Now he could meet Heatherpaw as much as he liked and no one would ever know! "That's a great idea! You're brilliant, Heatherpaw."

She purred and rubbed her muzzle quickly along Lionpaw's cheek, then turned away. "Follow me. I'll show you the cave."

Her paw steps disappeared into the darkness. Fear surged in Lionpaw's belly. He fought the urge to rush back out into the forest, and began to follow Heatherpaw. The blackness pressed in on him and suddenly he realized how Jaypaw must feel. He sniffed, searching for scents of fox, or rabbit or even badger, but smelled only damp earth. It was stale and musty as though no creature had walked here for moons.

"How come no one else uses this place?" he wondered.

"I guess no one's been lucky enough to find it." Heatherpaw's mew echoed eerily up ahead.

"Someone must have discovered it before."

"I've never smelled anything here except rock and water."

Uneasiness tugged at Lionpaw's pelt. "But it seems unlikely that we're the first—" Suddenly, the tunnel brightened and opened into a large cave. Lionpaw stopped dead and stared around in astonishment. The rocky walls were lit by moonlight filtering through a small hole in the roof, just like Heatherpaw had said. The floor was smooth, dusty stone, rippled here and there as if giant paw prints had left their shape. And most amazing of all, a river wound across the floor and flowed away into a low, broad tunnel, disappearing into shadow.

A river underground? How could that be?

"Isn't it brilliant?" Heatherpaw leaped up onto a rocky ledge. "It'll be like our own camp! We could be DarkClan. I'll be the leader and you can be my deputy!"

"Deputy? What if I wanted to be leader?" Lionpaw objected, scrabbling past her onto a higher ledge.

"I found the place, so I'm leader!" Heatherpaw jumped at him and knocked him off his perch.

Purring, Lionpaw landed lightly on the floor of the cave. "Okay, Heather*star*," he mewed. "What's the plan?"

"Lionpaw, wake up!"

Lionpaw felt a soft paw nudging him in the ribs. He jerked his head up, surprised to find rock walls surrounding him. Then he remembered. He was in the cave. Heatherpaw was sitting beside him, her eyes bleary with sleep.

"Look!" She jerked her head toward the gap in the roof. "We dozed off." The sky outside was pale with early morning light.

Lionpaw leaped to his paws. "I must go home!" He stared anxiously at the many tunnels opening around the walls of the cave. "Which one leads to ThunderClan?"

Heatherpaw padded to a narrow tunnel near the river's edge. "This way." She flicked her tail toward a wider tunnel in the facing wall. "I head up there." Her eyes glittered. "Will you come again tonight?"

"Yes." Lionpaw could hardly wait. "If I can get away."

Heatherpaw's farewell echoed behind him as he hurried away down the tunnel. His denmates must have noticed he wasn't in his nest. How would he explain it this time? Hollypaw was bound to be suspicious. He had to come up with a reason to be out of the camp this early or there was no chance he would be able to meet Heatherpaw that night.

The tunnel grew narrower around him and something brushed his pelt. It must be the walls closing in. Had Heatherpaw remembered the right route? Panic started to rise in his chest. What if he couldn't find his way out again? Something else brushed his pelt. It didn't feel like earth. It felt softer, like the pelts of cats pressing against his. Alarm shot through him. He began to run, hurtling into the blackness, fear crushing the breath from him.

Light glowed up ahead. Desperation and relief made his legs weak as he shot out of the hole. Dawn light flooded his eyes, making him blink as he glanced furtively around. No sign of any patrols. Ducking down, he scrabbled under the brambles and began to run for home.

I can't go back empty-pawed! The thought brought him sliding to a halt.

A sparrow flitted overhead. *No one can complain if I feed my Clan.* Lionpaw dropped into a hunting crouch. Still as a rock, he watched the sparrow flutter to the ground and waited as it hopped closer, fighting the urge to spring until it was within reach. The leaves rustled as it bobbed nearer. Lionpaw kneaded the ground with his hind paws. One more hop . . .

Got you! Springing forward quick as a snake, Lionpaw killed the bird with one swipe. He picked up the limp body in his teeth and bounded toward the camp.

"Hello, Lionpaw." Whitewing was still guarding the entrance. "I didn't see you go out."

Lionpaw's mew was muffled by his mouthful of feathers. "I went through the dirtplace tunnel." His tail pricked at the lie, but he had no choice.

"Looks like someone's going to have a nice early breakfast," Whitewing commented.

"Mmmm." Lionpaw nodded, whisking past her into the camp.

Hollypaw was lying beside the halfrock with Jaypaw. She looked up as Lionpaw entered the camp. Flicking his tail at her, he dropped his catch on the pile.

"You must have been up early," Jaypaw mewed as he clambered onto the smooth halfrock and began to wash.

"The birds make so much noise, I'm surprised you can sleep through them," Lionpaw replied, thinking fast.

Hollypaw narrowed her eyes. "After the hunt Brackenfur took me on yesterday, I'd have slept through anything."

Lionpaw wiped a paw over one ear. Inside, his stomach was a hard knot. He hated lying. He wasn't doing any harm by playing with Heatherpaw. But he knew his Clanmates wouldn't see it like that.

I'm loyal to my Clan, Lionpaw told himself. *I shouldn't have to prove it.*

But still, the bitter taste of his lie stung in his throat.

CHAPTER 6

Hollypaw yawned and stretched in the den entrance. The early morning sun felt warm on her paws. She looked over her shoulder. Lionpaw was still asleep in his nest.

Cinderpaw was already at the fresh-kill pile.

"Anything there?" Hollypaw called to her friend.

"Only a mouse." Cinderpaw pawed it uncertainly. "A bit stale, but not too bad."

Hollypaw padded toward her. "Perhaps we should see if Daisy wants it for the kits first."

"No, thank you!" Daisy was sunning herself outside the nursery while Ferncloud's kits tumbled around her. "They can wait for the dawn patrol to return and have something warm and fresh."

"I don't mind eating a stale mouse!" Foxkit offered.

"No," Daisy mewed, "you've got a cold. Only warm food for you."

"But I'm hungry!"

"Greedy, more like!" Icekit teased. The fluffy white kit cuffed her brother around his ear. He turned on her at once and pounced. She squealed and pummeled him with her hind legs.

Daisy moved her tail out of the way as they rolled past her. "It'll be a relief when they move into the apprentices' den," she mewed. Hollypaw knew that she didn't mean it. Ferncloud would move back to the warriors' den, and Daisy would be alone in the empty nursery. She'd always made it clear she wasn't cut out to be a warrior but, without kits to nurse, what would she be? Hopefully the spring would bring a new litter.

"Hollypaw! Cinderpaw!" Leafpool was looking out from the elders' den. "Come and clean out the bedding in here."

"Okay!" Cinderpaw bounded over to her, abandoning the mouse.

"I'll get fresh moss!" Hollypaw knew that Leafpool kept a fresh stock beside the medicine den. She raced to grab a wad of it, then carried it to the elders' den.

The honeysuckle that trailed over the elder bush where Longtail and Mousefur slept was bright with new leaf. Fresh tendrils swayed in the light breeze. Buds were forming that would flower come greenleaf and fill the hollow with a wonderful smell. Hollypaw ducked inside and dropped the moss. Cinderpaw was already busy scrabbling through the bedding, bundling out stale bits.

Leafpool looked up from where she was crouched at Longtail's side. "Longtail has an infected tick bite." The tangy aroma of herbs filled the den. "I'm putting a poultice on it, but I want the bedding freshened up so he doesn't get another one."

"Okay." Hollypaw nodded.

Mousefur sat up stiffly. "Good to see newleaf again."

Longtail winced as Leafpool washed more herbs into his wound. "The forest smells good," he meowed. "I've been thinking about going out."

Hollypaw blinked in surprise. Since he had lost his sight, Longtail rarely left camp.

"Only if I can come with you," Mousefur croaked. "You'll need someone to keep an eye out for foxes."

"Foxes!" Hollypaw tucked her tail close to her.

Cinderpaw tossed a wad of moss toward the entrance. "Foxes aren't that bad."

"Aren't that bad?" Hollypaw gasped. "What about the ones that chased me? They almost had my tail!"

"You were only a kit," Cinderpaw pointed out. "They wouldn't seem so scary if you met them now."

Hollypaw wasn't convinced.

"Foxes are just a nuisance," Cinderpaw went on. "It's badgers you have to watch out for." The gray tabby's eyes grew wide. "*They* are terrifying." The fur along her spine rippled. "I hope I never meet another one as long as I live."

"*Another* badger?" Hollypaw sat up. "You've never even met one."

Cinderpaw tipped her head to one side. Confusion clouded her gaze. "You're right." She reached out and tugged some stale moss from beside Mousefur. "I must have dreamed it."

Cinderpaw could be so mouse-brained!

As Hollypaw began to reach for fresh moss, she noticed Leafpool staring at Cinderpaw. The medicine cat's mouth was open as though frozen mid-lick. What had surprised her so much? It wasn't the first time Cinderpaw had been muddled.

Longtail started to fidget. "Have you finished, Leafpool?"

"No." Leafpool bent her head quickly. "Hold still, I'm nearly done."

Firestar's call sounded from outside the den. "Let all cats old enough to catch their own prey gather here beneath the Highledge."

"A Clan meeting?" Mousefur narrowed her eyes. "I hope everything's okay." She got slowly to her paws. Hollypaw glanced at Cinderpaw, excitement fluttering in her chest. Had something happened? She darted out of the den ahead of the others and saw Firestar leaping down the tumble of rocks from Highledge.

The fresh-kill pile was well stocked. "The dawn patrol's back," Hollypaw whispered to Cinderpaw as her friend caught up. "Perhaps they've brought news."

Stormfur and Brook settled at the edge of the clearing. Graystripe and Millie padded out from behind the warriors' den. Brambleclaw and Squirrelflight sat down in the shadow of Highledge while Lionpaw padded after Ashfur and settled beside his mentor. Daisy stayed by the nursery, whisking Icekit and Foxkit back with her tail as they tried to see what was happening.

Once the Clan had settled, Firestar sat down in the center of the clearing. He gazed around, his eyes shining.

"Doesn't look like anything bad," Hollypaw murmured to Cinderpaw.

"There is something I've wanted to do for a while," Firestar began. "And now that newleaf is here it seems like a good time for new beginnings."

Hollypaw leaned forward excitedly.

"It is time Millie became a ThunderClan warrior!"

Hollypaw froze. Millie had been a kittypet when Graystripe had met her. He'd given her some warrior training and she'd helped him on the long journey back to his Clan. But did that make her a warrior? Hollypaw didn't even know if Millie believed in StarClan.

Mews of approval rippled around the edge of the clearing.

"About time!" Whitewing called.

Birchfall kneaded the ground. "She has the heart of a warrior!"

Hollypaw stared at them in surprise. Surely it wasn't that simple? The daylight Gathering had helped to smooth the ruffled fur of the other Clans, but making a kittypet a warrior? Wouldn't that stir up hostility again? Millie was a good hunter and had proved her bravery and loyalty in battle, but to make her a ThunderClan warrior . . .

"Millie." Firestar beckoned the striped gray tabby.

She stepped forward, chin high. Hollypaw couldn't help admiring her. And yet she had never trained as an apprentice. How could she possibly have a warrior name? Hollypaw felt her chest tighten with anxiety.

"You have fought bravely in battle," Firestar meowed. "You have made sure the Clan has been fed through a bitter leafbare. No cat here doubts your loyalty or your skill. You have earned the warrior name I give you." He paused for a moment. "From this day on you shall be known as—"

"Wait!"

Mews of surprise rippled among the Clan as Millie interrupted Firestar.

She gazed steadily around the cats, her blue eyes glowing. "I'm privileged to be considered a ThunderClan warrior," she meowed. "I could ask for no greater honor. And I am grateful to Graystripe for rescuing me from my life as a kittypet." She blinked warmly at her mate. "If I'd stayed my whole life as a Twoleg companion, it would have been only half a life. But—"

Graystripe stepped forward. "Millie?" His eyes were clouded with anxiety. "You're not going to leave, are you?"

"Never." Millie padded toward him and brushed her muzzle against his. Then she turned back to Firestar. "You can rely on my loyalty until the day I join StarClan, and you must believe that I will live and die to protect ThunderClan. But I don't want to change my name. I have always been Millie, and I see no shame in it."

A shocked silence gripped the Clan. Ashfur flicked his tail. Sandstorm narrowed her eyes, studying the former kittypet. Brambleclaw's whiskers twitched.

Graystripe lifted his chin. "Millie is right. It doesn't matter what she's called. It only matters how she acts, and I know that she will always put the Clan first."

Hollypaw watched Firestar, wondering what he would do. The ThunderClan leader shifted his paws uneasily, glancing from Graystripe to Millie.

Suddenly, another mew sounded. "May I speak?"

Hollypaw spun around. Daisy was padding forward. The cream-colored queen slid between Spiderleg and Birchfall and stepped into the center of the clearing. Hollypaw pricked her ears. Daisy had never spoken at a Clan meeting before.

"I am glad Millie has chosen to keep her name," the she-cat began. Her soft mew trembled a little. "I am no warrior, but I am a ThunderClan cat. I stay in the nursery rather than hunt and fight because that is what I do best. I care for our young as though each kit were my own. This is my gift to the Clan, but I do it in my own chosen name."

"She is right!" Brook stepped forward. "My loyalty lies with ThunderClan, but I would never give up the name given to me by the Tribe."

Stormfur padded forward and ran his tail along his mate's flank. "Is there any cat here who would not trust Millie or Daisy or Brook to fight on their side?" He stared challengingly around the Clan.

"No!" Graystripe led the call and Brambleclaw, Cloudtail, Whitewing, and the others quickly took it up. Daisy's kits, Berrypaw, Hazelpaw, and Mousepaw cheered loudest of all.

Hollypaw watched uneasily.

Suddenly, Thornclaw's mew rose above the others. "Stop! What would the other Clans say if they could see us now?"

Dustpelt nodded. "ShadowClan has already tried to take territory from us because we are no longer a pure forest-born Clan."

Spiderleg narrowed his eyes. "Naming ceremonies are part of the warrior code. Can we ignore them and still keep the respect of the other Clans?"

Hollypaw swept her tail over the ground. Dustpelt and Spiderleg were right. Millie, Daisy, and Brook were important to the Clan, but unless they accepted all the customs of the Clan, how could they truly be part of it?

Firestar's eyes flashed. "Silence!" he snapped. "Don't forget you're talking about your Clanmates! I invited Daisy, Brook, and Millie to join ThunderClan because they make us stronger." He glared around the clearing. "You are happy to eat their fresh-kill and to have them fight beside you. Do you want me to throw them out because they have the wrong names? Do you want the other Clans to tell us what to do?"

"Of course not!" Graystripe meowed.

"Millie and Brook *are* warriors already," Brambleclaw put in. "Names make no difference."

That's not true! Hollypaw dug her claws into the earth. They had not had proper naming ceremonies; the Clan was ignoring a ritual that had been followed for countless moons. What would StarClan think? *We must live by the warrior code!* She stared at Thornclaw, willing him to speak, but he only dipped his head to their leader.

Firestar blinked at him and turned once more to Millie. "You may keep your name. We have seen your courage in battle and your skill at hunting. You are ThunderClan now. May StarClan recognize you as a true warrior."

"ThunderClan! ThunderClan!" Birchfall began the

chant and the others quickly joined in. Hollypaw watched in silence, noticing Dustpelt and Thornclaw exchange anxious glances.

"Don't you feel like cheering?" Squirrelflight had weaved her way to Hollypaw's side.

Hollypaw's whiskers quivered. "What if StarClan doesn't recognize her as a true warrior?"

"Do you really think StarClan is narrow-minded?" Squirrelflight murmured.

"We have the warrior code for a reason and this goes against it." Hollypaw's fur rippled along her spine. "Brambleclaw should have spoken out. He knows how important it is to follow the code."

Squirrelflight smoothed Hollypaw's fur with her tail. "Brambleclaw is Clan deputy. He must support Firestar." Her green eyes glittered. "And don't forget that Firestar was a kittypet once."

"But he still took a warrior name!" Hollypaw mewed hotly. "He followed the warrior path and trained as an apprentice." The cheers were dying away as the cats began to return to their duties. *He never tried to change the warrior code!*

"Hollypaw!"

Brackenfur's mew jerked her from her thoughts. He was standing beside Cloudtail and Spiderleg. Their apprentices, Cinderpaw and Mousepaw, were pacing back and forth.

"It's time we assessed your progress," Brackenfur told her. "I want you, Cinderpaw, and Mousepaw to go hunting. Catch as much prey as you can."

Squirrelflight's eyes glowed. "An assessment already?"

Hollypaw forgot her unease, excitement pulsing through her pelt. At last she would have a chance to show everything she had learned.

Brackenfur flicked his tail. "Don't forget I'll be watching, out of sight."

"Good luck!" As Squirrelflight padded away, nerves fluttered in Hollypaw's belly. What if she let Brackenfur down? *No!* She wouldn't let that happen.

Mousepaw and Cinderpaw hurried to join her.

"I don't know who I want to impress more—Cloudtail or Brackenfur!" Cinderpaw glanced anxiously at the two warriors. Brackenfur was her father.

"I'm going to show Spiderleg that I really can catch a squirrel," Mousepaw vowed.

"You may as well start now." Cloudtail padded over. "You must each hunt alone. We'll be keeping an eye on you, so do your best."

"Of course we will!" Hollypaw promised.

Cinderpaw shot away, Mousepaw hurrying after her. Hollypaw caught up with them as they raced through the thorn tunnel, each pushing to be first out. Hollypaw had never hunted alone before. Her whiskers twitched with anticipation.

"Where are you going to hunt?" she asked as they burst out of the camp.

"I'm hunting by the stream near the ShadowClan border," Cinderpaw announced. "There's always prey there."

"It's a bit open, isn't it?" Hollypaw mewed.

"I'm good at jumping," Cinderpaw reminded her. "Even in the open, the prey won't see me coming till it's too late."

"I think I'll stick to the undergrowth," Hollypaw decided. "I prefer stalking my prey." She glanced at Mousepaw. "What about you?"

"I'm with you," he announced. "Undergrowth is easier. But once I've caught a couple of mice, I'm going to get a squirrel."

"Come on, then!" Cinderpaw charged up the slope away from the camp.

Hollypaw and Mousepaw sped after her, leaves fluttering in their wake. As they neared the stream, Cinderpaw veered away toward the bank. Hollypaw headed for a small dip where the ferns grew thickly, and Mousepaw bounded away in the other direction.

Hollypaw halted at the edge of the dip. Steadying her breath, she dropped into a hunting crouch and crept down the slope. She wound her way through the thick fern stems, careful not to set any of them rustling. *Is Brackenfur watching me already?* she wondered as she drew herself forward, one slow paw step at a time. *Don't think about that. Concentrate on the hunt.* She focused her senses on the foliage ahead, opening her mouth slightly to taste the breeze. Rabbit scent hung stale in the air, but the smell of mouse was fresh. *Good!* She halted and pricked her ears. The ferns were shivering up ahead. Narrowing her eyes she peered through the lush stalks and saw a small brown shape dart across over the leafy earth. A shrew! It began rooting among the leaf litter.

She crept closer.

The shrew stiffened.

Mouse dung! Her tail had brushed against a leaf.

The shrew glanced around.

Don't move! Hollypaw held her breath and pressed her tail to the ground.

The shrew began rummaging again.

Good! It's busy looking for food.

Moving as slowly as a snail, Hollypaw drew herself forward. The shrew went on rummaging. One more paw step!

A twig cracked beneath her paw. The shrew darted away. Hollypaw sprung and shot out her forepaws, catching the shrew in her claws before it had time to escape. One quick nip to the back of the neck and it was dead. Heart pounding, she carried it to the roots of a beech and buried it quickly before turning back for her next catch.

Before long she had caught another shrew and a mouse. As she safely buried the last of her catch beneath the beech, she saw golden fur flash among the brambles at the top of the slope. How long had Brackenfur been watching her? She hoped he was impressed.

Ferns rustled and Mousepaw exploded from the woods behind her.

"I've caught my two mice," the gray-and-white tom declared. "Now for that squirrel!"

"Shh!" Hollypaw snapped. "You'll scare the prey away!"

"Sorry." Mousepaw flicked his tail. "Are you still hunting?"

"I think I've got enough," Hollypaw conceded.

"Any sign of Cinderpaw?" Mousepaw asked. "I hope she's done okay."

"I've done fine!" Cinderpaw emerged from the ferns, four water voles dangling by their tails from her jaws. She dropped them next to Hollypaw. "Can I bury them with yours?"

"Won't they get mixed up?"

"Cloudtail already knows what I caught."

"Have you spoken to him?" Hollypaw was surprised. Mentors weren't meant to help in an assessment.

"Of course not," Cinderpaw assured her. "But I could see him watching the whole time. It's hard to hide in anything but snow with a pelt as white as his." She purred with amusement.

"Mousepaw's still determined to catch a squirrel," Hollypaw told her.

"Really?" Cinderpaw stared at the gray-and-white tom in surprise. "Didn't you get enough mice?"

"I got plenty," Mousepaw mewed indignantly. "I just want to show Spiderleg I can catch squirrels, too."

"There are usually some upstream," Hollypaw suggested.

"I think I'll climb the Sky Oak," Mousepaw announced.

"No way!" Cinderpaw looked amazed. "It's the tallest tree in the forest!"

"There'll be squirrels in other trees," Hollypaw cautioned. Mousepaw was Daisy's kit, born outside the Clan, and keen to impress his Clanmates. But surely after the latest Clan meeting, he shouldn't feel he had anything to prove.

"I'm going to climb the Sky Oak!" Mousepaw insisted. "I've been practicing and I want Spiderleg to see how good I am now."

"Wow," Cinderpaw breathed, "that's brave!"

"Come on." Mousepaw darted among the trees. Cinderpaw, kicking up leaves, scooted after him. Hollypaw glanced once more at the beech to make sure she would remember where she had buried her catch, and raced after them.

At the base of the Sky Oak, Hollypaw gazed up through the branches. The trunk seemed to stretch up forever, the blue sky glinting between the bright green leaves. Mousepaw was staring up too, and Hollypaw felt sure she saw his tail tremble.

"You're scared," Cinderpaw teased.

Hollypaw dug her claws into the earth. *Don't dare him into doing something he doesn't want to do.* "Why not just catch a few more mice instead?" she suggested. "There'll be plenty around here."

The fur along Mousepaw's spine was spiked like a hedgehog. "No. I'm going to catch a squirrel," he muttered determinedly. He sprang up and stretched out his forelegs to grip the wide trunk with his claws. Dragging himself upward, he managed to clamber onto the lowest branch. "There!" he called. "Easy." He looked up, searching for his next perch.

Hollypaw suddenly heard paws pounding toward them.

"Mousepaw!" Brackenfur hurtled out of the trees. He was panting and his eyes were wide with alarm. "Get down!"

Spiderleg skidded after him. "Leave him alone!" he

snapped at Brackenfur. "If he wants to do it, let him!"

Cloudtail padded out from the trees. "I thought we weren't meant to help—" He stopped when he spotted Mousepaw scrambling up to the next branch.

"I really think you should tell him to come down," Brackenfur advised.

"Are you saying my apprentice isn't good enough?" Spiderleg flattened his ears.

"He's still young," Brackenfur argued. "I wouldn't let Hollypaw climb it."

"Hollypaw's not been training as long as Mousepaw," Spiderleg pointed out.

"Look, it's easy!" Mousepaw called. The branches were close together now and he was leaping nimbly upward.

"Not too high," Spiderleg cautioned. Even he was beginning to look worried as Mousepaw hopped from branch to branch.

Leaves rustled just above him. A squirrel was scrambling up the tree.

"Look!" Cinderpaw called excitedly. "There's one!"

Mousepaw darted after it. Hollypaw's neck began to ache from looking up. She could see leaves shivering far above as the squirrel kept climbing, staying just a few tail-lengths ahead of Mousepaw, almost as if it were enticing him upward.

Be careful, Mousepaw!

Suddenly, the squirrel leaped out of the Sky Oak and landed in the tree next to it, sending twigs showering down.

Mousepaw froze.

He was so far away he looked the size of a mouse. But even from this distance, Hollypaw could see that his fur was bushed out from nose to tail-tip. The gray-and-white apprentice was terrified.

"Good try. You may as well come down," Spiderleg called encouragingly.

"I can't!" Mousepaw's mew came out as a squeak. "I'm stuck!"

Brackenfur sighed. "What are we going to do now?"

"I could go up after him," Cloudtail offered. Every cat knew he was one of the best climbers in the Clan.

"He's not going to get down by himself," Spiderleg agreed.

"I'll fetch him!" mewed Cinderpaw.

"Wait!" Hollypaw yelped as the gray apprentice began to scramble up the tree trunk.

"Get down at once!" Brackenfur hissed at his daughter.

Cinderpaw paused on the lowest branch. "But I can see an easy route to get him down," she argued.

Cloudtail exchanged worried glances with Brackenfur.

"I'll go slowly," Cinderpaw promised when they didn't say anything. "And if I feel like I'm getting too high, I'll stop."

Brackenfur nodded. "Okay, but be careful."

Cautiously, Cinderpaw began to climb the tree, taking her time between jumps, making sure that she only reached up a little at a time. Hollypaw watched, her mouth dry. *She'll be all right,* she told herself again and again.

She felt Brackenfur trembling beside her. He was watching Cinderpaw with round, frightened eyes.

"She's nearly reached him," Cloudtail reported.

Cinderpaw was only a few branches from her denmate now. Mousepaw was watching her, his fur slowly flattening.

"It's okay, Mousepaw," Cinderpaw called up to him. "There's nothing to be frightened of."

Hollypaw held her breath as Cinderpaw began to guide Mousepaw down, one branch at a time.

"That's it," Cinderpaw mewed. "The next branch is really close. Just make sure you grip with your claws and you'll be fine."

The two cats were easier to see now, getting closer and closer to safety with every uneasy jump.

They're going to make it!

Suddenly, a bird shrieked and flapped out of the tree just below them. Mousepaw squealed in shock and slipped from the branch.

Quick as a flash, Cinderpaw lunged forward and reached for him. She caught him and hauled him back onto the branch, her hind legs scrabbling for a hold. Mousepaw grabbed at the branch and clung to the bark, his tail lashing in panic.

Relief flooded Hollypaw.

Then she saw Cinderpaw wobble. The gray tabby's hind paws were slipping over the back of the branch. Her forepaws churned desperately at the air. With a yelp she slid over the edge and fell. Hollypaw stared in horror as Cinderpaw dropped through the leaves like a stone and landed with a sickening thud.

"No!" Brackenfur's mew cracked as he darted forward. "Cinderpaw? Cinderpaw!" He crouched over the limp body lying awkwardly on the ground.

"Get Leafpool!" Spiderleg hissed in Hollypaw's ear.

Hollypaw glanced once more at her friend's twisted body before hurtling away through the trees. *Cinderpaw can't be dead! She mustn't be dead!*

CHAPTER 7

❧

"Ow!" Birchfall snatched his paw away from Jaypaw.

Jaypaw sighed. "If I don't get the thorn out it's going to hurt a lot more!"

Tentatively, Birchfall held out his paw again. Jaypaw leaned down and grasped the fat end of the thorn between his teeth. "It's not that big," he muttered out of the side of his mouth.

"That's because most of it is buried in my paw!" Birchfall complained. "It's amazing I made it back to camp at all."

Jaypaw braced himself and gave a fierce tug.

"Ow!" Birchfall leaped away, then hopped noisily around the medicine den.

Jaypaw dropped the thorn, spitting to get rid of the taste of blood.

"I told you it was huge!" Birchfall meowed triumphantly.

Jaypaw touched it with his pad. The curved barb felt like a claw. "Not exactly deadly, though," he mewed.

Birchfall lapped at his wound. "You're not very sympathetic for a medicine cat."

"I'm here to *heal* you. If you want sympathy, go to the nursery." Jaypaw padded to the back of the den. *Warriors!* They might be brave in battle, but one thorn and they squealed like kits. He picked up a mouthful of marigold and began to chew the leaves into a pulp. A poultice would make sure Birchfall's paw didn't get infected.

Suddenly, he stiffened. Paws were pounding toward the camp. He tasted the air. Hollypaw's fear-scent hit the back of his throat.

"Here, wash this into the cut!" He dropped the pulp at Birchfall's paws and pushed through the trailing brambles that screened the den from the rest of the camp.

Hollypaw exploded into the camp. "Cinderpaw's fallen out of the Sky Oak!"

Jaypaw gasped. "I'll fetch Leafpool!" He pelted for the nursery where she was tending to Foxkit's cold.

But Leafpool was already racing out. "Cinderpaw?"

Jaypaw skidded to a halt, narrowly avoiding her. She stopped, trembling, in the middle of the clearing. Horror pulsed from her like blood from a wound. *No, not again!* Her silent plea sliced into Jaypaw's thoughts, as clear as if she'd cried out loud.

"You have to come at once!" Hollypaw wailed.

"What's happened?" Firestar pounded across the clearing. Paw steps sounded on every side as the Clan came running to see what was wrong.

"Cinderpaw was helping Mousepaw down the Sky Oak and she fell!" Hollypaw's words came in great gulps.

"Leafpool, go to her!" Firestar ordered.

Come on! Jaypaw willed his mentor to move, but she seemed

rooted to the spot, her terror blocking out every other thought. "What herbs will we need?" he prompted. He could feel Hollypaw trembling behind him.

"Poppy seeds?" he pressed when Leafpool didn't answer.

Just as panic threatened to overwhelm him, Leafpool snapped out of her daze. He felt her mind clear, like rain lifting. "Poppy seeds, yes. Rushes and cobweb to bind any broken legs, and thyme for the shock."

"I'll fetch them," Jaypaw offered.

"Please hurry!" Hollypaw begged.

"Who's with her?" Leafpool demanded.

"Mousepaw, Ashfur, Cloudtail, and Brackenfur."

"Good. She'll need carrying."

Jaypaw pushed past Millie and Graystripe and raced to the medicine den, his tail bristling. He barged past Birchfall standing, fur spiked, in the entrance and darted to the herb storeroom. Lapping up several poppy seeds, he tucked them safely under his tongue, then grabbed a sprig of thyme and quickly wrapped it up in a fat wad of cobweb along with a pawful of rushes. He picked the bundle up in his jaws and hurtled back into the clearing.

"Got everything?" Leafpool asked.

Jaypaw nodded.

"Hurry!" Hollypaw called. She led them out of the camp at a run.

The forest floor felt soft beneath Jaypaw's pads. Hollypaw plunged up the slope, Leafpool on her heels. Jaypaw ran after them, every sense alert, dodging the trees only by a whisker.

A bramble tugged at his paw and he stumbled forward, dropping his bundle.

"Here, I'll carry that!" Leafpool turned and swiftly picked up the rushes before speeding away again. Jaypaw hurried after her, keeping close, following her paw steps as she weaved through the forest.

"I see the Sky Oak!" Hollypaw called. Her paws beat faster against the ground. "Watch out for the fallen tree!" she warned.

Her paw steps fell silent as she leaped over the log and landed with a thump on the other side. Leafpool followed her. Jaypaw didn't hesitate. Tensing, he leaped as high as he could, praying he had timed it right. He felt the rotting bark of the fallen tree brush his paws as he sailed over and landed lightly on the ground beyond.

"Over here!" Hollypaw had reached the others. Jaypaw felt Brackenfur's panic flash like lightning from his pelt. He could hear Ashfur pacing around the Sky Oak, could sense Mousepaw trembling.

"She's still breathing!" Cloudtail called.

"Good!" Leafpool dropped the bundle. Jaypaw crouched beside her as she leaned over Cinderpaw. He could hear the injured apprentice's breathing. It was quick and shallow. He touched her flank with his nose. She was as limp as a dead mouse. His belly tightened.

"She's in shock!" Leafpool pronounced. "Lick her chest while I give her the thyme."

Jaypaw spat out the poppy seeds and began to lick

Cinderpaw. Her heart beat rapidly beneath his tongue. He smelled the herbs as Leafpool tore open the bundle and chewed the leaves into a pulp that she could drip into Cinderpaw's mouth.

"Is she going to die?" Brackenfur's mew trembled.

"I won't let her," Leafpool snapped.

The medicine cat moved around to Cinderpaw's other side. "Lick more gently now," she ordered. Jaypaw began to lap Cinderpaw delicately, relieved to feel her heart slowing. He could hear Leafpool sniffing Cinderpaw's body, examining her. Suddenly, the medicine cat stiffened.

"What's wrong?" Jaypaw whispered.

Leafpool backed away as though stung by a wasp.

"What's the matter?" Brackenfur surged forward, nearly knocking Jaypaw over.

What had frightened Leafpool so much? Jaypaw stopped licking, and searched her mind. He felt dread there like darkness, threatening to overwhelm her. What could be so bad?

"Sh-she's broken a hind leg," Leafpool gulped.

"We can bind it with the rushes," Jaypaw suggested.

Leafpool didn't reply. *Not again!*

Fear and bewilderment sparked from Brackenfur. "She won't die of a broken leg, will she?"

Leafpool didn't move. Jaypaw focused on her mind, saw an image of a gray cat limping, felt grief sear Leafpool's heart.

"Here!" Jaypaw tugged one of the rushes free. He jabbed it at Leafpool. She jerked and then took it. Jaypaw felt a wave of relief as she laid it beside Cinderpaw's broken leg and took another. He passed her the cobweb, and she carefully began to bind the rushes to Cinderpaw's leg. "We need to secure it until we can get her back to camp," Leafpool muttered. "Then I can set the break properly."

When she had finished, Leafpool sat up. "Ashfur, Cloudtail, you help Brackenfur carry her back to camp. Make sure her leg moves as little as possible."

Cinderpaw let out a soft moan as Brackenfur, Cloudtail, and Ashfur lifted her.

"Careful!" Leafpool gasped.

Jaypaw could hear her paw steps dancing around the warriors, pushing aside brambles, fear sparking from her pelt. "Watch those roots! Take her around the fallen tree! Avoid that dip! Hold her more steadily!"

Hollypaw pressed against him. She was trembling. "I thought she was dead," she murmured.

"She's going to be okay," Jaypaw reassured her. "She's got a strong heart. And it's only her leg that's broken."

"*Only* her leg!" Leafpool's sharp mew took him by surprise. "A warrior needs four good legs!"

Hollypaw pressed her muzzle to Jaypaw's ear. "I've never seen her so upset," she whispered.

Jaypaw shook his head. "Me neither." He leaned against Hollypaw, letting her guide him through the undergrowth. He wanted to focus his attention on Leafpool. He could feel panic, anger, and regret seething in the medicine cat's mind. *Why?* She hadn't pushed Cinderpaw out of the tree.

It was just an accident.

Why did Leafpool feel so responsible?

Cinderpaw's fur swished against the sandy floor as the three warriors laid her gently down in the medicine den.

Sorreltail was in the den already, plucking at the ground with trembling paws. Grief and fear crackled from her pelt. Poppypaw and Honeypaw fidgeted beside Hollypaw, breathing in frightened gulps.

"Thank you," Leafpool mewed briskly to Brackenfur, Cloudtail, and Ashfur. "Leave us now."

"But—" Brackenfur began to protest, but Sorreltail interrupted him softly.

"I'll stay with her."

The brambles rustled as the tom followed Ashfur and Cloudtail out.

Jaypaw bent down and licked Cinderpaw between her ears. She was unconscious again. "We'll take care of you," he promised. He felt Hollypaw's gaze on his pelt.

"You'd better go too," he advised her. "Firestar's waiting." He could sense the ThunderClan leader's heavy presence outside the den. "He'll want to know what happened."

"You will make her better?" Hollypaw mewed.

"We'll try."

As Hollypaw padded from the den, Leafpool murmured to Sorreltail, "I'll do everything in my power to make her well."

"I know you will." Sorreltail's voice cracked with grief, but Jaypaw could still hear affection in her mew. She had been

Leafpool's best friend since before he was born.

Sorreltail's breath ruffled Cinderpaw's pelt. "May Star-Clan protect you," she whispered.

"She will be all right, won't she?" Honeypaw's frightened mew sounded beside Sorreltail.

"Don't let her die!" Poppypaw sobbed.

"Come on," Sorreltail encouraged them. "Let's go and see Brackenfur. He'll need company." She guided her kits out of the medicine den, leaving Jaypaw alone with Leafpool.

With the other cats gone, Jaypaw could feel Leafpool's anxiety buzzing like a swarm of bees. Suddenly, Cinderpaw stirred.

Leafpool swished her tail over the young cat's flank. "Don't be frightened," she soothed. "You are safely back at camp. You fell from the Sky Oak and you've hurt your leg. But we're going to fix it." Desperate hope flared in her mind, but her voice remained calm. "What were you trying to do? Did you think you were a bird? Did you think you could fly?"

Her mew was as gentle as a mother's. Jaypaw had never wondered if Leafpool felt sad she would never have kits of her own.

Cinderpaw let out a soft moan, then her breathing deepened. She was unconscious once more.

"Come on, Jaypaw," Leafpool mewed, suddenly brisk. "Let's get this leg set. First, we need to take this binding off."

Jaypaw began to help Leafpool to gnaw through the cobweb, releasing the rushes.

"Now, we need fresh rushes." Leafpool darted to the back

of the cave before Jaypaw could move and fetched three fresh rushes and another wad of cobweb. "If we place those two there, and hold another one here—"

Jaypaw reached out to help, but felt her paw already pressing the rush gently to Cinderpaw's hind leg while she used her teeth to wrap cobwebs around it. "This should hold it tight."

Jaypaw started to feel as if he wasn't needed. Was Leafpool showing him what to do, or just talking herself through it? "Shall I get some comfrey?" he offered.

"What?" Leafpool sounded distracted. "Yes, yes. Good idea."

Jaypaw collected a mouthful of leaves and began chewing them into a pulp. He could still hear Leafpool fussing over the dressing. "A bit more cobweb here should hold it just right," she murmured.

Cinderpaw twitched and let out a small whine.

"Perhaps we should leave her to rest," he ventured. "There's nothing more we can do for her now."

In an instant he felt Leafpool's hot breath on his face. "There's *everything* we can do for her!" she hissed.

Alarmed, Jaypaw backed away, ears flattened.

Anger flamed from Leafpool's pelt. "We can't let Cinderpaw lose the use of her leg!"

"I—I—" he stammered.

Leafpool backed off and Jaypaw felt guilt flood her mind. "I'm sorry, Jaypaw. I shouldn't have snapped. You've been a great help."

But you didn't let me do anything. Jaypaw bit back the words, wary of antagonizing her again.

Leafpool turned away. "I must go and talk to Sorreltail and Brackenfur." The brambles rustled as she pushed her way through them. Jaypaw stayed where he was. What had gotten into his mentor? He knew she cared deeply for her Clan-mates, but he'd never seen her *angry* that a cat had been hurt before. It was as though healing Cinderpaw was the most important thing she'd ever have to do. Was it because Cinderpaw was her friend's kit?

He checked Cinderpaw's heart, pressing his ear to her chest. It was beating too rapidly, her breathing too quick. He settled down beside her and let his warmth spread into her body. Speeding up his breath to match hers, he closed his eyes.

He was standing at the top of a ravine. Thick woodland crowded every side, and far below, trees and bushes hid the ground from view. *Is this part of StarClan's territory?* Fear clutched his heart. Was Cinderpaw dying? Had he been brought here to save her the way he'd done with Poppypaw?

A gray shape caught his eye below. Cinderpaw was leaping from boulder to boulder, down the ravine. She disappeared into the lush greenery.

Jaypaw started to panic. *I mustn't let her out of my sight!* He scrambled over the edge of the ravine, following the path Cinderpaw had taken, fighting to keep his balance on the tumble of rocks because he was unaccustomed to using sight to guide him. At the bottom, a dense wall of gorse blocked his way. Just in time he spotted the tip of Cinderpaw's tail disappear into it. He raced after her and found an opening in the gorse. He slithered through and found her standing in a sandy clearing at the bottom of the ravine. Bushes and ferns circled it protectively and at the far end, a jagged rock blocked the way out.

"Cinderpaw?" Cautiously, Jaypaw padded toward her, tasting the air. It didn't smell like StarClan territory, but there were definitely some scents that he recognized. A tree stump near the edge of the clearing seemed to smell of Firestar and Graystripe. The bramble bush beside him carried the scents of Dustpelt and Thornclaw.

Cinderpaw gazed around, wide-eyed, her tail twitching with pleasure. "It's just as I remembered! I haven't been here for such a long time."

What did she mean? This wasn't ThunderClan territory. How could Cinderpaw have been here? It didn't even feel like anywhere near the lake. The wind sounded different as it rustled the leaves in the trees at the top of the ravine. The air tasted warmer, filled with a damp fustiness that Jaypaw had never scented before.

"Look here!" Cinderpaw was padding over to the huge rock. "This is Highrock."

Then she turned and bounded over to the bramble bush that smelled of Thornclaw. "And this is the warriors' den. The elders' den is over there." She flicked her tail toward a fallen tree. "And over here"—she raced across the clearing to another bush—"is the apprentices' den. I used to sleep here before . . . " Her mew trailed away, her eyes growing misty. She blinked. "Then I moved to Yellowfang's den."

Yellowfang! The name seared Jaypaw's ears. Yellowfang had been ThunderClan's medicine cat before Cinderpelt. She was with StarClan now, and it seemed to Jaypaw that her main duty was to butt into his dreams. He could picture her, yellow eyes sparking, matted pelt bristling with impatience. . . .

"Come and see!" Cinderpaw's mew interrupted his thoughts.

An eerie feeling pricked his tail as she led him through a narrow tunnel to a much smaller clearing. A rock towered at the far end, split down the middle by a cleft big enough for a den.

Cinderpaw gazed wistfully into the shadowy cave. "Yellowfang kept her herbs in there."

"Yellowfang's dead," Jaypaw mewed. "She's in StarClan now."

Cinderpaw looked at him. "Of course she is! Where else would she be?"

"I don't understand. Why are you acting as if you lived here too?"

"Because I did. Many moons ago, before we left the forest."

"But you never lived in the forest!"

"Once I did." Cinderpaw's blue eyes sparkled with starlight. "But I have returned to tread a different path, the path of a warrior." She looked warmly at him, and when she spoke her voice seemed deeper, more wise, as if she'd aged in front of him. "Tell Leafpool that she has nothing to fear. I will recover this time. And tell her that I am proud of her. She has learned more than I could ever have taught her."

Jaypaw's pelt bristled. Vivid images were thronging in his mind: a young gray cat running through an unfamiliar forest, a monster screeching off a Thunderpath, agony piercing her hind leg, blood and the wails of her Clanmates; memories of learning herbs, limping after Yellowfang, of kits born in a river of blood, of fear and the forest being ripped apart by monsters, of a long hard journey through snow and ice and of snarling, vicious black-and-white creatures, jaws snapping, hungry for revenge and for death. . . .

Jaypaw took a gulp of air, his paws unsteady beneath him. "You're Cinderpelt, aren't you?"

He awoke with a gasp, his pads wet, his tail fluffed out. He jerked his head up, darkness filling his vision once more.

"Jaypaw?" Leafpool's breath stirred his fur. "Were you dreaming?"

Jaypaw struggled to his paws and leaned over the injured apprentice lying next to him. Cinderpaw's breathing was light and steady.

"Jaypaw?" Leafpool prompted. "You were dreaming, weren't you?"

"Yes." Jaypaw tried to catch his breath. The violent visions he had seen still flickered in his mind, red with blood and pain and fear.

"Will she get better?" Leafpool asked quietly.

"Yes."

Leafpool let out a relieved purr.

"She has been here before," Jaypaw whispered.

Leafpool touched his flank gently with her tail. "I thought so," she breathed. "She's Cinderpelt, isn't she?"

"She led me to the old ThunderClan camp," Jaypaw explained. "She seemed so happy to be there." He paused, suddenly aware of Cinderpaw's body resting beside them. "Do you think she knows?"

"No, not in her waking world," Leafpool murmured. "And we shouldn't tell her."

"Why not?"

"It's enough that StarClan have let her come back and tread the warrior's path she always dreamed of following."

Jaypaw pricked his ears. "Didn't she *want* to be a medicine cat?" *Then I am not the only one.*

"She only became a medicine cat after a monster crippled her. After the accident, there was no chance she could be a true warrior, so she served her Clan in a different way."

"But wouldn't she be happy to know that she is fulfilling her dream now?"

"If StarClan wants her to know, they will tell her." Leafpool's mew grew serious. "We should not try to shape her destiny."

"Do you think telling her would change it?" Jaypaw's mind began to race. Did Leafpool believe that destinies could be changed like that? Did that mean he was right to keep the secret of Firestar's prophecy from Lionpaw and Hollypaw? If he told them, would it make them act differently?

"Leafpool?" Cinderpaw stirred beside them. Her voice was hoarse.

"I'll fetch you some water," Jaypaw offered. He found a wad of moss and soaked it in the shallow pool at the side of the den.

"Here." He offered it, dripping, to Cinderpaw. She lapped at it eagerly, then murmured something he couldn't make out. He leaned closer.

"I'm hungry," she croaked.

He heard Leafpool purr with amusement. "That's more like the old Cinderpel—" She corrected herself. "Cinder*paw*. I'll fetch her something from the fresh-kill pile."

As Leafpool padded out of the den, Jaypaw heard Cinder-paw trying to stretch beside him. "Ow, my leg."

"It'll get better. You need to rest now."

"Where am I?" she murmured groggily.

"You're exactly where you belong." Jaypaw ran his tail along her flank. "In ThunderClan."

CHAPTER 8

"I name you Lionclaw, warrior of DarkClan!"

Lionpaw flexed his claws as Heatherpaw called down to him from the highest ledge in the cave. Moonlight, streaming through the gap in the roof, fell silver on her pelt.

She leaped down and touched her nose to his. "Congratulations."

Lionpaw's fur tingled.

"But first"—Heatherpaw's blue eyes flashed in the half-light—"you have to prove yourself a warrior by outrunning me."

"That's not fair!" Lionpaw flicked his tail. "WindClan cats are really fast; everyone knows that."

"If you want to be a DarkClan warrior, you've got to be as fast as me."

"In that case"—Lionpaw launched himself at her, stretching his paws around her to soften her fall, but pinning her to the ground—"you've got to prove you're as strong as me!"

"Hey! That's cheating! You didn't warn me!" she mewed.

"The leader of DarkClan must be prepared for anything."

"Like this?" She slithered from his grasp, darted behind him as fast as a blink, and grabbed his tail gently but firmly between her teeth.

"Hey!" he yelped, trying to reach around and swipe her away. She dodged and he found himself swiping at thin air, his tail still held firm. He twisted the other way, trying to reach her, but she dodged again. He could hear a rumbling in her throat and her whiskers were twitching.

She let go. "You looked so funny flapping your paws around! Like a fledgling just out of the nest!"

Lionpaw stared at her, happiness welling in his chest. Just the sight of her blue eyes and soft fur made warmth surge beneath his pelt. "I wish you were in ThunderClan."

She shuddered. "Under all those trees and closed in by stone walls? No, thanks! Besides," she went on, "we don't need to live in the same Clan when we've got this cave all to ourselves." She reached out a paw and batted something from the fur behind his ear. "Just a burr." She flicked it onto the ground.

"Thanks."

Heatherpaw was right about the cave. Lionpaw knew he wouldn't want to live on the moorland any more than she'd want to live in the forest. This cave was the perfect solution. They'd been meeting here for half a moon now, and none of his Clanmates suspected a thing. Not even his nosy sister.

"I wonder where some of these other tunnels lead?" Heatherpaw leaped over the river and began to sniff at one of the openings.

Lionpaw jumped after her. Dank, stale air seeped from the tunnel and he shivered.

"Do you think one leads into ShadowClan territory?" Heatherpaw wondered.

The fur along Lionpaw's spine lifted. "I hope not."

"We could explore."

Lionpaw backed away. "There's no hurry. We have enough fun here." He glanced around the cave. Getting here still made his paws quiver. There was something spooky about the tunnels and he was always relieved to find Heatherpaw waiting for him in the moonlit cave.

Heatherpaw's eyes sparkled. "There might be all sorts of terrible creatures down there with big teeth and sharp claws—"

Lionpaw nudged her. "Shut up!"

She darted away. "Come on!" she called. "You still have to prove you're a warrior!" She crossed the river with a graceful leap.

Lionpaw dived after her. As he landed, his hind paws slipped backward into the dark water. The splash echoed around the cave. Lionpaw's heart lurched as he felt the strong tug of the current and he scrambled forward, shaking droplets from his paws.

"Careful," Heatherpaw warned. "I don't want to lose you."

Lionpaw gulped at the thought of being dragged away into the tunnels by the river. Seeking comfort in Silverpelt, he glanced up at the gap in the roof. The sky outside was lightening. "We have to go."

Heatherpaw sighed.

"Tomorrow night?" Lionpaw mewed hopefully.

"Can't." Heatherpaw wove around him, brushing her light tabby pelt against his. "I have a training assessment the day after. I don't want to be too tired."

"Okay." Lionpaw shrugged; he understood. She had to put her Clan first. But he would still miss her.

"Bye."

They hurried away, each to their separate tunnel. Lionpaw was relieved that he knew the path well enough now to be able to run all the way. Jaypaw would be surprised to know how fast his brother could race through the blackness, using only his whiskers to guide him. He burst from the entrance, relieved to smell fresh air once more.

This is my part of the forest! He wriggled happily under the brambles and pulled himself out the other side. The older warriors acted like they had created ThunderClan territory because they had brought the Clans to the lake, but Lionpaw knew that they hadn't explored every paw step of it yet. The fact that he knew about the cave proved that there were still places left to find. It would be the young cats who would do that, who would make this land their own.

Through the leaves he could see that the star-studded sky was growing pale. He began to race through the forest. He had to get home before the camp woke.

"Greetings, Lionpaw." A deep mew sounded in his ear and fur brushed his flank.

Lionpaw bristled with alarm. He glanced sideways and saw the faint outline of a cat keeping pace with him. *Am I dreaming?*

"We have been watching you." The outline shimmered

beside him—a huge tabby tom with amber eyes which shone in the half-light. The tom's massive shoulders seemed strangely familiar.

Something brushed his other flank. Lionpaw turned, his heart pounding. Another shadowy cat was running beside him—a second tabby tom with ice-blue eyes, but the same massive shoulders.

"W-who are you?" he stammered.

"We are kin," answered the amber-eyed tom.

Lionpaw glanced anxiously from one to the other. "Are you from StarClan?"

"We were warriors once," the blue-eyed tom growled.

Lionpaw's tail pricked. "T-Tigerstar? Hawkfrost?" Why had they come to him?

Hawkfrost stiffened, jerking his huge head around to stare away into the forest. "Someone's coming," he warned.

Lionpaw ducked behind a hazel tree.

Paw steps beat the forest floor—real, solid paw steps. As Lionpaw crouched, hardly daring to breathe, Spiderleg raced past, stirring the air so that it tugged at Lionpaw's pelt. The long-limbed black tom bounded away, disappearing into a swath of ferns.

Lionpaw crept out from behind the hazel. "Tigerstar?" He glanced around. "Hawkfrost?"

The ghostly warriors had gone.

"Wait!" Lionpaw called in a whisper. "Come back." He had to know why they had chosen to appear to him.

The ferns rustled where Spiderleg had disturbed them.

Then the forest fell silent, except for the call of the birds, heralding the dawn.

Lionpaw crept, yawning, through the dirtplace tunnel. The camp lay in silence. Relief flooded his paws. Then guilt. Away from Heatherpaw's side he was suddenly aware how sneaky he was being. No cat was up. No sign of the dawn patrol preparing to leave yet. He shouldn't feel so pleased that he'd be able to creep to his nest unnoticed and get some much-needed sleep. He scooted around the edge of the clearing, clinging to the shadows, then slipped into the apprentice den. Stepping lightly, he began to tiptoe toward his nest.

"Lionpaw?" Hollypaw lifted her head. "Is that you?"

Panic seared his paws, then irritation. "Yes," he hissed.

"Where are you going?" she yawned.

Lionpaw hesitated. He couldn't use the dirtplace excuse again. She'd think he was ill. "Dawn patrol," he answered quickly.

Hazelpaw sat up groggily and blinked. "I thought I was doing that with Honeypaw?"

"I'm coming too," Lionpaw mewed, "just for the experience." His pelt burned. *So many lies!*

Hollypaw tucked her nose back under her paw. "Rather you than me," she murmured.

"We'd better get a move on." Hazelpaw prodded Honeypaw. "Wake up, sleepyhead. It's time to go."

Lionpaw glanced longingly at his nest, his paws as heavy as stones, but Hazelpaw was already brushing past him, leading the way out of the den. He padded after her, leaving Honeypaw stretching in her nest.

"You're up early, Lionpaw." Sandstorm, sitting by the entrance with Dustpelt, looked surprised to see him.

"I wanted to join the patrol," Lionpaw mewed.

"Good for you." Dustpelt looked up at the clear dawn sky. "It's going to be a great day for hunting. I think I'll take Hazelpaw out again once we've checked the borders."

Birds twittered noisily at the top of the ravine. Lionpaw stifled a yawn and stretched.

"Are you ready, Honeypaw?" Sandstorm asked. Her apprentice was stumbling from the den, blinking the sleep from her eyes.

Honeypaw nodded.

"Come on, then." Sandstorm padded out of the camp.

Back out in the forest, Lionpaw gazed longingly at every patch of moss, wishing he could lie down and rest. He trotted after the patrol, trying not to trail too far behind as they followed the ShadowClan border, renewing the scent markers.

"All clear here," Dustpelt meowed at last.

Great, now we can go home!

Sandstorm sniffed the air. "Let's check the WindClan border."

Lionpaw's heart sank.

The patrol turned and headed back through the forest. Lionpaw felt his eyes glazing with tiredness. Suddenly, a movement caught his eye. Far off through the trees, something was stirring.

Tigerstar! He scanned the forest, but it was only a fern flickering in the light breeze. Why had they come that morning? Tigerstar had said they'd been watching him. *They must know I've been meeting Heatherpaw.* His paws tingled. Did they think he was doing something wrong? But they had warned him about Spiderleg. Perhaps they only wanted to help him. But why?

The patrol neared WindClan's territory. A small gully marked the border, a stream trickling at the bottom between tangled ferns and brambles. Beyond it, the forest stretched farther before opening onto the moorland. Dustpelt stopped to mark a tree. Honeypaw clambered down into the gully for a drink, disappearing beneath thick brambles.

Hazelpaw stiffened. "Look!" she mewed, staring over the border.

Breezepaw and Harepaw were pelting toward the stream. Ahead of them raced a squirrel, its tail bobbing. The WindClan apprentices weaved skillfully through the thick undergrowth; it was strange to see them hunting in woodland.

Dustpelt padded to Sandstorm's side. "Why are they hunting here?"

"It *is* their territory," Sandstorm pointed out

"But WindClan don't eat squirrels!" Honeypaw had scrabbled up from the stream, alerted by Hazelpaw's warning.

Dustpelt narrowed his eyes. "Yes, I thought they only hunted rabbits."

Two more WindClan pelts appeared. Tornear and Whitetail were watching their apprentices from the edge of the moor.

"A hunting party so near to our border?" Dustpelt's mew was sharp with suspicion.

"They're still heading for us," Hazelpaw warned.

Breezepaw and Harepaw pelted after the squirrel; their eyes were fixed on their quarry.

"They're not slowing down," Dustpelt warned.

"They won't cross the border on purpose," Sandstorm reassured him.

"But they might do it accidentally," Dustpelt replied. "The stream's hardly visible here." He dropped into a crouch and crept to the edge of the gully, ducking behind the brambles that covered it.

Breezepaw's and Harepaw's pads thumped the ground as they hurtled nearer. They still weren't slowing.

"Stop!" Dustpelt reared up and yowled across the stream at the WindClan apprentices.

Breezepaw and Harepaw skidded to a halt, their eyes wide with alarm. The squirrel leaped the gully and disappeared up a tall birch.

"What in StarClan's name are you doing?" Tornear's angry mew rang through the trees. The WindClan warrior broke into a run, racing down to the border with Whitetail on his heels.

"How dare you frighten our apprentices?" Tornear halted at the edge of the gully and glared at Dustpelt.

"They were about to cross the border!" Dustpelt arched his back aggressively.

"How do you know?" hissed Breezepaw.

"You weren't even slowing down!" Dustpelt accused him.

"I'd have caught the squirrel in one more stride!"

Lionpaw curled his lip. "You were nowhere near it!"

Breezepaw bristled. "Was too!"

"Everyone knows WindClan can only catch rabbits!" Lionpaw spat back. "ThunderClan are the best squirrel hunters."

"Not anymore!" Harepaw squared his shoulders beside his denmate. "Every WindClan apprentice has special training in the woods so we don't have to rely on rabbits anymore."

Sandstorm's eyes grew round. "Really? Why?"

Tornear turned his glittering gaze on her. "It's none of your business!"

"Is it so you can invade our territory?" Dustpelt paced the borderline, lashing his tail.

Whitetail stepped forward, her ruffled fur smoothing. "We have woodland in our territory," she meowed evenly. "It makes sense to use it. And we don't want to be dependent on one sort of prey anymore. The elders still speak of the hunger WindClan suffered when Twolegs started poisoning the rabbits before the Great Journey."

That made sense. Lionpaw let his claws curve back into their sheaths. But it still felt odd to think of WindClan hunting ThunderClan prey.

Harepaw was nodding. "And there are sheep on the moorland now, with Twolegs and their dogs—"

Tornear silenced his apprentice by flicking his tail across his mouth. "That's none of ThunderClan's business either," he snapped. "So long as we stay on our side of the border, we can hunt what we like."

"But squirrels don't know about the border. They cross over it. You'd be eating our prey."

"If it's on WindClan territory it becomes our prey!" Tornear snapped.

"Squirrels have always been *ThunderClan* prey!" Dustpelt stopped pacing and let the fur stand up on his neck.

"Is that part of the warrior code?" sneered Tornear. He took a step forward, his eyes glittering.

Dustpelt dropped into a crouch, ready to spring. Blood pounded in Lionpaw's ears. He unsheathed his claws again; his tiredness forgotten, he was more than ready to show these pushy WindClan cats what happened to warriors who dare invade ThunderClan's hunting grounds.

"Leave it," Whitetail murmured to her Clanmate. "This isn't worth losing fur over."

Tornear dragged his gaze from Dustpelt and looked at Whitetail. Lionpaw held his breath, then Tornear nodded. "Okay. For now."

Dustpelt watched through narrowed eyes as the WindClan cats turned and padded away along the border, deliberately not hurrying.

"Come on." Sandstorm flicked her tail toward home.

Dustpelt didn't move. "Not until they've left the trees."

Sandstorm sat down and began to wash her face. "You three may as well see if you can find any prey to take back while we're waiting."

Lionpaw reluctantly stopped watching the dawdling WindClan patrol and followed Honeypaw and Hazelpaw over to a patch of brambles.

"Do you think WindClan are planning to invade?" Hazelpaw whispered.

Honeypaw's eyes stretched wide. "What makes you think that?"

"Chasing squirrels is what forest cats do. But they're moorland cats," Hazelpaw mewed. "It's a bit suspicious."

"Well, Dustpelt's acting like they are," Lionpaw commented.

Honeypaw glanced back over her shoulder. "But why would they want to take our territory?"

"Perhaps the Twolegs and their dogs are more of a problem for WindClan than we realized," Lionpaw suggested.

"They coped with it last newleaf," Hazelpaw pointed out.

Foreboding clawed at Lionpaw's belly. "It might be worse this time."

"Anything to report?" Firestar called down from Highledge as the dawn patrol padded into camp.

"WindClan are hunting in the forest," Dustpelt answered.

"In *our* forest?" Firestar leaped down from the ledge.

Lionpaw padded quickly to the fresh-kill pile and dropped the mouse he had caught, then hurried back to join Dustpelt. He was ready to defend his Clan's prey from any marauding WindClan cats, but what if one of those cats was Heatherpaw?

"Lionpaw!" Hollypaw stopped him halfway. "What's going on?"

Jaypaw was with her; his ears pricked with interest.

"WindClan were at the border," Lionpaw explained. He glanced at the patrol.

The ThunderClan leader had reached Dustpelt and Sandstorm. He was lashing his tail, clearly disturbed by Dustpelt's news.

"They haven't crossed the border," Sandstorm explained.

The tip of Dustpelt's tail twitched. "They almost did."

Brambleclaw emerged from the warriors' den. "What's going on?"

"Two WindClan apprentices near our border," Sandstorm meowed. "They were chasing a squirrel and nearly crossed the stream by mistake."

Hollypaw bristled. "A *squirrel*!"

"They should have known better," Dustpelt growled. "Unless they're so used to crossing the stream *by mistake* they don't notice anymore."

"There was no scent of WindClan in our territory," Sandstorm reminded him.

"But why is WindClan chasing squirrels?" Brambleclaw demanded. "They hunt rabbit."

Hollypaw hissed into Lionpaw's ear, "Exactly!"

"Not anymore." Hazelpaw kneaded the ground. "Breezepaw said that all the WindClan apprentices are being trained to hunt in woodland now."

Brambleclaw stiffened. "We must re-mark the borders!" he meowed.

"We've already done that," Dustpelt told him.

Sandstorm sat down. "Let's not make a big thing about this. It was just two young cats—"

Dustpelt cut her off. "Hunting *our* prey!"

"We should be on our guard," Brambleclaw advised. "It needs to be reported at the next Gathering."

Firestar plucked at the ground. "Did any WindClan cats cross the border?"

"No," Sandstorm replied.

"And there was definitely no scent of WindClan cats on our side of the stream?" Firestar pressed.

"None."

Dustpelt snorted. "The rain might have washed it clean."

"Or they've never crossed the border," Firestar pointed out. "I can't tell WindClan what to hunt on their own territory." He turned away. "We'll leave it for now and see what happens."

Jaypaw narrowed his eyes. "Not again!" he muttered.

Lionpaw glanced at his brother. "What do you mean?"

"Firestar didn't want to help RiverClan either," Hollypaw explained. "Even though Jaypaw dreamed they were in trouble."

"How are the Clans going to respect us if we never do anything?" Jaypaw complained.

Lionpaw frowned. "Does it matter? So long as none of them cross our borders."

"But there must be *balance*," Hollypaw protested. "If one Clan is too weak, we should help them; if one is too strong, we must react so we look strong as well."

Jaypaw scowled. "I don't know about balance," he mewed.

"It just seems like Firestar's wasted another chance to make ThunderClan look as if we can take care of ourselves." Flicking his tail, he padded away.

Hollypaw stared after him. "What do you think, Lionpaw?"

Lionpaw stiffened, suddenly picturing Heatherpaw chasing a squirrel toward the ThunderClan border. Was Hollypaw wondering the same? "What do I think about what?" he stalled.

"Should Firestar challenge WindClan at the next Gathering?" Hollypaw tipped her head to one side. Her clear green gaze was curious. Lionpaw shifted his paws, uncertain what to think about his leader's decision. If Firestar ignored every problem, ThunderClan might look weak. But the thought of fighting WindClan made his stomach churn. How could he go on meeting Heatherpaw if their Clans were at war?

Suddenly, a breeze ruffled his fur and a voice murmured in his ear. *Be honest, Lionpaw. Don't be afraid of the things you desire. You know what you think.*

Lionpaw's belly twisted with guilt, but Tigerstar was right. He knew exactly what he thought. A battle with WindClan was the last thing he wanted.

"We should leave WindClan alone," he mewed.

CHAPTER 9

The full moon rippled on the surface of the lake while clouds billowed on the horizon, gray against the blue-black sky.

Hollypaw shivered as she trekked around the shore to the Gathering. A cold wind was ruffling her pelt the wrong way, tugging at her downy fur. She ducked between Squirrelflight and Brackenfur to hide from the chill.

"It'll be warmer on the island," Squirrelflight promised, flattening her ears against the breeze.

Spiderleg and Mousepaw padded ahead, Dustpelt, Brambleclaw, and Squirrelflight beside them, while Thornclaw kept pace with Whitewing, brushing close against her as though shielding her from the wind. Firestar and Sandstorm headed the party while Lionpaw trailed behind with Ashfur and Leafpool. As they followed the edge of the lake, small waves slapped the shore and farther out, foamy crests glowed in the moonlight.

"Get off there!" Brambleclaw's impatient command rose above the wind.

Hollypaw slipped out from her sheltered spot to see who he was yowling at.

Berrypaw was padding along a log lying in the shallows. A gust of wind whipped in from the lake, flattening Hollypaw's whiskers against her face. Through narrowed eyes she watched as Berrypaw lost his balance and fell with a splash into the water. He fought his way to his paws and, shaking the water from his creamy pelt, raced back up the shore to join his Clanmates.

Brambleclaw cuffed him around the ears. "That was a mouse-brained thing to do!"

Berrypaw sneezed.

"And don't think you're missing any training if you've caught a cold!"

The sour smell of horseplace tainted the breeze as the cats neared the end of WindClan territory. The pebbly shore was narrow here, and the wind was blowing spray over it. Firestar led the party up onto the soft grass, skirting the fence. Beyond it the horses were whinnying in their field. Hollypaw felt a shiver of unease as she gazed at the great dark shapes shifting beyond the fence. *Perhaps they don't like the weather either.* The squally wind promised rain, and plenty of it.

Thud!

A horse stamped its foot close to the fence. Whitewing yowled in surprise, leaping sideways in alarm. She careered into Mousepaw, sending him tumbling down onto the pebbly shore.

"Watch out!" he spat, scrambling to his paws.

Whitewing stared down at him, appalled. "I'm sorry."

Why is everyone so jumpy and cross? Hollypaw gazed around at her Clanmates. Few words had passed between them since they had left the camp. Their fur was spiked against the wind, their tails flicking. She felt uneasy herself. Ever since WindClan had been discovered hunting squirrels, there had been rumors of prey-stealing and revenge and worries about invasion. Hollypaw wasn't convinced that WindClan's strange behavior had to end in battle. The warrior code didn't say what Clans could and couldn't hunt. But she hated the tense atmosphere. And she was still worried about River-Clan.

There had been no news since Jaypaw's dream at half-moon. She was desperate to speak to Willowpaw tonight, but her paws pricked with anxiety. What if things were so bad RiverClan didn't come at all?

Lionpaw brushed against her as she followed Brambleclaw down the sandy bank, back onto the shore. "I wish I'd stayed in camp with Jaypaw," he mewed.

She glanced at him. That didn't sound like Lionpaw. He looked sleepy.

"Are you okay?" Didn't he even want to see if Heatherpaw was going to be there?

"Just tired," he mewed. "Ashfur's been training me hard."

Part of her was relieved by his lack of interest in the WindClan apprentice. He must have put his friendship with her behind him at last. But still, it was strange that he'd rather be stuck in camp than going to a Gathering.

Dustpelt halted in front of them, ears pricked. "Wind-Clan!" he warned.

Hollypaw saw a swarm of dark shapes moving against the heather, heading down to the shore. "Do you think Firestar will mention the squirrel-hunting tonight?"

Lionpaw shrugged. "Who knows?"

The WindClan cats streamed onto the shore a little ahead of ThunderClan, and headed onto the marshy shore of RiverClan territory. Hollypaw wrinkled her nose as muddy water squelched between her claws. Firestar had veered closer to the water, hurrying his Clan forward so that they pulled ahead of WindClan.

"Squirrel thieves!" Dustpelt muttered, glancing sideways at the WindClan cats.

"Squirrel thieves!" Berrypaw echoed more loudly.

The insult rippled through the ThunderClan party until it rang above the blustering wind. Hollypaw tensed. They couldn't fight tonight! She glanced warily at the WindClan cats. Tornear's eyes blazed in the moonlight; Breezepaw curled his lip in a menacing scowl. But Onestar padded calmly on, eyes fixed on the fallen tree ahead. He reached it first but signaled with his tail for his Clan to step back. They watched with glittering eyes as Firestar led ThunderClan past and jumped onto the tree-bridge.

Firestar gazed down at the WindClan leader. "Thank you, Onestar."

Onestar dipped his head.

The ThunderClan cats filed across the tree-bridge. When Hollypaw's turn came to scramble up through the tangle of roots, she caught the first scent of RiverClan. It was strong, fresh scents mixed with stale. *They're here!* Relief washed her pelt. Things couldn't be too bad if they'd made it to the Gathering. She picked her way along the gnarled trunk and leaped down onto the shore. Kneading the sand beneath the pebbles to keep warm, she waited for Ashfur and Leafpool to follow.

"Is everyone over?" Firestar meowed.

Brambleclaw nodded; Firestar signaled with his tail and plunged into the undergrowth. Hollypaw darted after him into the brambles. *I must speak to Willowpaw!* A barb stabbed her nose, but she pushed on into the softer ferns and emerged ahead of her Clanmates.

The clearing was packed! Gray pelts glowed in the moonlight like stones among tortoiseshell and brown pelts. Striped fur mingled with mottled. Large toms, slender she-cats, lithe young cats. Some sat in groups exchanging hushed words, some lay at the edges gazing warily around. Small cats wove around larger cats, some so small Hollypaw could hardly believe they were old enough to be apprentices.

She sniffed the air. No sign of ShadowClan.

"How come there are so many RiverClan cats here?" Lionpaw had caught up to her. He sounded out of breath.

Hollypaw shook her head. Her pelt was bristling with unease. Every cat in the clearing was RiverClan.

"Some of them are a bit old to be here." Lionpaw was staring at a thickset tabby tom, whose muzzle was specked with white whiskers. A dark tabby she-cat sat beside him, her fur matted as though she could no longer wash herself properly.

"Swallowtail!" A very young cat was hurrying toward the elderly she-cat. Its eyes were wide with fear. "I can't find Graymist or Sneezekit."

"Don't worry, Mallowkit." Swallowtail swept her tail around the little cat. "Your mother will be back in a moment. Sneezekit's probably with her."

"Did she say *kit*?" Lionpaw asked in surprise.

Hollypaw didn't reply. She was staring at Willowpaw. The RiverClan apprentice was laying out some herbs in front of a heavily pregnant queen. Alarm flashing in her paws, Hollypaw zigzagged through the busy clearing to Willowpaw's side. "What's going on?"

Willowpaw looked up, her eyes filled with panic. "Hollypaw!"

"What in StarClan has happened?"

Before Willowpaw could answer, WindClan burst into the clearing. Mews of surprise rippled from them as they squeezed among the RiverClan cats.

"Graymist? Graymist?" A tiny tortoiseshell kit was wailing in the middle of the chaos.

"Sneezekit! What are you doing away from your mother?" Swallowtail darted forward and plucked up the tiny kit in her jaws. She winced as though the weight were too heavy for her stiff limbs and padded back to Mallowkit.

"Why are there kits and elders here, Willowpaw?" Hollypaw turned back to her friend.

"We had to—"

Firestar's mew cut her off. "Leopardstar, what's going on?"

The ThunderClan leader was padding toward the Great Oak, where Leopardstar sat among the roots.

Onestar was hurrying across the clearing. "It looks like you've brought the whole of RiverClan!" he growled.

Leopardstar blinked. "I have."

"What?" Onestar stumbled to a halt beside her, eyes wide.

Hollypaw leaned forward. *What had happened to RiverClan?*

Blackstar's angry mew sounded from the edge of the clearing. "What's going on here?"

ShadowClan had arrived.

Firestar plucked at the earth. "Let's start the meeting. Then we can all find out." He leaped onto the lowest branch of the oak, Leopardstar following. Blackstar and Onestar climbed up beside him. Below, the Clans jostled as they struggled to find space to settle.

Willowpaw stayed beside the pregnant cat.

"Is everything all right?" Hollypaw hissed.

"Join your Clanmates." Willowpaw pawed at the ball of herbs, avoiding her friend's gaze. *"Please!"*

Hollypaw nodded and fell in behind a group of RiverClan warriors padding toward the oak. Their heads were high, their tails flicking fretfully. A gray RiverClan queen pushed past her, heading in the other direction.

"Sorry!" Hollypaw swerved out of the way, but the queen didn't seem to notice her.

"Graymist! You're here!" Swallowtail's mew was filled with relief as the queen reached her. The kits hurried to greet their mother, but Graymist shooed them back and followed

Swallowtail to a clump of ferns where RiverClan elders and kits were already sheltering. Their eyes glowed warily from the shadows.

Hollypaw hurried to join her Clanmates. Berrypaw flinched as she squeezed past him. "Watch my tail!"

"Careful!" Dustpelt warned as she stepped on his paw.

"Sorry!" Hollypaw slid gingerly around Lionpaw, making sure she only put her feet on solid ground.

"Did you find anything out?" he hissed.

"No."

"Just sit down and keep quiet," Brackenfur ordered.

Hollypaw blinked a silent apology and looked up at Leopardstar.

The RiverClan leader gazed steadily from the oak. A kit wailed and was quickly silenced. "We have a small problem on RiverClan territory," Leopardstar began.

Small? Hollypaw's heart pounded. *Then why are you all here?*

"We've had to leave our camp."

"Leave your camp?" Blackstar's eyes glittered with interest.

"Only for a short time," Leopardstar meowed quickly. "We're sorting the trouble out. We shall move back as soon as it's fixed. Until then we'll be staying on the island."

What about Gatherings? Hollypaw glanced up anxiously at Silverpelt. Gatherings were governed by the warrior code; they took place on land shared equally by the Clans. Surely this broke with the tradition laid down by their ancestors?

"Where are you hunting?" Onestar stared accusingly at the RiverClan leader.

Russetfur stood up, the fur pricking along her spine. "There can't possibly be enough food on the island for the whole Clan."

Leopardstar glared at the ShadowClan deputy. "We have the lake!"

"Is that enough?" Crowfeather called. "What will you do when you have fished out the shallow waters around the island?"

Mistyfoot bristled. "We're not eating *rabbit*, if that's what you're worried about!" The RiverClan deputy curled her lip as though rabbit was the last thing she'd dream of swallowing.

"What about Gatherings?" Firestar gazed calmly at Leopardstar.

"We hope to be back in our camp by the next full moon," Leopardstar meowed.

"And what if you're not?" Blackstar demanded. "It's not fair if you outnumber every other Clan at the Gatherings."

Thornclaw stood up. "No cat ever lived at Fourtrees," he pointed out. "It was special to all the Clans, like Mothermouth."

Leopardstar met his gaze. "We would not be doing this if we had another option."

"What if you can never return to your camp?" Onestar's claws scratched the bark underneath him. "Where will you go then?"

"Will you move to new territory?"

"Will you invade another Clan's land?"

Anxious mews sounded from the clearing.

Leopardstar's gaze swept the cats. "You are worrying about something that will never happen!"

Blackstar's tail was twitching. "But what if it does?" he hissed.

"Three territories can't support four Clans!" Onestar meowed.

Smokefoot, a ShadowClan warrior, lifted his chin. "One Clan will have to go!"

Silence gripped the clearing. Nervous glances flashed from one cat to another.

Hollypaw's belly tightened. Could one Clan really be driven from the lake? *No!* There had to be four Clans! That was the way it was meant to be.

"We have to believe Leopardstar," Firestar's mew rang over the clearing. "We must give RiverClan a chance to return to their territory."

"At least until the next Gathering," Sandstorm put in. The Clans muttered, but no cat argued.

Firestar nodded. "If RiverClan is still living on the island next full moon, we can decide what to do." He stared at the other leaders. "Does that seem fair?"

Blackstar nodded curtly.

Onestar flicked his tail. "I guess," he muttered.

"Then it's settled." Firestar gazed out over the Clans. "ThunderClan has little to report. One of our apprentices was wounded, but she is recovering well." He glanced at Onestar. "And newleaf has brought plenty of prey to the forest."

Hollypaw dug her claws into the earth. *He's hinting about the squirrels.*

Onestar narrowed his eyes. "WindClan is healthy. And prey is running well on our lands too."

Hollypaw felt Berrypaw's breath ruffle her ear. "He said *prey*, not rabbits," he whispered fiercely.

"Why doesn't Firestar mention the squirrels?" Spiderleg hissed.

"Is he too scared to speak?"

Hollypaw jerked around to see which ThunderClan warrior had muttered the question. Thornclaw was glaring at Firestar.

But he's right not to stir up more trouble! There's enough tension here already.

"Blackstar?" Onestar was prompting the ShadowClan leader. "Anything to report?"

"A few Twolegs by the lake," Blackstar revealed. "But none near our camp."

"Good." Firestar nodded. "If there's no other news, I think we should leave RiverClan in peace."

Whispers rustled through the uneasy crowd, but Firestar jumped down from the Great Oak. Leopardstar followed him. The Gathering was over.

Hollypaw felt a wave of relief as she watched WindClan and ShadowClan disappearing into the undergrowth. She hurried back to Willowpaw. "What's really going on?" she demanded. "Why did you leave your camp?"

Willowpaw's mouth was full of herbs. "I can't talk now,"

she mumbled. "Not with every cat listening."

"I understand." Hollypaw could see the desperate plea in her friend's eyes. "I'll come back later. You can tell me then."

Willowpaw spat the herb pulp onto the ground. "Please don't get into trouble!"

"I won't," Hollypaw promised. She *had* to hear the whole story. Firestar might be able to help RiverClan. The future of the Clans could depend on what she could find out. She spotted Brackenfur disappearing into the undergrowth with Brambleclaw and Squirrelflight. Lionpaw was beckoning to her with his tail.

"I've got to go." Hollypaw touched her muzzle to Willowpaw's cheek before darting away.

"Did she say anything?" Lionpaw asked as she reached him.

"No, not really." Hollypaw began to hurry through the ferns. Her heart ached for her unhappy friend.

They caught up with their Clanmates at the tree-bridge. WindClan and ShadowClan were already padding away on the far shore.

"What does this mean for ThunderClan?" Mousepaw was asking anxiously as he scrabbled onto the trunk.

Squirrelflight jumped up behind him. "Nothing."

"How can you be sure?" Spiderleg stopped in the middle of the bridge.

Dustpelt narrowed his eyes. "If RiverClan can't stay in their own territory, they might try to invade WindClan or ShadowClan. If that happens, none of the borders will be safe."

"But we're over on the other side of the lake!" Mousepaw mewed. "It won't affect us." He followed Dustpelt through the branches and hurried in his paw steps along the trunk.

"I just hope you're right," Dustpelt muttered darkly.

"I suppose this explains why WindClan has started training their apprentices to hunt in woodland," Spiderleg growled.

Hollypaw shivered. Could he be right? Was WindClan planning to invade ThunderClan territory?

"Lionpaw!" Ashfur's urgent call woke Hollypaw. She looked up from her nest. Lionpaw was already halfway out of the den.

"Is something wrong?" she asked. Most of the nests were already empty; only Honeypaw slept on.

"Battle training!" Lionpaw replied over his shoulder.

Hollypaw got to her paws and stretched. Brackenfur hadn't called for her. Perhaps she'd get a chance to visit Cinderpaw before training.

Outside she could hear paw steps hurrying and excited mews. Everyone seemed very busy this morning. Intrigued, Hollypaw padded from the den. The sun was only just beginning to creep into the hollow, but the clearing was buzzing like a nest of bees. The fresh-kill pile was well stocked. Mousepaw and Berrypaw were practicing battle moves by the halfrock. Graystripe and Millie were dragging brambles toward the half-finished den. Firestar was talking with Thornclaw and Brambleclaw below the Highledge.

Outside the elders' den, Mousefur was stretching in the sun. Longtail sat beside her, his face lifted to the sky. "Hollypaw? Is that you I smell?" the blind warrior called across the clearing.

"Yes." Hollypaw went over to him.

"I hear trouble's coming." Longtail dug his claws into the ground. "I wish I could help defend my Clan."

"There's no trouble," Hollypaw answered quickly. "RiverClan just has a few problems, that's all."

"Sounds like there's going to be a new marking-out of territory," Longtail went on. "I'd like to see any Clan try to take a piece of what belongs to us!"

He's enjoying this! Alarm bristled along Hollypaw's spine. She was relieved to see Brackenfur padding toward her. Surely he would be too sensible to be caught up in all this talk of battle?

"We're going hunting," he announced.

Good! Something normal.

Brackenfur went on. "If there's going to be a battle, we need to be well fed."

Hollypaw stiffened. *Not Brackenfur, too!* "Can I visit Cinderpaw before we leave?"

"Go ahead," Brackenfur agreed. "But don't be long."

Hollypaw padded across the clearing and poked her nose through the trailing brambles that covered the medicine den entrance. "Can I come in?"

Cinderpaw was sitting up in her nest, her rush-bound hind leg stuck out awkwardly in front her. She was reaching forward to chase a ball of moss around the edge of her nest with her forepaws.

Leafpool was soaking dried horsetail stems in the pool at the side of the den. She looked around. "Hi, Hollypaw!"

Hollypaw thought she detected relief in the medicine cat's mew. She pushed through the brambles.

"I'm glad you're here. Cinderpaw could do with some company." Leafpool glanced at her fidgeting patient. "She's finding it hard to keep still."

Cinderpaw patted the moss ball so that it flew across the den and landed beside Hollypaw. "Toss it back so I can catch it!" she pleaded.

"Don't you dare!" Leafpool leaped over and grabbed the ball in her teeth. "You've got to keep still if you want your leg to mend straight!"

Hollypaw purred with amusement as Cinderpaw rolled her eyes. Then she noticed Jaypaw at the back of the den. He was busily wrapping up herbs in leaf parcels and piling them against the den wall. He seemed totally absorbed in his task and didn't look up to greet his sister.

"What are you doing, Jaypaw?" she called across the den.

"Preparing herbs," he muttered. "What does it look like?"

"That's a lot of herbs." Hollypaw could smell horsetail and marigold. She remembered enough of her medicine training to know that he was preparing for combat wounds. She felt sick. It seemed as though the whole Clan had accepted a battle was coming.

"What's up?" Cinderpaw called from her nest.

Hollypaw padded to her side. "Has anybody told you what

happened at the Gathering?"

Cinderpaw shook her head. "Leafpool and Jaypaw were whispering about something when Leafpool got back, but they haven't said anything to me."

"RiverClan is living on the island!"

Cinderpaw's eyes widened with shock. "*Living* there?"

"They can't use their camp for some reason and all the other Clans think they'll have to find new territory."

Cinderpaw gasped. "But that would mess everything up."

"I know." Hollypaw glanced at Jaypaw, still busy at the back of the den. "And it seems as if everyone is expecting a fight."

Cinderpaw plucked at the moss in her nest. "I just hope I'm better in time to join in," she mewed.

Hollypaw stared at her crossly. "There doesn't need to *be* a battle!"

"But if everyone wants one—"

Hollypaw cut her off. "Everyone's just scared about what RiverClan will do. If we can help RiverClan, then everything will go back to normal."

She padded out of the den and stared around the clearing. Foxkit and Icekit were play-fighting outside the nursery; Longtail and Mousefur were drawing battle plans in the sandy earth. Firestar was still talking with Brambleclaw.

She couldn't let her Clanmates get caught up in a battle before they had tried to find a different way to solve the problem. If she could just find a way to help RiverClan, maybe there would be nothing left to fight about.

CHAPTER 10

❧

Jaypaw heard the brambles swish. "Hollypaw's gone?" He blinked. Hollypaw had only been in the den a few moments.

"She must've remembered something she had to do." Cinderpaw sighed.

"Oh." Jaypaw went back to wrapping his marigold and horsetail poultices in leaves, preparing for a battle that might never happen. Why hadn't StarClan warned him? It was not like they were shy about interrupting his dreams.

Suddenly, he felt his pelt begin to warm under Cinderpaw's gaze. She was staring at him, her mind tingling with curiosity. Irritation made his claws itch. How long was she going to stay here? She was obviously bored and Jaypaw missed the peace and privacy of the empty medicine den. He turned and faced her. "Something wrong?" he asked.

"No." Cinderpaw sounded oddly thoughtful. "I just think I had a dream about you, and you could *see*."

Jaypaw's ears twitched. She remembered her dream! How much? The camp in the ravine? Being Cinderpelt? He waited for sparks of alarm to flash from Leafpool's pelt, but the medicine cat was busy soaking horsetail stems in the pool, her mind focused on her task.

Jaypaw padded forward. "What was I doing in your dream?" he asked casually.

"I don't remember. I was just surprised you could see." Cinderpaw fidgeted in her nest.

"Where were we?"

Cinderpaw hesitated. "Some bit of the forest, I think. You were following me and . . . "

"And what?" Jaypaw leaned close to her.

"I don't remember."

Jaypaw flicked his tail. What would happen if Cinderpaw worked out she had been Cinderpelt? Surely all the old medicine cat's memories must be buried somewhere in the apprentice's mind?

"Time for Cinderpaw's medicine," Leafpool called from the pool.

"Okay." Excitement sparked in Jaypaw's belly. This could be his chance to find out if any trace of Cinderpelt remained.

He darted to the back of the cave, ignoring the comfrey that would help Cinderpaw's bones to heal, and picked up some of the sweet-smelling mallow leaves instead. The mallow would do nothing but soothe her belly. If any of Cinderpelt's knowledge lingered inside her, she would know it was the wrong medicine and say something.

"Here you are," he announced, dropping the mallow leaves in her nest.

"These smell nice," Cinderpaw mewed.

"It's mallow," Jaypaw told her. He nudged them closer.

"Great for broken bones." He searched her mind for any doubt, but nothing stirred except gratitude.

"Thanks, Jaypaw."

"What are you doing?" Leafpool whisked past and snatched the mallow leaves away. He felt suspicion pricking in the medicine cat's pelt as she brushed against him. "You should be giving her comfrey."

"I must have picked up the wrong leaves," Jaypaw lied.

"Be more careful next time." Irritation flashed from Leafpool. She didn't believe him. Had she guessed he had been testing Cinderpaw? "Get back to making poultices," she snapped. Her voice softened as she spoke to Cinderpaw. "Sorry, Cinderpaw. It's not like Jaypaw to be so distracted."

Jaypaw padded mutinously away to the back of the den. It was so unfair! Leafpool had no patience with him these days, and yet she put up with Cinderpaw's boredom and fidgeting with unending kindness. He flicked his tail petulantly at the stems soaking in the pool. "Is that horsetail ready yet?" He knew full well that they'd need soaking overnight for the juices to be fully restored.

"Of course not!" she meowed. "Use the ones I soaked yesterday!"

"Okay!" He hooked a soggy stem from a nearby pile and began to gnaw crossly at one end.

Leafpool padded over to join him. Comfrey scent filled the air as she collected a few leaves for Cinderpaw. "What's the matter with you?" she hissed.

"What's the matter with *you*?" he snapped back.

"I'm not the one giving Cinder*paw* the wrong medicine."

"I only wanted to see if she would know the difference."

"She's Cinder*paw*, not Cinderpelt!"

"But there must be something there."

"If there is, it's not up to us to find it!" Jaypaw felt Leaf-pool's breath on his cheek. "We have to let Cinderpaw find her own destiny!"

"What's wrong with helping her along? Surely Cinderpaw deserves to know that she's been sent back by StarClan to be a warrior."

"If StarClan wants her to know, they'll tell her," Leafpool mewed.

"So you're happy to leave it in the paws of StarClan."

"Of course!" She sounded shocked. "And so should you."

Jaypaw went back to chewing. The stem's bitter juice made his whiskers twitch. Why was Leafpool so totally in awe of her ancestors? He'd met them; they seemed no different from cats who were still alive. Did Leafpool really think that dying made a dumb cat wise? They could walk in other cats' dreams, but so could he. That didn't mean he knew the answer to everything.

"Jaypaw!" Cinderpaw's mew rang around the den.

Jaypaw blinked open his eyes. "Are you okay?"

"I'm fine." Cinderpaw sounded wide awake. Jaypaw lifted his muzzle and sniffed. It smelled as though dawn had only just arrived. Couldn't she sleep a little longer? Or at least let *him* sleep a little longer?

"Leafpool's gone to check on Foxkit," she mewed. "I thought we could have a game while she's gone."

Jaypaw struggled to his paws, yawning. He could feel the lively energy coming off Cinderpaw in waves.

"I wish I could move my leg," she complained. "I feel fine apart from that."

"You have to keep it still if you want it to mend properly," Jaypaw told her.

"I know, I know." Cinderpaw sighed. "But I'm so bored!"

Jaypaw felt a wave of sympathy for her. Newleaf had set the forest atwitter and the scent of fresh life called out like a friend begging to play. Something whistled through the air and bounced softly off his shoulder. A moss ball.

"Okay," he conceded. "But you're not allowed to move from your nest. I'll throw it to you."

"But you can't see me."

"Yes," Jaypaw agreed. "But since you never shut up I can always hear exactly where you are." He hooked the moss ball up with his paw and lobbed it at her.

Her nest scrunched as she stretched to catch it.

I must throw it lower next time.

The moss ball hissed through the air once more. Judging its distance exactly, Jaypaw leaped and dived, rolling over as he caught it.

"Wow!" Cinderpaw purred. "Impressive." She was suddenly still. "What's it like?"

Jaypaw tipped his head to one side. "What's *what* like?"

"Being blind."

"What does it feel like being able to see?"

"I don't know, I guess it feels normal."

"Well, being blind feels normal to me."

"But isn't it hard not being able to tell where everything is?"

"But I *can* tell." Jaypaw appreciated Cinderpaw's honesty; most other cats acted like if they didn't talk about his lack of sight, he'd forget he was any different. "Everything smells or makes a sound, and sometimes I get a"—he searched for the right word—"a *sense* of things."

"So you never get frustrated?"

"Only when I get treated like I'm different," Jaypaw replied. "I don't *feel* any different, so it's really annoying when anyone makes a fuss about my blindness. It's like they feel sorry for me when there's nothing to feel sorry about."

He flicked the ball into the air, then swiped it toward Cinderpaw. Her nest rustled under her.

"What in StarClan?" Leafpool's furious mew sounded at the entrance. She darted across the den and whisked the moss ball into the pool, then rounded on Jaypaw. "What are you doing, making her stretch up like that?"

"It was my idea!" Cinderpaw mewed at once.

Leafpool ignored her. "You should have known better!"

Jaypaw bristled. "I told her not to move from her nest."

"That's not good enough! Her leg must heal *properly*!" Leafpool's mew dropped to a whisper. "She *must* train as a warrior this time."

"Why must she?" Anger exploded in Jaypaw's chest. "Why would it be such a disaster if she had to take a different path? *I* had to!"

Leafpool froze for a moment, then slowly replied, "You are *blind*."

Jaypaw's rage fell away. Did Leafpool think he was a lost cause? Did she only fight to save the cats who could be saved? He turned away from her, too wretched to say anything.

Leafpool hurried away to Cinderpaw's nest and began fussing with her cobweb binding.

Jaypaw padded out of the den. He could hear the Clan, busy in the clearing. Graystripe and Millie chatted to each other as they wove the roof of the new den into place. Lion-paw was chasing Foxkit and Icekit around the nursery. Fern-cloud was sharing tongues with Dustpelt below Highledge.

I'm more than just a blind medicine cat! Jaypaw flexed his claws. *I'll show them!*

The brambles swished behind him.

"We need to fetch herbs." Leafpool's mew was matter-of-fact, as though nothing had passed between them. He searched her mind for some lingering anger or guilt, but her thoughts seemed to be carefully shielded. "The marigolds should be flowering by the lakeshore," she went on as she led him out of camp.

Jaypaw didn't speak. He sulked in silence as they trekked up the slope and over the ridge. As they emerged from the trees, a chilly wind cut through his fur. It smelled of rain.

Leafpool headed down the grassy slope to the shore. "I can see some." She veered into the wind.

Jaypaw narrowed his eyes as it blasted his face. This was a pointless journey. "You know we've already got a pile of marigold in the den, don't you?"

Leafpool slowed her pace to match his. "If there is to be a battle, we must be prepared," she told him. "Our first duty is to heal the Clan." Jaypaw felt her willing him to speak. "Don't you think?" She sounded anxious.

Grudgingly, he let himself be drawn into conversation. "Yes," he conceded. "But what about sharing with StarClan? That's part of our duty too. Why didn't they warn us a battle was coming?"

"StarClan doesn't always tell us everything that's going to happen."

"Do we just have to wait until we're told?" Jaypaw bristled with frustration. "We can walk among them in our dreams. Surely we can find out for ourselves?"

"Are you questioning the wisdom of StarClan?"

Jaypaw bit back his reply—that he couldn't figure out why being dead made StarClan so wise.

"There's more to being a medicine cat than sharing with StarClan," Leafpool went on. "You still don't know every herb, for example." She halted and sniffed loudly. "What's this one?"

Jaypaw tasted the air. A sharp tang bathed his tongue. He reached down and touched small soft leaves. Tight flower buds bounced against his nose.

"Do you recognize that?" Leafpool prompted.

"Feverfew," Jaypaw mewed. "Good for aches, especially headaches." He turned away, adding, "But it's no good to us now because the flower won't be out for another moon." Why was she treating him like a mouse-brained idiot? How many times did he have to prove himself?

Another scent caught his attention. Something tastier than feverfew. He dropped into a hunting crouch. The grass ahead was shivering and he could hear a tiny snuffling. The image of a vole formed in his mind; he could see it as clearly as if he were dreaming. It was trembling.

Quick as a flash, Jaypaw shot forward, diving through the grass, paws outstretched. The vole darted sideways, but Jaypaw veered and cut off its escape route. It careered into his paws and he hooked it easily, killing it with a sharp nip. Padding back to Leafpool, he dangled his catch under her nose.

"Very good," she meowed.

He flung it at her paws, the morning's frustrations suddenly swamping him. "Now do you believe that I don't need eyes to see?"

He waited for anger to flash from her, for her sharp rebuke to sting his ears. Instead, he felt her tail sweep his flank, gentle as a breeze. "Oh, Jaypaw," she sighed. "I have *always* believed in you."

Emotion swelled from her, sentimental and oppressive, filling his mind like a sticky cloud. Taken aback, he edged away and darted down onto the shore. Ahead, a stream was babbling as it flowed out of the forest and into the lake. This was where Mousepaw had lost the squirrel. And it was where he had found the stick. He hadn't realized that they had come this far around the lake.

His paws tingled with excitement.

The stick.

He picked his way over the shore, careful not to trip on the twigs and Twoleg rubbish washed up by the lake. A large drop of rain landed between his shoulder blades. He shook it off, ducking as another hit his nose. He could smell the stick now, its strange scent calling to him like a kit mewling for its mother. He hurried to where he had left it tucked behind the tree root and dragged it out onto the shore. He wanted to run his paws over it again, feel the scars in its smooth surface. His pads felt warm as they stroked it, his heart suddenly as full as a well-fed belly.

"Is that the same old stick you found last time?" Leafpool had caught up to him.

Jaypaw nodded.

"Why are you so interested in it?" Leafpool was puzzled.

"It feels important!" He rested both paws on the wood, as smooth as spider's silk. A gentle murmuring filled his mind, like softly lapping waves. His paws traced the etching on the wood. They lingered on the uncrossed marks, and he felt sadness spike into his pads. *These marks are untold stories.*

Rain was spattering on the leaves overhead and splashed in great drops onto his back.

"We should get back," Leafpool decided.

"What about the stick?"

Thunder rolled in the distance. Wind whipped in off the lake, buffeting and pushing like a bad-tempered badger.

"We must get back to camp." Leafpool sounded worried. "I can see the storm clouds coming. We shouldn't be out in this."

Jaypaw's fur bristled. He felt lightning prickle in the air. A blast of wind pushed him sideways, knocking him away from the stick.

"Come on!" Leafpool urged.

Waves were pounding the shore now, beaten in by the rising wind.

"What about the stick?" Jaypaw called.

But Leafpool was already hurrying away. "Come on!" she ordered.

There was no time to drag it back to the safety of the root. The wind was tearing at his fur, blowing back his ears. Pelting rain stung his eyes. Ducking down, Jaypaw darted after his mentor and raced back to the safety of the camp.

The rain had stopped but the wind still roared above the hollow.

Jaypaw lay in his nest and listened to the forest creaking high above the medicine den. The leaves swished like waves upon a shore. But Jaypaw hardly heard them. His ears were filled with whispering. His claws itched as he imagined the earthy scent of the stick. He rolled over in his nest and flattened his ears, but the whispering still breathed in his ears. He stretched out and pummeled restlessly at the moss underneath him.

"Why don't you go for a walk?" Leafpool murmured from her nest. "Before your fidgeting wakes Cinderpaw as well."

"Okay." Jaypaw sat up. His paws ached to be outside. He wanted to touch the stick once more.

He pushed his way through the brambles. Outside, the wind was stirring up the restless scents of newleaf so that the whole forest seemed to be swaying and fidgeting with impatience. Instinctively, Jaypaw knew that the sky was clear and the moon was shining. He could feel its cold light wash his pelt. As he headed for the camp entrance, the thorn barrier quivered.

"Jaypaw?"

Lionpaw was squeezing though the dirtplace tunnel.

"Hi, Lionpaw," Jaypaw greeted him curiously. His brother's pelt pricked with guilt and alarm. And it smelled of the wind.

He's been out in the forest!

"I was just making dirt." Lionpaw was lying.

Jaypaw narrowed his eyes. *Does every cat in the Clan have secrets?* "I was just going out." He sensed weariness in his brother's paws and decided to test him. "Will you come with me?"

"If you want," Lionpaw mewed warily.

He feels too guilty to refuse.

Birchfall hailed them from the camp entrance. "Who's there?"

"Only us," Jaypaw called back. He padded toward the thorn tunnel. "We're just going out into the forest."

Birchfall purred. "A midnight adventure," he meowed. "That reminds me of my apprentice days." He sounded wistful, even though he'd been a warrior for only a few moons. Jaypaw didn't say anything; Birchfall always liked to pretend he was vastly wise and experienced compared with apprentices but Jaypaw hadn't forgotten the fuss he'd made over getting a thorn in his paw.

The warrior stepped aside, and Jaypaw felt the wind whisk down the tunnel. He beckoned to Lionpaw with his tail. "Coming?"

Lionpaw followed Jaypaw through the barrier.

"Watch out for foxes!" Birchfall called after them.

Jaypaw shivered. The memory of the fox springing from the undergrowth while he and Brightheart trekked through the forest made his belly tighten.

"Don't worry," Lionpaw reassured him. "I can handle foxes now."

They padded up the slope and onto the ridge.

"Where are we going?" Lionpaw asked.

"The lake."

Lionpaw made no comment. No interest sparked from his pelt. Jaypaw could feel a dark cloud hovering in his brother's mind, absorbing every other thought like quicksand. He tried reaching into it but felt nothing but uncertainty.

As they left the trees and headed down the grassy slope, the wind whipped at Jaypaw's ears and whiskers. He lashed his tail, excited by the stormy weather and the thought of touching the stick once more. He could smell the lake now and pictured it—a vast Moonpool, ruffled and reflecting a shattered moon.

The scents of RiverClan, WindClan, and ShadowClan clashed and mingled on the breeze. Was there really going to be a battle?

"Do you think WindClan is planning to invade us?" he mewed.

Lionpaw pressed against him, steering him around a rabbit hole. "It wouldn't make sense." Jaypaw thought he heard hope in his brother's mew. "It's RiverClan they should be worried about, not us."

"But what about the squirrel-hunting?"

"Why shouldn't they hunt squirrels? The woods belong to them on that side of the gully." Lionpaw sounded more like a warrior than an apprentice; as though he knew something Jaypaw didn't.

As their paws crunched on the pebbles around the edge of the lake, Lionpaw hesitated. "Why are we here?"

"I left something here," Jaypaw explained. "I need to drag it into the trees. I want to keep it safe from the lake."

"What?"

"A stick."

"A *stick*?"

"Yes!" Jaypaw sniffed the air, hoping to detect its scent. "It has markings on it." His tail pricked with anxiety as he smelled nothing but windblown water. "I left it here."

"What does it look like?"

"No bark," Jaypaw mewed. "Just smooth wood. With lines scratched into it."

"Okay," Lionpaw mewed. "You check where you left it. I'll search the top of the shore in case the wind's carried it up there."

Jaypaw hurried to the place where he had abandoned the

stick. His heart began to pound. He was certain it was gone, and not just because he couldn't scent it. There was a dark emptiness in his chest that told him the stick was no longer here.

He was right.

The pebbles were bare.

Fighting the fear that jabbed his belly, Jaypaw zigzagged over the shore, sniffing at the pebbles, trying to trace where the stick had gone. Why had he let the storm chase him away? He should have made sure the stick was safe before he ran home like a fox-hearted coward!

"Have you found it?" Lionpaw's mew was muffled by the wind.

"No!" Jaypaw felt panic rising in his chest. He couldn't have lost it.

"Is this it?" Lionpaw called suddenly.

Jaypaw charged toward his brother. He tripped over a piece of driftwood, bruising his paw, but he ignored the pain and limped desperately toward Lionpaw.

He knew even before he reached it that it was not the stick. "Where are the scratches?" he snapped. "I told you, it has *scratches*!"

"Okay, okay!" Lionpaw flashed with resentment. "I'm just trying to help."

"I have to find it." Jaypaw wandered away, stumbling over the pebbles and debris. *I'm sorry. I'm sorry.* He felt as if he had let someone down, though he had no idea how or who. His paw was throbbing now but he didn't care. Had the lake reclaimed the stick?

He headed down the beach until water lapped his paws and paddled into the shallows. He had to find the stick. Cold water rippled against his belly fur. It dragged at his paws as he waded deeper. He remembered falling from the cliff, sinking, floundering beneath the waves. Crowfeather had saved him then, but the fear of the lake had stayed with him. It screamed at him now, warning him to turn back.

Jaypaw!

A voice rang in his head. Something tugged his fur, drawing him farther out. The waves lapped over his spine and he lifted his chin to keep it dry.

This way!

With each paw step he had to reach down farther to feel the pebbles. But he had to find the branch.

Suddenly, his paw knocked something beneath the water.

That's it!

Taking a great gulp of air, he ducked his head beneath the waves and grabbed the end of the branch in his teeth. Tugging desperately, he began to drag it up the beach. He let go and took another gulp of air before diving again to grab the branch. He dug his paws into the pebbles, scrabbling to get a grip. The stick was so heavy! He pulled and pulled, his lungs bursting as he tried to drag it out of the water.

Suddenly, it moved more easily. Almost weightless, the stick began to float toward the shore; Jaypaw only needed to guide it with his teeth. Relief surged in his paws as his head finally broke the surface. He gasped and coughed, still gripping the stick in his teeth, water dripping from his whiskers.

He had reached the shallows.

"What in StarClan were you doing?" The branch slapped down in the water as Lionpaw let go of the other end. "I saw you disappear under the water and I thought you were trying to drown yourself. Then I realized you were dragging this! I don't know how you thought you were going to get it out on your own."

The water lapped around the stick. Jaypaw ran his paw over it, searching out the scratches. He wished the stick was not so big, that he could take it back to camp with him. "Look," he breathed, running his paw over the marks.

"You half drown yourself in the middle of the night for a stick with claw marks on it!" Water sprayed from Lionpaw as he shook himself. "You're crazy."

"I'm not," Jaypaw snapped hotly. "It's important."

Thank you, Jaypaw. We'll be remembered as long as you guard us.

"Come on," he mewed. "Let's get this tucked under a root and get back to camp."

CHAPTER 11

"For StarClan's sake!" Ashfur bounded from the ferns and glared angrily at Lionpaw. "How did you miss it?"

The wagtail, which had whisked away from Lionpaw's outstretched paws only moments earlier, perched on a branch above the training hollow and called an alarm before fluttering away into the trees.

Lionpaw hung his head. He should have caught it, but his paws felt like stones. "Sorry." The midnight trek to the beach with Jaypaw had left him exhausted. He quivered with irritation. He had left Heatherpaw early last night so he could catch up on his sleep. Why had Jaypaw dragged him out to the lake instead of letting him rest?

"You're lumbering around like a badger today," Ashfur scolded.

Spiderleg and Mousepaw padded out of the ferns with Honeypaw and Sandstorm.

"More like a hibernating hedgehog!" Mousepaw teased.

Lionpaw glared at his denmate.

Honeypaw flicked her tail at Mousepaw. "It wasn't long ago you missed a squirrel," she reminded him.

Lionpaw's ears grew hot. He didn't need Honeypaw to defend him.

"Honeypaw's right." Spiderleg nudged Mousepaw's shoulder with his muzzle. "And your climbing could use some practice."

Mousepaw flattened his ears. "Well, let's go practice, then!"

"You'd better not try the Sky Oak!" Honeypaw called out as the two cats headed for the trees. Mousepaw's tail quivered with annoyance as it disappeared into the undergrowth.

Sandstorm turned to her apprentice. "Come on, Honeypaw, we'll see if there are any mice around the old beech."

"Can we come too?" Ashfur looked pointedly at Lionpaw. "I don't think we'll find many birds around here now."

"Of course." Sandstorm bounded up the slope out of the hollow and then headed into the trees. Ashfur hurried to catch her up.

"Don't worry," Honeypaw whispered, falling in beside Lionpaw. "I missed a sparrow yesterday."

Lionpaw snorted and hurried ahead of her, bristling.

The ground beneath the beech was littered with empty husks. This was a great place for hunting mice attracted by the ready supply of beechnuts. Lionpaw pushed ahead of Honeypaw into the ferns that ringed the open ground beneath the tree. Ashfur and Sandstorm were waiting for them, sat beneath the arching fronds.

"Let's hope we manage to catch something *here*," Ashfur meowed. "We don't want the Clan to go hungry."

"They won't!" Lionpaw snapped. Why couldn't Ashfur

give him advice instead of pointing out his mistakes?

"Look!" Honeypaw jerked her head toward the clearing. A mouse was sitting between the snaking roots of the beech, a nut between its forepaws. It was busy nibbling at the shell. "That'll be easy to catch." She blinked encouragingly at Lionpaw. "It doesn't even know we're here."

"Why don't you catch it, then?" he hissed.

Honeypaw's eyes clouded. "I thought you might want the chance."

"I don't need help!" Lionpaw snapped. Did she think he was a helpless kit?

Honeypaw dropped her gaze and he felt guilty. She had only been trying to help. He turned and peered out of the undergrowth. He'd catch the mouse to show her he was sorry.

But it had gone.

Something else was stirring the leaves only a few tail-lengths away. Lionpaw dropped into a hunting crouch. Willing away the tiredness that made his limbs feel as heavy as wet wood, he began to creep forward. The leaves moved again and a tiny nose peeked out. Tensing every muscle, Lionpaw prepared to leap.

"Keep your tail down!" Ashfur hissed.

Lionpaw pressed his haunches down harder to the ground. Then he darted forward.

He wasn't fast enough. The vole scuttled beneath a root. Lionpaw glanced at Ashfur, expecting some comment, a word of advice or even disappointment, but his mentor turned away without saying anything.

* * *

Brambleclaw looked up as Lionpaw followed Ashfur into camp. The ThunderClan deputy's eyes narrowed as Ashfur dropped two mice and a sparrow onto the fresh-kill pile. Lionpaw had nothing to offer.

"Prey still running?" Brambleclaw padded over to them.

"There's certainly plenty around," Ashfur commented.

Lionpaw waited for Ashfur to tell Brambleclaw how useless he had been today. He blinked in surprise when Ashfur meowed, "Lionpaw's hunting is coming along fine. He just needs to work on his crouch."

Why didn't he tell Brambleclaw the truth? Had Ashfur given up on him? Or was he being soft on him because his father was deputy?

Brambleclaw cuffed Lionpaw softly around the ear. "I thought you'd mastered the hunting crouch before you left the nursery."

Didn't anybody care? Irritation pricked his paws. He had been floundering for days, but nobody had mentioned it. Why weren't they taking his training seriously? With all the talk of battle, surely it was more important than ever that he was doing well. He glanced at Brambleclaw, but the ThunderClan deputy was already padding away with a mouse in his jaws.

"You might as well have something to eat too," Ashfur meowed. "It's been a long morning."

"What about training?"

"Rest first." Ashfur began to head across the clearing. "We'll do some battle training later."

It looked as if Ashfur really had given up on him. Maybe his mentor thought training was a waste of time. Lionpaw felt a flash of indignation, but it died as he stared wearily at the fresh-kill pile. He was too tired to eat. All he wanted was to curl up and sleep. He headed for the apprentice den, ducking beneath the low branch of the bramble bush. With a sigh of relief, he coiled down into his nest and closed his eyes.

"Lionpaw!" Berrypaw's voice woke him. "Time for battle training!"

Lionpaw struggled awake like a drowning cat fighting its way to the surface. Berrypaw was standing over him, shaking his shoulder with a paw.

"Okay, okay!" Lionpaw mewed. "Put your claws away! I'm awake." He shook Berrypaw away and heaved himself to his paws. A fog filled his brain, and his body felt as though it was weighted down with boulders. His nap had only made him feel more tired.

"Ashfur and Brambleclaw want us to do some battle training together."

Lionpaw sighed.

"What's the matter?" Berrypaw leaned forward. "You normally can't wait to try and beat me." His whiskers twitched. "Are you scared?"

"No!" Of course he wasn't scared. *I just want to sleep!*

He stumbled out of the den after Berrypaw and blinked in the afternoon sun. Ashfur and Brambleclaw were already waiting by the camp entrance. They nodded at Lionpaw and headed out of camp.

Slow down! Lionpaw felt hardly awake as he hurried after Berrypaw and the two warriors. He stumbled through the forest in a daze of tiredness, tripping over brambles and stifling yawn after yawn. He half slid down the slope into the mossy training hollow where Berrypaw was waiting with Ashfur and Brambleclaw. Stretching his claws, Lionpaw padded to join them. He shook himself, hoping to jerk himself awake, but a numbing fog still clouded his mind.

"Let's get started," Brambleclaw meowed. "Berrypaw, I want you to pretend you're defending your territory." He flicked his tail. "Lionpaw, attack him."

Berrypaw dropped into a crouch, hackles bristling and tail lashing. His eyes were narrowed to slits and his chin glided back and forth over the ground like a snake's.

"Come on, Lion*kit*!" he teased.

Anger flashed in Lionpaw's pelt. Without thinking he rushed at Berrypaw, his sleepy paws stumbling over the ground. He hurled himself at his denmate, forelegs splayed. Berrypaw reared up and caught him under the chin, flinging him backward. Before Lionpaw could roll out of the way, Berrypaw sprang on top of him. Lionpaw struggled but the other apprentice's weight pinned him to the ground.

Berrypaw looked up triumphantly at Brambleclaw. "That was easy!"

As his attention slipped, Lionpaw darted out from underneath him. He butted Berrypaw's creamy flank with his head, but Berrypaw hardly flinched. Instead, he rounded on

Lionpaw and swiped at him with a forepaw. Lionpaw only just managed to duck in time. *What now?* His mind was sluggish with sleep. Working on instinct, he dived beneath Berrypaw's belly and tried to leap up and unbalance him. But he hadn't bargained for Berrypaw's greater weight. Berrypaw merely dropped on top of him and squashed him to the ground.

Lionpaw, defeated, went limp. Every move he had made had been badly thought out. Berrypaw stepped off Lionpaw and sat down beside Brambleclaw, curling his tail over his paws.

Ashfur stared down at his apprentice. "Was that the best you could do?"

Lionpaw shot to his paws, his ears burning. He was wide awake now, his body tingling with anger. "It's not my fault you taught me all the wrong moves!"

Shock flashed in Brambleclaw's eyes, but Ashfur's gaze remained calm. "Do you think *anyone* would believe I taught you that clumsy display?"

"Well, if you had it would be the first thing you've taught me today!"

That managed to ruffle Ashfur's pelt. The gray warrior's eyes blazed.

Brambleclaw stepped forward. "A warrior never blames his Clanmates for his own mistakes, Lionpaw." He turned to Ashfur. "I think you need to speak with your apprentice. Come on, Berrypaw. Let's carry on training over there."

The fur along Ashfur's spine quivered as he watched Brambleclaw pad to the other side of the clearing. Lionpaw suddenly felt cold as his anger slid away. He had gone too far. "I'm sorry," he mewed.

Ashfur swung his head around and glared at Lionpaw. "I have tried to make you the best apprentice in your den," he growled, "but lately it's been like training a slug. You only seem to hear half of what I tell you and the things you do hear, you forget. You used to have an instinct for hunting and fighting, but it's gone and I don't know where."

Lionpaw's whiskers trembled. He couldn't deny that he had been distracted lately, but he thought no one had noticed. "I promise I'll try harder."

"You'll have to if you don't want to get left behind in the apprentice den and watch Foxkit and Icekit become warriors before you!"

"I will!" Fear squirmed in Lionpaw's belly, not of Ashfur, but of failure. Everything had come so easily before. The idea that he might struggle to keep up filled him with dread.

"Good." Ashfur nodded curtly. "Let's start again."

Lionpaw squared his shoulders. "Okay."

"We'll try the badger defense."

Lionpaw blinked. "B-but that's one of the hardest."

"I know." Ashfur crouched. "Watch carefully." He reared up and leaped forward, high enough to clear a badger's back. He landed without dropping onto his forepaws and spun around so fast that Lionpaw marveled at how he kept his balance. Then he ducked down, back onto four paws, and twisted to the side, snapping his jaws as though clamping them into a badger's hind leg.

"Now you do it," he ordered. "And don't forget, a badger is twice as big as a cat, so make the leap as high as you can. You don't want to end up on its back. If it rolled over, it could crush you."

Heart pounding, Lionpaw reared up. He tried to leap forward, but lost his balance and fell to one side, slamming his forepaws onto the ground.

"Again!" Ashfur demanded.

Lionpaw pushed himself up and tried to leap forward once more. This time he managed to spring a little way, but he toppled over and fell down onto four paws again.

"Put more power into your jump," Ashfur meowed. "Most of your strength is in your hind legs—use it!"

"But I can't get my balance," Lionpaw protested.

"Then keep trying until you can!"

"Ashfur!" Brambleclaw called from the other side of the clearing. "I want to try out a double attack on Berrypaw. Can you come and help?"

Berrypaw was ready to take on *two* warriors? Lionpaw's pads tingled with jealousy. *They'll never let me try that!*

Ashfur narrowed his eyes. "Keep practicing," he commanded and bounded away to join the ThunderClan deputy.

Lionpaw felt despair drag at his paws. Why had Ashfur given him something so impossible to practice? Was he trying to make him look even more useless? Halfheartedly, he reared onto his hind legs. He staggered even before he tried to jump, the forest swaying in front of him. Frustrated, he dropped onto four paws. *I'll never get this!*

"Of course you will!" A pelt brushed his, nudging him so roughly that it sent him sprawling across the wet moss.

Lionpaw scrambled crossly to his paws. "What are you—?" He broke off.

Brambleclaw, Ashfur, and Berrypaw were still on the far-side of the clearing.

Who pushed me?

"Keep your eyes fixed on something in front of you," a voice growled. "It's the only way to keep your balance."

Lionpaw stared in alarm. Two eyes burned against the background of the forest. A hazy outline moved like mist against the ferns.

"Tigerstar!" Lionpaw glanced nervously toward his Clan-mates. Could they see him?

"Only you can see me." Tigerstar seemed to read his mind. "I'm not here as far as they're concerned."

"Why *are* you here?" Lionpaw shivered.

"To help you." Tigerstar narrowed his eyes. "It looks like you need it."

Lionpaw felt hot with shame.

"I'll be the badger." Tigerstar crouched in front of him.

Lionpaw frowned. How would he be able to tackle this ghostly warrior? He could hardly see him.

"Try it!" Tigerstar commanded. "And don't forget to keep your eyes on something solid."

Lionpaw took a deep breath and stared at a birch at the edge of the clearing. Concentrating hard, he reared onto his hind legs. He was balancing! He tensed the muscles in his

hind legs and sprang up and over Tigerstar, landing behind
him. He turned and began to feel himself falling to one side.
Tigerstar shifted fast as a snake and pushed him back up so
that he could complete the turn. Lionpaw regained his balance, ducked, and twisted to nip Tigerstar's hind leg.

"Not bad." Tigerstar dodged away. "But you won't always
have me to prop you up."

At least I was better than before! Lionpaw padded back to his
starting place while Tigerstar crouched in front of him again.
This time he tensed every muscle in his body before pushing
up with his back legs and leaping forward. He landed perfectly and ducked, baring his teeth to nip Tigerstar's hind leg.

But Tigerstar was already up and pacing. "That's more like
it," he growled. "But you should slash out with your forepaw
as you spin. That way, you could scratch the badger as well as
bite it."

Lionpaw's heart was pounding with excitement. He hadn't
felt this awake in days. "Let's try it!"

He managed it perfectly the first time.

Tigerstar dodged to avoid being raked by Lionpaw's fast
forepaw slash.

"Much better!"

"How are you getting on?" Ashfur's call made Lionpaw
jump. He spun around guiltily, and saw his mentor padding
toward him. He glanced nervously over his shoulder.

Tigerstar was gone.

Ashfur narrowed his eyes. "You have been practicing,
haven't you?"

"Yes," Lionpaw mewed quickly.

"Show me."

Lionpaw performed the move even better than he had with Tigerstar. He finished in a perfect crouch and glanced up at Ashfur. His mentor's eyes were glowing. "You might make a warrior, after all." He beckoned to Brambleclaw with his tail. "Come and watch this."

Brambleclaw bounded to join them, Berrypaw on his heels.

"You be the badger, Berrypaw," Ashfur ordered.

Berrypaw crouched, and Lionpaw reared up and leaped over him. He spun and flicked out a claw that parted Berrypaw's fur, then finished by grazing Berrypaw's hind leg with his teeth.

"A badger wouldn't stand a chance!" Ashfur meowed proudly.

"He could have jumped higher," Berrypaw mewed.

"It would have slowed him down," Ashfur argued.

"Brambleclaw?" Lionpaw was itching to know what his father thought. "Was it okay?" A troubled look seemed to be clouding the ThunderClan deputy's gaze.

Brambleclaw blinked. "It was great," he meowed. He turned to Ashfur. "Did you teach him the move with the claw?"

"No, he came up with that by himself."

"Did you?" Brambleclaw's gaze seemed to burn into Lionpaw's.

Lionpaw nodded guiltily. Had his father recognized Tigerstar's move? "Did you like it?"

"It's a nice touch." Brambleclaw stroked his tail along Lionpaw's flank. "Let's get back to camp."

The ThunderClan deputy padded out of the mossy clearing, his striped tail disappearing into the ferns. Berrypaw made a face at Lionpaw before following his mentor into the undergrowth.

"Are you coming?" Ashfur meowed.

"In a moment." Lionpaw wanted to see if Tigerstar would come back. He wanted to know why the dark warrior was taking so much interest in him. Jaypaw was the one who spoke with their ancestors. As Ashfur slipped into the ferns, Lionpaw scanned the clearing. There was no sign of Tigerstar, not even a scent. The tabby warrior had vanished.

Lionpaw shook away the doubt pricking in his pelt. He should be grateful. Tigerstar seemed to care more about his training than his mentor did.

"Thanks, Tigerstar," he whispered into the trees, and followed his Clanmates home toward camp.

CHAPTER 12

❧

"Watch out!"

Graystripe's warning was muffled by the bramble stem clasped in his jaws. Hollypaw hopped backward as the trail of brambles swished past her. Millie scurried by, trying to guide Graystripe's prickly load safely across the clearing.

"I thought the den was finished," Hollypaw mewed to Hazelpaw, flicking her tail at the addition to the warriors' den. Its walls were thick and its roof pressed firmly into place. *Why do they need even more brambles?*

"It's not for the warriors' den." Hazelpaw shook her gray-and-white head. "They're reinforcing the nursery."

Hollypaw's heart sank. Why was everyone so sure there was going to be a battle?

Ferncloud began shooing Foxkit and Icekit away from the nursery while Graystripe and Millie wrapped the brambles around the already densely tangled bush.

Hazelpaw nodded toward the fresh-kill pile where Mousepaw was choosing his midday snack. "Are you coming?"

Hollypaw shook her head. She wasn't hungry. Anxiety had been churning in her belly since the Gathering. Besides, she was hunting with Brackenfur later; she could eat then. She watched Hazelpaw pick a mouse from the pile and settle down beside Mousepaw, their fluffy gray pelts merging into one.

Suddenly, the honeysuckle quivered and Brightheart rushed from the elders' den. The one-eyed cat was snapping instructions over her shoulder. "Quick, this way!"

Longtail shot out behind her, Mousefur limping after him.

"I don't see why we have to practice," Mousefur coughed. "I know the drill."

Brightheart halted at the bottom of the tumble of rocks. "You need to know it by heart in case there's an attack at night."

Longtail paused beside Brightheart. "Dark or light, it makes no difference to me." His sightless eyes sparkled teasingly.

Mousefur padded stiffly past him. "I've been in this camp long enough to know the way." Hollypaw could hear her begin to wheeze as she clambered up the rocks toward the safety of Highledge. Longtail followed closely, nudging her forward whenever her paws slipped. Greencough had left Mousefur weaker than any cat would admit—Mousefur especially. It wasn't fair to make her drill like this, especially for a battle that might never happen.

Thornclaw and Whitewing padded past Hollypaw. Thornclaw glanced at her. "Shouldn't you be helping reinforce the defenses?"

"I'm training with Brackenfur soon," Hollypaw explained.

"Good." Thornclaw halted beneath Highledge where

Stormfur and Brook were sharing tongues. "We need our apprentices sharp."

Brook looked up. "Are you so sure the battle will happen?" There was anxiety in her husky mountain mew.

"We can't be too careful," Thornclaw growled.

Stormfur sat up. "It doesn't make sense," he meowed. "Why would WindClan attack us?"

"Yes!" Brook's eyes brightened. "RiverClan's the one they're going to have trouble with."

"What happens to RiverClan will affect us all," Whitewing meowed.

Thornclaw flicked his tail. "If RiverClan is driven from their territory, where will they go?"

"They'll need to settle somewhere," Whitewing pointed out.

Stormfur sighed. "None of the borders will be safe."

Hollypaw's pelt pricked with anxiety. How could the four Clans survive if RiverClan lost their territory?

"Hollypaw?" Brackenfur was heading toward her.

"Are we going hunting?"

"Change of plan." Brackenfur nodded toward Mousepaw and Hazelpaw. "We'll be battle training with your denmates instead."

Battle training!

He started to hurry away. "I'll meet you at the training hollow."

Hollypaw padded halfheartedly to the camp entrance. She didn't want to train for a battle that might lead to the end of four Clans living around the lake. Stormfur's words rang in her ears: *None of the borders will be safe.*

She had to stop this!

She turned and almost crashed into Mousepaw. His green eyes were shining. "Did Brackenfur tell you?"

Hazelpaw clawed the ground behind him. "We're battle training!"

Hollypaw stared at them. "Go ahead without me," she whispered.

"What are you doing?" Mousepaw asked.

"It doesn't matter," she mewed. "I'll catch up with you when I've finished."

"But what will we tell Brackenfur?"

Hollypaw didn't answer Hazelpaw's anxious question. She had already pushed past her denmates and was halfway across the clearing. Brackenfur had stopped to talk with Stormfur. Hollypaw quickly ducked behind the elders' den.

"Imagine thinking I couldn't find my way up to Highledge." She heard Mousefur's croaking mew from inside. "They'll have us practicing washing next."

"Well, at least we're ready now," Longtail mewed soothingly.

"I was *born* ready!" Mousefur grumbled.

Hollypaw's pelt bristled with anticipation as Brackenfur finally nodded to Stormfur. "See you later." The golden warrior headed away toward the camp entrance.

Hollypaw slipped out from behind the honeysuckle and scurried up the rocks to Highledge. "Firestar!" She rushed into the cave, blinking against the sudden darkness.

Firestar's eyes flashed in the shadows. Sandstorm was

plucking the feathers from a sparrow carcass on the other side of the cave.

"What is it, Hollypaw?" Firestar sat up straight.

"You can't just let it happen!" Hollypaw mewed.

Sandstorm padded to Firestar's side. "Let what happen?"

"The battle that everyone's preparing for!"

"The battle might not happen." Firestar meowed calmly. "There's nothing wrong with being prepared."

"But why are we getting ready to fight WindClan when we should be helping RiverClan?" Hollypaw stepped forward, her paws trembling. "When I spoke to Willowpaw at the Gathering, she was so upset! All the RiverClan cats were. They need our help. But all we're doing is getting ready to attack WindClan!"

Firestar curled his tail over his paws. "I have no intention of attacking WindClan," he meowed. "But we must be ready if they attack us."

Hollypaw couldn't understand how Firestar could be so stupid. "WindClan won't attack. It's RiverClan who is in trouble!"

"If RiverClan is forced into WindClan territory, then WindClan may try to take some of ours," Firestar explained.

"RiverClan would never want to live on the moorland!" Hollypaw's whiskers quivered. "They'd want to stay by the lake where they can fish."

Sandstorm leaned forward. "Clans can adapt to anything if they have to."

Firestar nodded. "Look how WindClan is getting used

to hunting in woodland."

Hollypaw angrily flicked her tail. "Why don't we try to solve the problem before it turns into a fight?"

Firestar lifted a paw, warning her to calm down. "RiverClan must be allowed to solve their own problems."

"But what if they can't?"

Paw steps sounded outside. Hollypaw glanced around to see Leafpool padding into the cave.

"I thought I heard you in here." The medicine cat blinked at Hollypaw.

Firestar dipped his head to Leafpool. "Hollypaw's worried about the battle."

Fresh frustration flared in Hollypaw's pelt. "There doesn't have to *be* a battle!"

"Of course there doesn't," Leafpool assured her. "When I spoke to Mothwing at the Gathering, she said that RiverClan was dealing with their problem. But if they can't solve it, we have to be ready."

"But if we helped them," Hollypaw mewed, "then they'd be okay."

Leafpool shook her head. "We must trust RiverClan to sort it out themselves."

"Leafpool's right," Firestar meowed. "Besides, helping RiverClan would mean crossing WindClan territory."

"Or ShadowClan's," Sandstorm added.

Leafpool ran her tail down Hollypaw's flank. "And that would only make things worse, wouldn't it?"

Hollypaw shied away from Leafpool, bristling. She didn't

need to be soothed, like a kit having a bad dream! Why couldn't they take her seriously?

"Isn't Brackenfur waiting for you?" Sandstorm prompted.

"You mustn't fall behind with your training," Firestar reminded her.

Hollypaw turned and stamped out of the cave. Pebbles clacked under her paws as she bounded down the rocks to the clearing.

"Wait!"

Hollypaw glanced backward.

Leafpool was hurrying after her. "I can see you're upset."

Hollypaw turned on her. "Why won't any of you listen?"

"You must remember," Leafpool soothed, "we all have more experience than you. You have to trust us to know what's right."

"StarClan would want us to help RiverClan," Hollypaw mewed.

"You can't be sure of that." Leafpool blinked. "I know you're worried about Willowpaw, but you're training to be a warrior now. It's not appropriate to have such close friends in other Clans."

Hollypaw glared at her. *This isn't about Willowpaw. This is about the future of all four Clans!* She searched Leafpool's gaze and found only a gentle concern. *I'm wasting my breath!*

"Go and find Brackenfur," Leafpool suggested. "He's heading for the training hollow."

"I know where he is," Hollypaw hissed through gritted teeth.

"I'm sure he must be expecting you." Leafpool touched Hollypaw's cheek with her nose, then padded away.

Hollypaw flexed her claws. If she could find out exactly what was happening in RiverClan, perhaps *then* she could convince Firestar to help, and the Clans wouldn't need to fight.

She had to talk to Willowpaw.

She darted through the entrance tunnel, thorns scraping her pelt. Outside the camp, she glanced around. No one was there. She hurried into the trees, away from the training hollow, and headed up the ridge toward the WindClan border.

"Squirrel!"

Birchfall's excited yowl pierced the air. Hollypaw dived into a patch of ferns, pressing her belly to the ground. Paw steps were pounding toward her. She peeped through the green fronds and saw Birchfall and Ashfur skidding down the slope. Lionpaw was racing behind them, his tail fluffed out. She ducked back into the foliage and held her breath. The ferns rustled around her as the patrol whisked past less than a tail-length away.

Hollypaw screwed her eyes shut. *Don't let them see me!*

Heart pounding, she heard their paw steps fade into the forest. Relief washed her pelt and she crept from her hiding place and started up the slope. Ears pricked and nose twitching, she ran over the top of the ridge and headed down, out of the trees, and across the bumpy grass to the WindClan border. Her paws trembled as the tang of WindClan hit her nose. This border had been recently marked.

Hollypaw scanned the heather-swathed slope that rose

up to the high moorland.

No sign of any patrols.

Tail trembling, she padded across the scent line. Rain was beginning to fall from the dove-gray sky. *It'll help cover my scent*, she thought, relieved as the drops began to soak her fur. She padded through the heather, heading downhill toward the lake, and scrambled down from the peaty earth onto the pebbly shore. Keeping low, she scooted to the water's edge. Just to be on the safe side, she waded through the shallows. The water would disguise her scent even more. She shivered with cold as the waves lapped her belly fur, but at least WindClan wouldn't suspect a ThunderClan cat had trespassed on their territory.

The rain fell harder, hissing against the surface of the lake. Droplets streamed from her whiskers. Hollypaw glanced toward the moorland rising from the shore, praying that, if a patrol appeared from the heather, her black pelt would appear only as sodden driftwood against the gray water. She saw reeds begin to dot the shore up ahead; she was nearing RiverClan territory. She quickened her pace. She could hide more easily among the rushes. Pebbles turned to mud beneath her paws and she smelled the strong scent of RiverClan. Padding out of the shallows she crept into the reed bed, thankful to be out of the water and hidden by the towering rushes.

Suddenly, a yowl sounded ahead.

Hollypaw froze and sniffed the air. Fresh warrior scent. A hunting party?

She dropped into a crouch, trembling with cold and fear as she spotted the stone-colored pelt of Mistyfoot through the reeds. The RiverClan deputy was stalking something. Hollypaw backed away as Mistyfoot drew nearer. She pressed herself against the earth, hoping that her drenched pelt was too wet to betray her scent.

Suddenly, Mistyfoot sprang forward, paws outstretched. A moment later she straightened, her whiskers twitching with triumph and a water vole dangling from her jaws. Hollypaw sighed with relief as the RiverClan deputy turned and padded away. Mistyfoot looked thin and her usually glossy pelt was dull. Clearly, RiverClan was going hungry.

Hollypaw waited a few moments before she began to pad on gingerly. The island was not far ahead now, the tree-bridge distinct on the shoreline. How would she cross it without being seen? She stiffened herself against the anxiety that nagged at her bones. *I've come this far.* . . . Slipping from the cover of the reeds, she darted over the marshy shore and dived among the tangle of roots at the foot of the tree-bridge. Pressing herself into them she scanned the shore, blood pulsing in her ears. She sniffed the air.

No sign of any cat.

Cautiously, she clambered up through the roots and hauled herself onto the tree-bridge. Keeping low, she crept along the trunk, gripping the slimy bark with her claws. Hardly daring to breath, she pricked her ears, listening for an alarm call. She reached the other side, shaking with relief, and slid down through the branches onto the shore.

Which way now?

This wasn't a Gathering. She couldn't just push through the undergrowth and head for the clearing. How was she going to find Willowpaw?

Hope tingled in her paws when she realized that, not far along the shore, the beach was overtaken by undergrowth. The trees reached the water here, their roots snaking into the lake, and ferns and brambles tumbled over the lip of the island.

Hollypaw took a deep breath and raced across the small stretch of open beach. She dived under the cover of a clump of ferns. The fronds spilled into the water, forming a tunnel around the edge of the island.

Where in StarClan is the medicine den? Hollypaw prayed she would detect Willowpaw's familiar scent soon. But what if it led her inland, toward the heart of RiverClan's new camp? She crept through the fern tunnel, clambering over tree roots and hauling herself through clumps of bramble, her paws occasionally slipping off the muddy bank and into the cold lake.

Suddenly, the undergrowth ended. Rocks stretched ahead of her, rough and flat and black against the water. They reached into the lake, forming a small causeway that ended in a rocky outcrop, jutting up from the water. Hollypaw lifted her head, ears pricked, and tasted the air. She could hear the sounds of RiverClan drifting from the center of the island: queens talking, kits mewling, an elder complaining about ticks. No sound of warriors or apprentices, though. Hollypaw frowned. At the Gathering, the island had been teeming with RiverClan cats. Where were the rest of them now?

No time to worry about that!

Where was Willowpaw?

Hollypaw shivered. She was freezing. Her wet pelt clung to her. She was far from home. Panic started to rise in her chest. What if she couldn't find her friend?

Then she heard a squeal. A kit was wailing somewhere up ahead. "That hurt!"

The soft mew of a queen soothed it. "It'll only hurt for a bit."

Hollypaw could smell herbs. Someone was treating the kit with marigold!

She crept out onto the rough, flat causeway, following the scent. It was coming from the rocky outcrop. Crouching lower than ever, Hollypaw slithered around the edge and peered through a gap in the stones.

"We'll need more marigold soon."

Willowpaw!

The RiverClan medicine cat apprentice was crouched in a hollow in the heart of the outcrop, crushing leaves against the rough stone floor with her paws. "The kits keep getting pine needles stuck in their pads."

Mothwing sat on a ledge nearby, licking herbs into the mewling kit's paw. A white she-cat held the kit in her paws as it struggled against Mothwing's lapping tongue.

"Try to keep her out of the pine needles, Icewing," Mothwing advised.

"It's not easy," the queen sighed.

"I know," Mothwing agreed. "I'll come back to the nursery with you and sweep some of the needles away from the entrance."

The queen lifted the kit by its scruff and began to carry it, still mewling, out from the sheltering rocks and along the causeway that led back to the island. Mothwing followed her.

When she was sure there was no other cat close enough to hear, Hollypaw hissed through the gap in the rock. "Willowpaw!"

The medicine cat apprentice froze. "Who's that?"

"It's me, Hollypaw!"

Hollypaw quickly clambered back around the jutting rocks and slipped into the hollow beside Willowpaw. There was more space inside the outcrop than she had imagined. It was a cave, hollowed out by countless moons of wind and water, protected from the wind and rain by a low roof.

Willowpaw crouched at the back, her eyes round with shock. "What are you doing here?"

"I promised I'd come," Hollypaw reminded her.

"Does anyone know you're here?"

Hollypaw shook her head. Then she tensed. Mothwing's scent was wafting into the cave.

"Hollypaw?" Mothwing's mew was sharp.

Hollypaw spun around.

"I came back for poppy seeds." The RiverClan medicine cat was standing in the cave entrance. Her bones looked sharp beneath her pelt. "Hollypaw! What are you doing here?"

"I had to do something!" Hollypaw mewed desperately. "ThunderClan are getting ready to fight WindClan. Everyone's scared about what will happen if RiverClan is driven out of its home."

Mothwing looked at her. "RiverClan is not going to be driven out of anywhere."

"How can you be sure?" Hollypaw gazed back at her thin frame, unconvinced. "You're half starved, and you're still living on the island."

Willowpaw brushed against her. "It won't be for long."

Hollypaw glanced at the rows of herbs carefully stacked against the cave wall. It looked like RiverClan was planning to be here for some time. "But you've brought everything from your old camp," she pointed out.

The RiverClan medicine cat sighed. "You'd better show her."

"Really?" Willowpaw looked surprised. "Now?"

Mothwing nodded. "Just don't let yourselves be seen."

Willowpaw nodded and streaked from the cave. Hollypaw hurried after her, pelt ruffled with curiosity. She followed Willowpaw across the tiny causeway and back around the shoreline.

"Let's swim across to the mainland," Willowpaw mewed. "It'll be easier to stay out of sight."

Hollypaw's wet fur spiked in alarm. "I know I'm soaked, but there's no way I'm swimming!" The tree-bridge lay only a few fox-lengths ahead of them.

"Okay, okay," Willowpaw mewed impatiently. "But we'd

better disguise you somehow. Your scent's seeping through."
She scanned the shoreline, whiskers twitching. "Follow me."

The medicine cat apprentice pushed her way among some
clumps of grass that grew half in, half out of the water.
"Here." Before Hollypaw could complain, she scooped up a
pawful of brown muck and smeared it over Hollypaw's pelt.

Hollypaw gagged. "What's that?" The goo clung to her fur,
sticky and smelly.

"Otter dung," Willowpaw mewed. "It should hide your
ThunderClan scent."

Hollypaw coughed. "You're kidding!"

"You can wash it off later," Willowpaw hissed. "Just be
quiet and keep still."

She smeared another few pawfuls along Hollypaw's flank.
Hollypaw began to wish she had never come. Then Willowpaw reared up and scanned the shore on both sides of the
lake.

"Quick!" She scrambled across the beach and up onto the
tree-bridge.

Hollypaw followed, swallowing the nausea that rose in her
throat at the smell of the otter dung. "Are you sure this stuff
will disguise me?" she hissed as they crossed the bridge. "It's
so strong, I bet *ThunderClan* can smell me."

"Certain." Willowpaw leaped down from the tree, crossed
the shore, and dived into a forest of reeds. Hollypaw followed, struggling in the soft ground. Mud clung to her legs
and coated her belly fur. Willowpaw seemed to be hopping
among the clumps of reeds, staying free of the mud.

Hollypaw watched her closely and began to follow her path exactly, relieved to find that, so long as she kept to her friend's paw steps, she kept her paws and belly dry.

At last the ground became firmer and Hollypaw felt grass underpaw. Willowpaw was leading her up a slope. There were trees here and the undergrowth grew thick and lush. The slope grew steeper until Hollypaw found she was scrambling up a red sandy cliff. She followed Willowpaw as the RiverClan apprentice leaped up and up, using rocks that jutted from the earth to haul herself higher. At last the two cats clawed their way onto the grassy bank at the top. Panting, Hollypaw looked down. The lake shone far below, glimmering through the fresh green leaves.

"Where are we going?" Hollypaw panted.

"You'll see in a moment." Willowpaw headed up the bank and disappeared into a swath of long grass.

Hollypaw hurried after her.

"Look." Willowpaw had stopped.

Hollypaw crept to her side as Willowpaw gently parted the grass. She peered through. Below them, a wide stream followed the line of the slope. An island rose in the middle, parting the water abruptly so that eddies swirled where the stream was forced to divide. The island was crowded with small trees and bushes, green amid the rolling brown water.

"That's our old camp," Willowpaw explained.

Hollypaw heard the clatter of rocks and stiffened. "What's that?"

"The warriors are working."

"Working?" Hollypaw blinked.

Suddenly, she spotted the pelts of RiverClan warriors and apprentices weaving through the grass on either side of the stream. On the near side, she recognized the apprentices Pouncepaw and Minnowpaw. They were helping Reed-whisker and Voletooth to shift stones, pushing them toward the stream and tipping them over the edge so that they fell with a loud splash into the water.

"What are they doing?"

"Blocking the stream to make it deeper and wider," Willowpaw replied.

Blackclaw, a muscular, broad-shouldered black tom, called from the far side of the stream. "Hurry! Grab what you can!" He stood near the water's edge, calling orders to warriors who were bravely leaping across the channel with wads of mossy bedding dangling from their jaws.

"We need to rescue as much stuff as we can," Willowpaw explained. "The pine needles on the island are no good for making the nests weatherproof."

"But why are you doing all this?" Hollypaw couldn't understand what was going on. The old camp looked safe enough, almost as well protected by the divided stream as ThunderClan was by the cliffs of stone.

A warning yowl sounded upstream and Minnowpaw came hurtling down the bank. "They're coming!"

Every RiverClan cat instantly dropped whatever they were carrying or pushing and scrambled away from the island, heading down toward the lake.

Hollypaw's fur bristled. "What's the matter?"

"You'll see," Willowpaw mewed.

Tramping through the grass, along the far side of the stream, came a gang of Twoleg kits. They were sweeping jagged branches through the grass and mewling loudly to one another. As Hollypaw watched, the largest of the kits hopped from the shore and onto a stone that barely broke the surface of the stream, then onto another and another. Balancing precariously on one leg, it leaned toward the island, and began to poke the bushes with its stick. The other kits yelped their approval and encouraged him by waving their hairless paws in the air.

Hollypaw stared at her friend in dismay.

Willowpaw lashed her tail. "Now do you see why we had to leave?"

CHAPTER 13

❧

"*It was Blackclaw's idea to push* the stones into the stream," Willowpaw explained as they picked their way down the sandy cliff.

Hollypaw put her head on one side. "But that will stop the water flowing."

"Exactly, so the stream above gets deeper and wider, and the island will be better protected."

Hollypaw was impressed. "But will it be enough to keep the Twoleg kits away?"

"Once the stream's flooded, we're going to put up barricades of gorse." Willowpaw stopped to catch her breath. "The Twolegs aren't trying to hurt us. I think they're just playing." She bent her head to wash the red sand from her pads. "They're like our kits. If we make it too hard for them to get near the island, they'll give up and play somewhere else."

"And then you can move back to the island!" Hollypaw guessed. RiverClan had no intention of moving onto WindClan territory. Her paws tingled. She couldn't wait to get back to her own camp and tell Firestar. WindClan's borders were perfectly safe, and they'd have no need to try to take any of ThunderClan's territory. There wasn't going to be a battle after all!

Willowpaw bounded down the rest of the slope and wove in among the reeds.

Hollypaw hurried after her. "But why didn't Leopardstar just tell the other Clans what was going on?"

"And look weak because we'd been driven out of our home?"

"But the other Clans might have helped."

"RiverClan can sort out their own problems!"

Hollypaw lowered her gaze. "I didn't mean to say that you couldn't, but—"

Willowpaw's pelt was bristling. "It's hard living on the island. There's not enough fish because the boats scare them away, and we can't hunt in the rest of our territory until we get rid of the Twoleg kits. The Clan is hungry and hungry warriors don't win battles."

Hollypaw remembered Mistyfoot's dull pelt and the way Mothwing's bones jutted out on her hips and along her spine.

"Do you really think Leopardstar can trust the other Clans not to take advantage?" Willowpaw went on, pushing her way through a clump of marsh grass. "We need all our strength to rescue our camp from the Twolegs."

"I won't tell ThunderClan that you're hungry," Hollypaw promised. "Only that you'll be back in your old camp soon and there's no reason to think you'll have to leave your territory."

Willowpaw blinked gratefully. "But first you have to get

home," she reminded her. "Your Clan must be wondering where you are."

Hollypaw felt a twinge of guilt. Had her Clanmates noticed she was missing yet? "I'll just go back the way I came."

Willowpaw stretched up on her hind legs and peered above the spiky grass. "The shore's quiet," she announced, dropping down onto four paws. She began to weave through the marsh toward the firmer ground inland, where bushes and ferns crowded the shoreline.

"Let's head up there," Willowpaw suggested. "It'll be easier to hide." Her eyes sparkled mischievously. "And the otter dung will stop any cats from noticing your scent."

"Wasn't there anything else you could have used?"

"Tansy might have worked," Willowpaw admitted. "But our supplies are a bit low." She pushed her way past a clump of ferns, and Hollypaw padded after her.

They followed the shoreline until Hollypaw began to smell the scent of horseplace. "We're near WindClan territory," she whispered. "You can leave me here."

Willowpaw's eyes clouded with worry. "Not till we reach the border."

The brown fences around the horseplace loomed larger and the ferns began to thin out as the lush foliage of RiverClan's territory gave way to WindClan moorland. Willowpaw paused behind a stunted bramble bush at the edge of a stretch of open grass lay. "There's the border." She pointed with her tail.

The wind raced down from the moors, tugging at

Hollypaw's pelt. She could smell the WindClan scent-line only a few fox-lengths ahead.

Willowpaw rested her tail-tip on Hollypaw's shoulder. "Promise you'll be careful."

Suddenly, stones clattered on the shore. Willowpaw whipped around.

A RiverClan patrol was haring toward them.

Hollypaw stiffened, fear shooting through her like lightning. Then she felt Willowpaw's teeth grab her scruff and drag her behind the bramble.

"Did they see us?" Hollypaw whispered, trembling.

"I don't know." Willowpaw flicked her tail over Hollypaw's mouth. "Keep quiet!"

Hollypaw peered through the leaves. Reedwhisker headed the patrol, his apprentice, Pouncepaw, racing behind him. Voletooth was at Reedwhisker's heels with Minnowpaw at his side. The young she-cat's dappled fur was slicked back by the wind, her whiskers blown against her cheeks, running as though her life depended on it.

"Are they hunting?" Hollypaw asked.

Willowpaw glanced around the empty shore. "Hunting what?"

"Well, are they coming for us?"

"Doesn't look like it," Willowpaw replied as the patrol streaked past the bramble without even looking at it.

Hollypaw realized that the RiverClan cats' eyes had been stretched wide with terror. Her pelt bristled. "Something's wrong."

Willowpaw hissed, flattening her ears. "Look!"

A rough-haired black-and-white dog was hurtling after the RiverClan patrol. Its eyes were wild, its lips drawn back to show shining white fangs.

"The horseplace dog!" Willowpaw yowled. "Run!" She pelted after her Clanmates.

Before Hollypaw could move, the black-and-white dog spotted her and skidded toward her, howling with excitement. Hollypaw shrieked and shot after Willowpaw. Her claws threw up clods of soil as she tore over the grassy slope. The RiverClan patrol had swerved off the beach and was racing up the slope toward the WindClan border.

Reedwhisker's eyes widened when he saw Willowpaw. "Stay near us!" he ordered. He raced up the slope, dodging a gorse bush and leaping a low clump of heather.

Willowpaw pelted after him. She screeched over her shoulder at Hollypaw. "Hurry up!"

Hollypaw pushed harder against the peaty soil. She skidded after the RiverClan cats through a thick swath of heather and out onto the grassy slope.

"Stop!" Reedwhisker gave the command and Hollypaw scrambled to a halt with the others. Panting and terrified, she glanced over her shoulder.

The dog stood by the fence at the bottom of the slope and gazed around, tongue lolling. Then it shook itself and squeezed under the fence. Hollypaw watched it trot across the field, heading for the Twolegplace.

"It must be going home," she guessed.

"Shh!" Willowpaw gave her a warning look but it was too late.

"What are *you* doing here?" Minnowpaw's shocked mew made Hollypaw jump.

Reedwhisker stared at her, his black pelt bristling. "You're a ThunderClan cat, aren't you?" His stern gaze flashed accusingly at Willowpaw.

Minnowpaw wrinkled her nose. "And why do you smell so bad?"

Voletooth padded toward her and leaned in close, his tabby muzzle only a whisker from Hollypaw's. "Are you spying on us?"

Hollypaw backed away. "No, no, I wanted to see if I could help!"

"Help?" Reedwhisker stared at her in disbelief.

"It's true!" Willowpaw padded, tail trembling, between her Clanmates and Hollypaw. "She's here by herself. She was worried about me after the Gathering. She just came to see if—"

"Mouse dung!" Reedwhisker's yowl cut Willowpaw off. The black tom was staring up the slope, his eyes round with dismay.

A WindClan patrol was streaking toward them.

Hollypaw tasted the air. The musky scent of WindClan bathed her tongue. The dog had chased them right across the border.

"Should we run?" Minnowpaw whispered, her tail stiff with fear.

"There's no use." Voletooth sighed. "We've come too far."

"We'd better just stand our ground," Reedwhisker meowed.

Pouncepaw stepped closer to Minnowpaw.

As the WindClan patrol neared, the deputy Ashfoot flicked her tail. Crowfeather, Heatherpaw, Whitetail, Torn-ear, and Breezepaw fanned out. Hollypaw felt Willowpaw's pelt brush against her flank as the WindClan cats slowly encircled the patrol. Their eyes were blazing.

"What are you doing on WindClan land?" Ashfoot demanded.

Reedwhisker met her gaze, the fur on his shoulders twitching. "We were being chased by that mouse-brained dog from the horseplace."

Crowfeather stepped forward. "Where is it now?"

Voletooth nodded toward the Twolegplace. "It went home."

"And we're meant to believe that?" Tornear sniffed the air, his whiskers quivering. "All I can smell is dung!"

Hollypaw wished she could sink into the ground. Wind-Clan were angry enough without finding a ThunderClan cat among the intruders. What if they thought RiverClan and ThunderClan had formed an alliance? There would be a bat-tle for sure, and it would all be her fault.

Hollypaw fought her rising panic. Breezepaw was staring at her. She lowered her gaze, praying he wouldn't recognize her, finally grateful for the otter dung that disguised her black pelt and drowned her scent.

"What happened to you?" Breezepaw's eyes glittered with contempt. "Don't they teach RiverClan kits to wash?"

Rage surged in Hollypaw's throat. She wanted to spit at the arrogant fox-face. But at least he didn't seem to know who she was.

"Get off our land!" Ashfoot hissed. "You may have lost your own territory but you're not having ours!"

Voletooth bristled, baring his teeth. "We haven't lost our territory!"

"Then why are you here?" Tornear demanded.

"Looking for prey?" Crowfeather hissed.

Reedwhisker lashed his tail. "No!"

Hollypaw tensed. Every cat was bristling, ready to leap. She unsheathed her claws. This was not her Clan, but she would fight if she had to.

Pouncepaw hopped forward, his short tabby tail flicking angrily. "We wouldn't eat rabbit if we were starving!"

Ashfoot hissed. "Get off our land *now!*"

Tornear and Whitetail moved apart to let the RiverClan cats through.

Slowly, Reedwhisker and Voletooth began to back away. Pouncepaw and Pebblepaw turned and padded uneasily past the WindClan cats. Hollypaw hurried after them, keeping her eyes fixed on the ground.

"There'll be extra patrols along the border from now on!" Ashfoot called after them.

"And they'll be battle ready!" Tornear growled.

They walked slowly to the border, refusing to be rushed by the threatening hisses from the WindClan patrol. Hollypaw crossed the scent-line with a shiver of relief. *But this isn't my territory!*

"I have to get home," she whispered.

Reedwhisker rounded on her. "No, you don't! You have to

explain what you're doing here!"

"I did explain!" Hollypaw retorted. "I was worried about Willowpaw."

"There's no way we're letting you set one paw on Wind-Clan territory now," Voletooth mewed. "You'll have to come back to the island with us."

Despair dropped like a stone in Hollypaw's belly. She gazed across the lake. Night was falling and the ThunderClan forest looked like shadows against the distant hills. She scanned the shoreline, hoping to see the familiar shape of one of her Clanmates—Jaypaw was always fiddling around by the water—but it was too dark and too far to see anything clearly.

"Okay," she sighed.

"But first you can wash off that awful-smelling dung!" Reedwhisker ordered.

He walked her down to the lake and stood at the edge while she splashed around in the freezing water. Willowpaw waded in to help, rubbing Hollypaw's pelt with her paws until it was clean.

Shivering with cold, Hollypaw padded back along the marshy shore after the RiverClan patrol. Willowpaw walked beside her.

"Sorry if I got you in trouble," Hollypaw whispered.

"I'll be okay," Willowpaw pressed against her and the two friends, still dripping from the lake, shared their warmth.

Hollypaw's pelt prickled under the curious gaze of the RiverClan cats as she followed Reedwhisker into the island clearing. Gradually, the camp went quiet as they drew closer to the Great Oak. She tried to stop her paws from trembling when she saw Leopardstar squeeze out from among the giant roots at the bottom of the oak.

"Don't be scared," Willowpaw murmured in her ear. "Leopardstar's always fair."

Hollypaw lifted her chin and faced the RiverClan leader as bravely as she could.

Leopardstar's eyes glowed in the twilight. "Reedwhisker tells me you've been spying on RiverClan territory," she accused.

"I was just trying to help," Hollypaw explained. "Thunder-Clan is worried that WindClan will attack us if you're forced into their territory. Everyone's preparing for battle. I just wanted to stop it."

Leopardstar blinked. "That's a big ambition for such a small apprentice."

Offended, Hollypaw fluffed out her fur.

Were Leopardstar's whiskers twitching?

"I presume Willowpaw has shown you enough to put your mind at rest?" meowed the RiverClan leader.

"Just the old camp—" Hollypaw stopped herself too late. She had betrayed her friend.

Leopardstar's gaze flicked to the RiverClan medicine apprentice. "You took her all the way there?"

Willowpaw dipped her head. "I only wanted to reassure her."

Leopardstar sighed. "Well, Hollypaw," she meowed, "you had better stay here on the island."

Hollypaw's heart lurched. "But my Clan will be worried about me."

"You should have thought of that before you came here." Leopardstar gazed around her Clan. The RiverClan cats had gathered under the oak tree, their ears twitching with interest. "We can't spare the warriors to escort you home and even if we could, I don't want to antagonize WindClan or ShadowClan by crossing their territory."

"But the warrior code says I can safely travel two foxlengths from the lake," Hollypaw pointed out.

"If it was time for a Gathering, I would agree," Leopardstar argued. "But as things stand, our neighbors would want a very good reason for finding RiverClan or ThunderClan scent on their land." She narrowed her eyes. "Plain nosiness is not good enough."

"But—" Hollypaw desperately searched for another argument. She had to get home before her Clanmates thought something dreadful had happened to her.

Leopardstar turned away. "You can stay with Mothwing and Willowpaw until it is safe for you to return."

"Come on." Willowpaw nudged her. "Let's get warm and dry in the medicine cave."

Paws heavy as stone, Hollypaw followed her friend to the edge of the island and over the causeway to the rocky outcrop.

Mothwing was waiting with a pile of herbs beside her. "I thought I told you not to be seen," she greeted them.

Willowpaw lowered her head. "Sorry."

Mothwing pawed the herbs toward them. "Eat these," she ordered. "They'll help warm you up."

Hollypaw's belly rumbled. She'd prefer a fresh, juicy mouse.

"It's all we have to spare at the moment," Mothwing told her.

Hollypaw leaned down and began to chew one of the leaves. It was sticky and warmed her tongue as she chewed it. "What is it?" she whispered to Willowpaw.

"Dried nettle, smeared with honey," Willowpaw replied.

"Not bad."

When they had finished eating, Willowpaw led her to a mossy nest at the back of the cave. They washed themselves dry and squeezed together onto the soft bedding. Hollypaw was grateful for Willowpaw's warmth. The cave was drafty and rain was starting to batter the rocks and hiss over the lake. She yawned, suddenly feeling bone-tired. "You know Leopardstar is just keeping me here because I know too much," she murmured.

"Yes." Willowpaw laid her tail across her friend's paws. "But would Firestar act any differently?"

Hollypaw sighed. "I guess not." She closed her eyes. How long would she have to stay here? She was going to be in big trouble with her Clanmates when they found out she was being held by RiverClan, suspected of being a spy.

CHAPTER 14

❧

Rain pattered on Jaypaw's pelt as he crossed the clearing. He held a bundle of watermint and juniper berries in his jaws and their pungent scent filled his nose.

Millie trotted beside him. "I told him not to eat another sparrow!" She stopped beneath Highledge where Graystripe was groaning.

"How was I supposed to resist?" Graystripe gasped. He let out another low moan. "It's been moons since there's been so much prey."

Jaypaw dropped his bundle of herbs. He rested a paw on Graystripe's round belly as he lay fidgeting with pain.

"Keep still." Jaypaw felt the hardness beneath Graystripe's flank. "You've just given yourself gas."

"I told you so," Millie meowed.

Jaypaw rolled the juniper berries toward Graystripe's muzzle. "These will help," he mewed. "Then eat the watermint."

"I thought a warrior would know that you have to start slowly after leaf-bare," Millie went on. "All those moons on an empty belly. You can't just stuff yourself as soon as the prey starts to run. You have to get used to it."

"Don't go on," Graystripe pleaded.

Millie's tongue lapped Graystripe's pelt. Jaypaw felt her affection for her mate like warm air around him. His whiskers twitched with amusement. It was funny to hear a warrior being lectured by a kittypet. *But she's a warrior now,* he reminded himself quickly.

Paw steps hurried into the camp. Jaypaw tasted the air. Mousepaw and Poppypaw. From the mossy scent on their pelts, he could tell they had been in the training hollow.

"Have you seen Hollypaw?" Poppypaw called as she bounded toward Highledge.

Jaypaw felt Poppypaw's anxious gaze burning his pelt. It darted away, awkwardness pricking from the apprentice.

"I didn't mean *see*," she corrected herself quickly. "I meant hear or scent—"

"She means, do you know where she is?" Mousepaw's impatient mew chipped in.

Jaypaw's pads tingled. He hadn't seen Hollypaw since this morning. He let his awareness spread around the camp, feeling for her presence in the same way he would grope for poppy seeds among the herb store. Nothing. No sense of Hollypaw in the camp or near it. He shook his head.

Graystripe scrambled to his paws. "How long has she been missing?" he demanded.

"She was supposed to be training with us, but she didn't turn up," Poppypaw mewed.

"Brackenfur figured she'd been kept in camp for some reason," Mousefur added. "So we just did the training without her. We thought she'd be here when we got back."

"But she's not!" Poppypaw's shrill mew rang around the camp.

Brackenfur came bounding from the thorn tunnel. "She's not here?"

Spiderleg and Ashfur were on his heels.

"Her scent is in the tunnel, but it's stale," Ashfur reported.

"She must have left camp when I told her to," Brackenfur guessed.

"But she didn't make it to the training hollow," Spiderleg concluded.

Jaypaw felt the interest of their Clanmates pricking around the clearing.

Brightheart hurried over. "Perhaps she's hurt!"

"Who's hurt?" Sorreltail called.

"No one's hurt!" Graystripe explained. "But Hollypaw seems to be missing."

Jaypaw was starting to get squashed by the warriors pressing around him. Thornclaw and Whitewing had joined them.

"Perhaps WindClan has captured her!" Thornclaw declared.

Alarm flashed from the warriors and apprentices.

Cloudtail pushed his way to the front. "Why would they do that?"

Jaypaw smelled Brook's mountain scent. "Has WindClan ever taken hostages before?" she asked.

"No, but they've never hunted squirrels before either!" Dustpelt pointed out.

Sorreltail gasped. "I hope they don't hurt her!"

Jaypaw felt torn between alarm and irritation. Everyone was panicking far too quickly. But what if Hollypaw *had* been captured?

Only Brook remained calm. "It wouldn't make sense for WindClan to give themselves an extra mouth to feed."

"But they have extra prey now that they hunt in the forest," Brightheart meowed.

"They might think it's worth it." Sorreltail's voice was taut with worry.

"We should send a patrol to rescue her!" Thornclaw announced.

Brambleclaw joined his Clanmates. "Rescue who?"

Jaypaw felt relief wash his pelt as he sensed Squirrelflight at his father's side. She licked him between the ears. "What's going on, Jaypaw?"

"Hollypaw's missing."

Squirrelflight stiffened. "Since when?"

"I spoke to her at midday," Brackenfur explained. "She was supposed to come to the training hollow, but she never arrived."

"WindClan must have captured her!" Brightheart meowed.

"Do we know that for sure?" Brambleclaw asked.

No one replied.

"Well, in that case, let's not assume the worst," the ThunderClan deputy urged.

"Knowing Hollypaw, she's just gone off by herself," Squirrelflight meowed.

Jaypaw nodded. Hollypaw had wandered off more than once when she needed time to think.

"But would she deliberately miss training?" Sorreltail fretted.

"She's never missed it before." Firestar's mew sounded above them. He was on Highledge. The cats shuffled backward to look up at their leader. Jaypaw was relieved to have some space but he could feel guilt and anxiety flooding from Firestar. What did he have to feel guilty about?

"We can't assume that WindClan have taken her," the ThunderClan leader went on.

"But we know they want to attack us," Thornclaw called. "This might be their way of provoking a battle."

Worried mews rippled around the Clan.

"We don't know for sure they want to attack," Firestar reasoned. "And as Squirrelflight pointed out, Hollypaw is perfectly capable of going off by herself. She's always been independent. Don't forget she went fox-hunting when she was still a kit!"

Firestar's mew was light but Jaypaw could sense the leader's thoughts churning. Meanwhile, his Clanmates' ruffled pelts began to smooth. Of course Hollypaw was all right. Disappearing for the day was just the sort of thing she'd do. Jaypaw wasn't convinced. Firestar knew more than he was letting on. He tried to probe the ThunderClan leader's mind, but a fretful cloud obscured any clear thoughts. Perhaps he should just ask him outright? Jaypaw shrugged away the idea. Firestar clearly wanted to keep his fears to himself.

Jaypaw slipped past Brook and Brightheart and headed toward the medicine den. As he neared it, he heard the brambles at the entrance rustle. Leafpool had just darted inside. She must have been listening. He padded into the cave, a little taken aback by the wave of emotion flooding from Leafpool's pelt.

"Is it true?" Cinderpaw's anxious mew sounded from her nest. "Has Hollypaw disappeared?"

"You know Hollypaw," Jaypaw soothed. "She's probably gone off to think."

"I guess." Cinderpaw's nest rustled as she settled back down, but Jaypaw could sense the tension in her muscles.

Across the den, alarm pulsed even more fiercely from Leafpool.

"What's the matter?" he hissed, hurrying to his mentor's side. He focused on her thoughts and found her mind chaotic with worry and guilt, just as Firestar's had been. They both knew something!

"I spoke to Hollypaw before she left the camp," Leafpool admitted quietly.

Jaypaw pricked his ears. "Did she say where she was going?"

"No, but she was upset." Leafpool's voice was hoarse. "She'd just asked Firestar to help RiverClan."

"And he said no," Jaypaw guessed, remembering how Firestar had reacted to his dream.

"She couldn't possibly believe she could help RiverClan by herself!" meowed Leafpool.

"Hollypaw wouldn't be that mouse-brained," Jaypaw agreed.

"But maybe she thought that if she couldn't reason with Firestar, she might be able to convince Onestar not to fight," Leafpool went on reluctantly.

A dark pit seemed to open in Jaypaw's stomach. Hollypaw always thought the world was neatly divided into right and wrong. And if she thought Firestar was making a mistake, she might be stubborn enough to try and mend things on her own. He shook the thought away. She wouldn't be that reckless. Would she?

He felt Leafpool's paw pressing his. "You must try to dream!" she meowed. "You have to find out where she is!"

Her urgent plea set his fur bristling with indignation. Not so long ago she'd begged him to keep his dreams a secret; now she wanted him to use them to find Hollypaw. Was this all he was to her? A quick way to get answers from StarClan when she wanted them, and a danger to the Clan when she didn't?

"Please!"

"I'm not tired!" Jaypaw objected. "I can't just dream when I like."

"Just close your eyes and try," Leafpool begged.

"I'll dream when I'm ready!" he snapped.

He padded toward the entrance and felt Leafpool's pelt brush against his. She was blocking the way!

"You have to try now!" Leafpool hissed.

Jaypaw's pelt bristled. "But she's probably just gone off by herself for a bit." What was wrong with Leafpool? She sounded more worried than Squirrelflight!

Cinderpaw's nest rustled. "Is something wrong?"

Leafpool turned to reassure her patient. "Don't worry," she soothed. "Keep still and rest your leg."

So that was what she was worried about. Not Hollypaw. Just her precious patient. Jaypaw's ears burned with rage. He pushed past her and stamped out of the den.

The camp was calmer now. Firestar had jumped down from Highledge to talk to Brambleclaw and Squirrelflight.

"The sunset patrol can keep an eye open for any trace of her," Firestar was meowing. "We'll see what they report and then send out a search party."

"I want to be on the sunset patrol," Squirrelflight meowed at once.

"And the search party," Brambleclaw added.

"Of course," Firestar agreed. "You must lead them both."

Jaypaw let his ruffled fur relax. A search party was much more sensible than Leafpool's desperate plea for dreams. She was as edgy as a deer these days. If Hollypaw didn't turn up, then of course he'd try and use his powers to find her, but he wasn't going to sleep all afternoon just because Leafpool ordered him to. He wanted to get away from her, away from the camp, away from everyone. He began to squeeze through the thorn tunnel.

"Where are you going?" Squirrelflight called after him. Anxiety was pricking from her pelt. Was she worried about losing another kit? One that every cat believed couldn't take care of himself?

"For a walk."

"Don't be long."

I'll be as long as I like! Jaypaw headed into the trees. The damp air promised rain, and the forest smelled musty. He found his paws heading up the slope toward the lake. He sniffed eagerly for the scent of the open water, quickening his pace as he topped the ridge and headed down and out of the trees. This route would take him straight to the shore where he had left the branch. He began to hurry, whiskers twitching, paws following the familiar path down to the shore.

He scrambled down onto the beach and paused. Unlike the forest, which never seemed to change, the ground around the edge of the lake was always different. The pebbles seemed to shift so that they never felt the same underpaw, and debris came and went, washed up, then washed away again. Jaypaw loved the challenge of the shore. Just so long as he could steer clear of the water. He padded cautiously forward, muzzle outstretched, sniffing for driftwood or rubbish that might trip him. But his mind was fixed on the stick, hopefully still tucked safely behind the tree root. He weaved his way toward it, his heart beating faster as he neared it. He reached out a paw. It was there! Still safe.

Happily, he dragged it from its hiding place and ran his paws over it, feeling the warmth of the wood and welcoming the jarring ripples as his pads bumped over the scratches. The swishing of the waves and the murmuring of the wind drifted away. He was aware only of the branch beneath his pads and the sharp etches cut into it. A voice breathed in his ears, too soft to hear. It was husky like the voice of an old cat and it seemed to be listing names, as though counting them off. Jaypaw felt his heart quicken as his paw neared the end of the branch. The uncrossed scratches lay there. His belly tightened. He strained to hear the voice. But when his paw touched the first uncrossed mark the voice choked and fell silent.

Disappointed, Jaypaw lay down beside the stick and rested his cheek on the smooth wood. He closed his eyes, soothed by the lapping of the lake, and began to dream.

Sandy earth shifted beneath his paws. He blinked open his eyes. A wall of jagged rock loomed ahead of him. Rolling heather rippled behind him in the wind. The sky overhead was black, studded with stars. At the top of the rock wall, he saw cats silhouetted against the night sky. None looked familiar and when he sniffed the air, Jaypaw recognized the scent only from those he had smelled at the Moonpool, when ancient Clans had brushed pelts with him on the paw-worn path to the pool.

Suddenly, one cat broke away from the others and bounded down the steep slope, a young tom with muscular shoulders beneath his sleek ginger-and-white pelt. A she-cat scrambled after him. The others remained at the top, their tails flicking nervously.

"Take care," the she-cat called, landing lightly on the sand.

The tom brushed muzzles with her. "I will see you at dawn, I promise." He turned to face the cliff and, for the first time, Jaypaw realized there was a crack in the rock immediately behind him.

The tom padded toward it. Jaypaw tried to step out of the way but the tom stepped through him as though he wasn't there. As their spirits crossed, Jaypaw felt a shudder of foreboding. This cat had never entered the rock before. He was frightened. As his tail disappeared into the shadows, Jaypaw's belly fluttered with excitement. He had to know where the cat was going. Quickly he slipped in after him.

Darkness swallowed him and for a moment Jaypaw wondered if he had woken up and was blind once more. But then he heard the soft pad of the tom's paws ahead and Jaypaw sensed space opening into the hillside, a narrow passageway that led straight into the rock.

Fear spiked the air. Yet determination rippled out from the tom's pelt too. The pounding of his heart seemed to make the air around them tremble and it grew louder as the tunnel opened into a cave. Pale light glowed overhead, streaming through a small gap in the roof. The arching walls were filled with more openings; the tunnels must spread like roots beneath the moor. Rushing water echoed around the rocks. Jaypaw saw with surprise that there was a river cutting through the cave and flowing away into yet another tunnel, the water black as night.

"Fallen Leaves?"

Jaypaw jerked his head up. An old cat was calling to the tom from a high ledge near the moonlit gap. *Fallen Leaves?*

The tom jumped.

"I can feel your surprise," the old cat croaked.

Jaypaw stared at the ancient cat. Its pelt was nothing but a few tufts of fur, its eyes were white and bulging and stared sightlessly down.

I hope my eyes don't look like that!

Fallen Leaves knew this cat would be here—Jaypaw could sense understanding and recognition between the two cats—but the young tom had clearly not expected him to be so ugly.

The old cat ran a paw over something smooth and pale—a bare branch clasped beneath his twisted claws.

Jaypaw stiffened. *My stick!* He strained to hear what the ancient cat was saying.

" . . . I must stay close to our warrior ancestors; those who have taken their place beneath the earth."

"And for that we thank you," Fallen Leaves murmured.

"Don't thank me," the old cat growled. "It was a destiny I was bound to follow. Besides, you may not feel so grateful to me once your initiation has begun." He ran a long claw over the lines scratched into the branch.

Fear pulsed from the young tom and swept Jaypaw like an icy wind. What was he so afraid of? Jaypaw looked back up at the ledge.

The old cat was shaking his head. "I cannot help you. To become a sharpclaw, you must guide yourself through these tunnels and find your own way out. I can only send you on your way with the blessing of our ancestors."

A sharpclaw? Was that like a warrior? Jaypaw suddenly understood the young tom's fear and his determination. It wasn't just the darkness he faced, but his future.

"Is it raining?" the old cat asked suddenly.

Jaypaw saw Fallen Leaves stiffen.

"The sky is clear." But Jaypaw sensed doubt flicker in the young cat's mind.

The old cat ran his claw once more over the lines etched in the branch. "Then begin."

Fallen Leaves leaped across the river and headed into the tunnel that opened beneath the old cat's ledge. Jaypaw bounded after him, relieved that he could see. He wouldn't want to cross the river blind. He shuddered as he imagined falling in and being sucked into the tunnel. Forcing away the thought, he followed Fallen Leaves into blackness once more.

This way leads up!

Jaypaw felt the realization cross Fallen Leaves's mind as clearly as if he'd said it out loud. Jaypaw weaved after him through the darkness. The rocky tunnel was smooth beneath his paws. What had made it so slick? It wound upward, narrowing and then widening, turning first one way, then the other.

Jaypaw's breath quickened. He could hardly believe he was walking with an ancient Clan cat, watching him cross the border from kithood to cathood. The surface of the moor couldn't be far away now, and then Fallen Leaves would be safe. Safe and a sharpclaw, just like he wanted. A puddle of moonlight splashed the floor ahead of them; Fallen Leaves dashed through it, glancing up. Jaypaw followed and saw a narrow gap above them, too high to reach.

Suddenly, the tunnel narrowed and began to slope downward.

Downward? But they'd nearly reached the open moor!

Doubt bristled in Fallen Leaves's pelt, but Jaypaw sensed him push it away. The tunnel twisted and Fallen Leaves's pelt brushed the wall as he swerved to follow the snaking passageway. Jaypaw was impressed how this cat coped with the darkness, much better than any ThunderClan cats would; he must have been trained to find his way with scent and touch alone.

The slope continued downward. Fallen Leaves halted, and Jaypaw sensed uncertainty. The tunnel ahead split. Which way should he take? Fallen Leaves padded slowly into one, then backed up. Jaypaw felt the tom's tail slide through his formless body. He jerked as it sent a jolt of doubt like lightning through his fur. He scrabbled backward. The young tom was losing his nerve.

Fallen Leaves darted forward, hurrying on once more. He had chosen the other tunnel, though it sloped downward. Jaypaw could smell heather; Fallen Leaves was following the scent of fresh air. Hope flashed in Jaypaw's chest. This must be the right way. He saw another pool of moonlight flood the tunnel in front of them. Could they get out here?

Fallen Leaves quickened his pace. Jaypaw felt hope flare in the young tom and then plummet as he reached the moonlight. Jaypaw looked up. The hole was wide but a long way out of reach. And in the shaft of moonlight, drops of rain flickered, spattering down into the tunnel.

Alarm blazed from Fallen Leaves's pelt. It swept away his disappointment like a cold wind clearing mist. He was scared of the rain! He shot onward, moving faster now, bumping into the sides of the tunnel more often in his desperation to find a way out. Jaypaw skidded as he followed Fallen Leaves around a sharp bend. The tunnel floor was growing slippery with raindrops. He flicked his tail, recovering his balance, frightened he might lose sight of Fallen Leaves.

The floor was growing wetter and wetter. Rain dripped faster through each hole they passed. A storm must be battering the moor above.

Suddenly, Fallen Leaves skidded to a halt. The tunnel had stopped at a smooth gray wall. He spun around and raced through Jaypaw.

Jaypaw's fur stood on end.

Fallen Leaves was struggling to keep his terror under control. He raced away, veering down an opening in the side of the tunnel, and Jaypaw's claws skittered over the floor as he turned and pelted after him. The tunnel dipped sharply. Jaypaw gasped as water lapped his paws. He followed Fallen Leaves as the tunnel began to slope upward, but still the water came, rushing down the passage, washing up against Jaypaw's belly.

The tunnels were flooding!

Fallen Leaves swerved through a new opening. It was narrower than the previous tunnels, and the walls pressed in on either side. A hole let in a glimmer of light, but it was too far up to climb out.

Fallen Leaves skidded to a halt. Jaypaw could smell peaty water and hear it sloshing ahead. He peered through the darkness and saw Fallen Leaves recoiling, his forepaws engulfed. The tunnel sloped down sharply in front of him and disappeared into water so deep it lapped the roof. Jaypaw turned around even before Fallen Leaves began to double back. He was leading now, scrambling back the way they'd come. Perhaps they could make it to the cave!

Fallen Leaves ran faster, clearly remembering the route, pulling past Jaypaw and taking the lead.

Please StarClan, let him find the cave!

Blood pounded in Jaypaw's ears. Unbridled terror pulsed from Fallen Leaves.

Jaypaw heard a roaring. Wind surged behind him, tugging his fur as it swept over him. He glanced back over his shoulder and saw water skidding toward them, splashing around the walls and roof.

Hurry! Jaypaw was running for his life.

Fallen Leaves glanced backward too, his eyes shining with terror. For the first time, he seemed to see Jaypaw.

"Save me!"

As Fallen Leaves cried out, the water lifted Jaypaw, swallowing his tail, his belly, and finally engulfing all of him so that he was tossed and swirled by cold clutching waves. Water filled his ears, his eyes, his mouth, and he struggled against it, not knowing which way was up, lost in the darkness, drowning. His sight faded, his ears roared, and he let his body go limp.

Jaypaw blinked open his eyes, gulping for air, and leaped away from the branch. Rain was pelting down, drenching his fur, and waves pounded the shore, driven across the lake by a fierce wind. He wanted to go home, back to the shelter of the camp.

Fallen Leaves!

Gingerly he reached out for the branch, feeling for the last uncrossed mark.

Now he knew what it meant. Fallen Leaves had gone into the tunnels, but he had never come out.

CHAPTER 15

Lionpaw leaped and twisted in the air, diving forward as he landed with his claws raking the ground.

Perfect! In battle, that would have beaten even the fastest ShadowClan warrior. *Did you see how well I made the turn, Tigerstar?*

Tigerstar had only taught him the move that afternoon. Lionpaw had mastered it quickly. He sat back on his haunches now, panting, and sniffed the air. *Heatherpaw's late.*

The cave was dark, the moon hidden by the rain that had been falling since sundown. Jaypaw had returned to camp just after dark, drenched to the skin. The mouse-brain had fallen asleep by the lake! Leafpool had hurried him away to dry off in the medicine den. There was still no sign of Hollypaw. The search party had followed her scent down to the shore where it bordered WindClan territory, and now Thornclaw was even more convinced that she had been captured by a WindClan patrol.

"Did you think I'd forgotten about you?" Heatherpaw's mew sounded from the tunnel entrance.

Lionpaw leaped to his paws happily. "You're late!"

"Sorry." Heatherpaw was out of breath. "I caught Gorsetail's kits following me. I had to take them back to camp."

"They didn't go near the tunnel entrance, did they?"

"No, but it was close." Heatherpaw flicked her tail. "They kept themselves well hidden. I didn't spot them till it was almost too late."

Lionpaw's pads pricked. What if their secret had been discovered? "I nearly didn't come myself," he confessed.

Heatherpaw widened her eyes. "Why not?"

"Hollypaw's missing."

"Missing?"

"A search party followed her trail as far as—" Lionpaw stopped. He didn't want to let Heatherpaw know that Hollypaw might have crossed the WindClan border. Anxiety spiked his belly. He couldn't be honest with her without feeling like a traitor to his Clan. The realization stung. At least she might give him some clue about where his sister had gone. "Have you seen her?"

Heatherpaw shook her head.

Lionpaw gazed into her blue eyes. "Are you sure?"

Heatherpaw blinked. "Of course I'm sure!"

Guilt tickled in his tail. Heatherpaw wouldn't lie to him. Clearly WindClan hadn't captured Hollypaw after all. Lionpaw narrowed his eyes. How could he tell his Clanmates without letting them know how he had found out?

"What are you thinking about?" It was Heatherpaw's turn to sound suspicious.

"I was just wondering where Hollypaw could be," Lionpaw lied.

"She'll be okay," Heatherpaw mewed, winding around Lionpaw. The touch of her fur soothed him.

"It's just odd that she didn't come back before dark." It had been strange creeping out of the apprentices' den without having to worry if Hollypaw had one eye open. He had felt guiltily relieved that he didn't have to have an excuse ready in case she'd asked him where he was going.

"I bet she'll be back at first light," Heatherpaw mewed.

"I hope so." Lionpaw sighed.

"So what have you been doing while you were waiting for me?" Heatherpaw sat back with her head on one side.

"I was practicing some new battle moves." He plucked the ground excitedly. "Watch this one!"

Flicking his hind legs into the air, he spun around on his forepaws and leaped backward, then reared up and raked the air with each paw before tucking his head down and doing a neat forward roll.

"Impressive!" Heatherpaw pricked her ears. "Did you make it up yourself?"

"Yes." Lionpaw couldn't tell her that Tigerstar had taught him. She'd never believe him.

"It'd be perfect for a DarkClan warrior," Heatherpaw mewed. "Teach me how to do it!"

Lionpaw demonstrated the move again and Heatherpaw copied him.

"Nearly," he mewed. He crouched in front of her. "Try again, but this time aim your paws at me."

She flicked out her hind legs, spun, and reared at him.

Lionpaw dodged as she lashed out with her paws, shouldering her away before she could dive into the roll. She fell sprawling onto the cave floor.

Lionpaw's heart lurched. He had forgotten for a moment that he was stronger than her. He darted to her side and pressed his muzzle against her cheek. "I didn't hurt you, did I?" Tigerstar's training had made him even quicker and tougher than before.

"You only caught me because you knew what my next move was going to be!" she mewed. She twisted away from him and gave her shoulder a quick lick. "I just hope I never have to go into battle against you." Her eyes glowed with affection as she looked back at him. "Not that I ever could."

Lionpaw blinked. She was staring at him expectantly. Did she want him to make the same pledge? He couldn't do that, not when it meant promising to be disloyal to his Clan. "We'll just have to hope we never have to," he mewed, glancing away.

"Dawn's coming."

Lionpaw stretched and blinked open his eyes. Heatherpaw was sitting beside him, looking up at the gap in the roof where the sky was growing pale. He got to his paws, feeling his muscles protest. Teaching Heatherpaw the battle moves he'd learned from Tigerstar had tired him out. It seemed like only a few moments since they had dozed off.

"We'd better go," Heatherpaw told him.

"Will you meet me here tonight?"

Heatherpaw flicked her tail. "Of course, even if Crow-feather makes me run to the top of the moor and back again in our training session." She pressed her nuzzle against Lionpaw's cheek, then trotted away toward her tunnel. "See you later."

Lionpaw's paws tingled. "Bye." He headed in the opposite direction and raced for the open air.

The forest was damp, washed by a light rain. Lionpaw wriggled under the brambles and headed home through the half-light of early dawn. The trees and bushes cast eerie shadows across the pale forest floor. A light wind rustled the leaves.

"Traitor!"

Lionpaw halted and jerked around, fur spiking.

A familiar outline shimmered against the ferns.

"Tigerstar?"

"What do you think you're doing?" It was Hawkfrost. Lionpaw looked for Tigerstar but Hawkfrost was alone. His eyes blazed as he padded toward Lionpaw.

"What do you mean?" Lionpaw protested. Hawkfrost knew about his nightly visits to the tunnels. Why was he challenging him now?

Hawkfrost curled his lip. "You were teaching battle moves to the enemy!"

"Heatherpaw's not an enemy!" Lionpaw retorted. "She's my friend!"

"She belongs to another Clan!" Hawkfrost hissed. "That makes her an enemy! What if she uses the moves you just taught her against you one day?"

"Heatherpaw would never do that!"

"Wouldn't she?"

Lionpaw stiffened, trying to imagine facing Heatherpaw in battle. Surely she wouldn't take advantage of him like that? "I thought you and Tigerstar didn't care about me seeing Heatherpaw."

"We liked your independence," Hawkfrost growled. "We assumed it was just a harmless kit-friendship."

"It *is* harmless!" Lionpaw bristled. "But it's not just a kit-friendship! It's more important than that. That's why I know she'd never use those battle moves against me!"

"Then you're a mouse-brain!" Hawkfrost snarled. "I thought you wanted to be a great warrior!"

Lionpaw lifted his chin. "Of course I do!"

"Then why can't you see what those tunnels mean?"

Lionpaw blinked. The tunnels meant he could meet Heatherpaw without upsetting his Clan.

Hawkfrost snorted. "You don't understand anything, do you?"

"I do!"

"Then why haven't you figured out that those tunnels could be used for a surprise attack on WindClan?"

"Why would we want to attack WindClan?"

"The same reason WindClan might one day use the tunnels to attack ThunderClan!"

Lionpaw stared at Hawkfrost. He wasn't making any sense to his tired ears.

Hawkfrost rolled his eyes. "What if you need more territory or extra prey?" he meowed slowly, as though explaining a battle move to a kit. "Would you wait at the border for a passing WindClan patrol and beg for it?"

"But we have enough territory and enough prey," Lionpaw argued.

"Things change!" Hawkfrost snapped. "Clans change! Look how different WindClan is now that they have Onestar as leader. ThunderClan is terrified of them!"

"No, we're not!"

"Really?" Hawkfrost pricked his ears. "Then why is Firestar too scared to ask them what's happened to Hollypaw?"

Lionpaw's eyes grew round. "Do *you* know?"

"I know enough not to sit around the camp sending fruitless search parties to the borders and no farther!"

"Tell me!"

But Hawkfrost had turned away.

Lionpaw padded after him. "Where is she?"

"Let the great Firestar find her!" Hawkfrost glanced over his shoulder. "Meanwhile you'd better think about whether you want to be a warrior or whether you plan to live your life as a loner. Because if your Clanmates find out that you've kept the tunnels a secret from them, that's what you'll become!"

"No!" Lionpaw felt sick. That couldn't be true! He stared after Hawkfrost. "Come back!"

The tabby warrior's outline shivered and disappeared. Lionpaw was alone again.

His heart felt like a stone in his chest. He had taught Heatherpaw battle moves. She might not use them against him, but what about his Clanmates? Suddenly weary, he padded through the trees and headed down the curve of the hollow, toward the camp. Thanks to Tigerstar's training, he had begun to think that he would achieve his ambition to become a great warrior after all. Now he felt like a fox-hearted traitor. What if WindClan did use the tunnels to attack and had the advantage because ThunderClan knew nothing about them? He would have betrayed his Clanmates just so he could see Heatherpaw. Was their friendship really worth that?

As he trailed miserably toward the thorn barrier, he saw it quiver. Paws were thundering through the tunnel. Lionpaw flattened his ears in surprise as Dustpelt exploded from the entrance, fur bristling. On his heels were Ashfur and Stormfur. Lionpaw leaped out of the way as they raced past him. Thornclaw, Hazelpaw, and Poppypaw pelted after them.

"Come on, Lionpaw!' Hazelpaw called as she whisked past.

Alarm set the blood pounding in Lionpaw's ears. He fought off his weariness and chased after his Clanmate, panting as he caught up with her.

"What's going on?" He was fighting for breath, summoning up the dregs of his energy to keep up.

"Two WindClan apprentices chased a squirrel right over the border." Hazelpaw swerved around a fern. "They caught it and killed it on ThunderClan territory. The dawn patrol saw them do it! They sent Mousepaw back to fetch us. The

WindClan cats are saying it was their prey, no matter where they caught it!"

Lionpaw's spine bristled. How dare they? It was bad enough they were hunting squirrels at all! He pulled ahead of Hazelpaw and caught up with Ashfur. The gray warrior glanced at him. "Where were you? I looked in the apprentices' den when the alarm was called, but you weren't there."

Lionpaw stared ahead. What could he say? "I—I went out early," he mewed.

Ashfur narrowed his eyes.

"I couldn't sleep," Lionpaw offered.

Screeching split the air.

Through the trees, Lionpaw could see the pelts of his Clanmates. He recognized the angry yowling of Spiderleg and saw Brook's pelt streak across the forest floor. Brightheart was wrestling with Whitetail. Tornear, Ashfoot, Owlwhisker, and Weaselfur screeched and hissed, their claws flashing in the dawn light. The ThunderClan cats were outnumbered by the WindClan patrol.

As Dustpelt hurtled from the undergrowth, Spiderleg spun around in surprise and relief. "Thank StarCl—"

His yowl was cut off as Tornear knocked him to the ground. Ashfoot reared up behind the ThunderClan warrior and sunk her claws into Spiderleg's shoulder. Brook was grappling with Owlwhisker. The mountain cat screeched in pain as the pale tabby tom pinned her to the ground and let Weaselfur clamp his jaws around her tail.

Dustpelt pointed his nose to a gap in the trees where the

ground sloped down toward the stream that marked the border. "Spread out and drive them down there!" he ordered.

Thornclaw swerved toward Ashfoot. He butted the WindClan warrior with his head, knocking her away from Spiderleg. As Spiderleg scrambled to his paws, Thornclaw reared up and hurled himself at Ashfoot again. Sending leaves and earth spraying across the forest floor, Spiderleg spun and dived at Tornear.

Dustpelt darted in the other direction, skidding around Brook and flying at Weaselfur. The brown WindClan warrior let go of Brook's tail and turned to face Dustpelt, darting beneath his forepaws. Dustpelt dug his claws into the earth and held his ground, wrestling Weaselfur to the floor while Brook turned and knocked Owlwhisker flying with a back-kick.

"Let's take those two!" Poppypaw nudged Lionpaw and flicked her bushed-out tail toward Harepaw and Breezepaw, who were swiping at Brightheart as she wrestled with Whitetail.

Lionpaw nodded. "I'll take Breezepaw," he hissed. He pelted forward and flung himself at the black apprentice.

Caught off guard, Breezepaw rolled onto the ground. Lionpaw leaped on top of him, using his hind legs to brace himself as he slashed out with his forepaws. But Breezepaw was quick. He ducked out of the way, leaving Lionpaw flailing at thin air. Lionpaw spun in time to see Breezepaw lunge at him. Remembering Tigerstar's move, he flicked his hind legs into the air, spun on his forepaws, and leaped backward, then reared up and raked Breezepaw's astonished face with each paw, before tucking his head under and doing a neat forward roll.

Satisfaction flooded him. *Did you see that, Tigerstar?*

Then he froze. He had spotted a pale tabby pelt among the fighting cats.

Heatherpaw?

His heart lurched. He looked closer and sagged with relief when he saw that it was just Owlwhisker hurtling away from Brook. Suddenly, his ear burned; Breezepaw had caught him with a thorn-sharp claw. Lionpaw's ear grew wet as blood pulsed from the wound. Angrier than ever, he hurled himself at Breezepaw. The WindClan apprentice fell backward and Lionpaw reared up to rake him with his forepaws, but Breezepaw rolled neatly out from under him.

"Not fast enough," the WindClan apprentice sneered.

Suddenly, Hazelpaw streaked past and butted Breezepaw with her head. The WindClan apprentice fell over, winded, and Lionpaw raked his claws down his flank.

"Never stop to gloat!" Hazelpaw hissed at Breezepaw and clamped her teeth into his tail.

Yowling, Breezepaw scrambled to his paws and kicked Hazelpaw away with his hind legs. He stared into Lionpaw's eyes. "Can't take me by yourself?"

"Do you want to bet?" Lionpaw leaped at him, grabbing Breezepaw's head between his forepaws and using his hind paws to sweep his legs from under him. Another Tigerstar move! The WindClan apprentice rolled down the slope and disappeared over the edge of the gully.

Ashfur had Weaselfur pinned to the ground a tail-length away. The WindClan warrior managed to struggle from his grasp, but Ashfur caught him under the chin with a well-aimed blow that sent him sprawling back against a clump of brambles. Weaselfur screeched in pain and, struggling to free himself from the thorny branches, scrabbled backward onto WindClan territory.

Brook was driving Owlwhisker steadily down the slope, balancing on her hind legs while she aimed slash after slash at his retreating muzzle. Poppypaw clung to Whitetail's back while Brightheart raked the ears of the WindClan warrior.

Harepaw was already fleeing across the stream, with Hazelpaw yowling after him. "Run back to the nursery, Harekit!"

"Retreat!" Ashfoot ordered.

Tornear looked up from pummeling Thornclaw's back with churning hind paws. At once Thornclaw slithered from his grasp and scrambled to his paws, aiming a vicious blow at the tabby's head. Tornear reeled, hissing, then turned back, eyes narrowed with rage. But the other WindClan cats had already fled.

"This isn't finished!" Tornear leaped the gully and halted beside his Clanmates. They huddled together, scratched and bleeding, flanks heaving, and stared furiously at the ThunderClan cats.

"Stay on the moor from now on!" Dustpelt hissed.

Ashfoot glared at the dark brown tabby warrior. "Firestar

gave us these woods! If you have a quarrel about us hunting on them, take it up with *him*!"

Dustpelt flexed his claws. "I'll take it up with any WindClan cat—warrior or apprentice—that I catch hunting ThunderClan's prey!"

Lionpaw fluffed out his fur and hissed at Breezepaw. "No more squirrels for you!"

Breezepaw lashed his tail. "Don't be so sure!"

Thornclaw leaned toward the border. "Go home!" he snarled.

Dustpelt bristled, blood staining his muzzle. "This isn't the end." He turned and, muttering angrily, led his Clan-mates limping into the trees. "Is anyone badly hurt?" He swung his head around to look at them.

"My tail hurts," Brightheart meowed. "But it'll mend."

Lionpaw licked his paw and ran it over his scratched ear. He could feel the nick that split the top. He would carry this battle scar forever, he thought proudly.

"Brook?" Dustpelt narrowed his eyes at the mountain cat. "That looks like a nasty scratch on your flank."

"It's not deep," Brook reassured him, though fresh blood was still welling at one end.

"I'll take her back to camp," Stormfur offered.

Dustpelt nodded. "Thornclaw, Spiderleg, and I will re-mark the border. The rest of you go back with Stormfur."

"Can I stay and help?" Lionpaw asked.

"You look like you've had enough for one day," Ashfur told him.

Lionpaw dropped his gaze. Did his lack of sleep show that much? Reluctantly, he followed Stormfur and Brook as they headed into the trees.

Hazelpaw caught him up. "Wasn't that great?"

"I feel like a real warrior now." Poppypaw fell in beside them.

"Me too!" Lionpaw felt a sudden surge of happiness. Hawkfrost was wrong if he thought Lionpaw would never make a great warrior!

As the patrol headed down into the hollow, Brambleclaw shot out of the thorn tunnel to meet them. "Did you drive them off?"

"It was easy," Stormfur meowed.

"No serious injuries?" Brambleclaw asked.

"Just some scratches." Brightheart flicked her tail and winced.

Brambleclaw touched Lionpaw's head with his muzzle. "That ear looks sore."

"It's okay," Lionpaw assured him.

"Lionpaw fought like a warrior," Stormfur meowed.

Lionpaw lifted his chin as Brambleclaw ran his tail along his spine. "I'm sure he did," the ThunderClan deputy purred.

"Is he hurt?" Squirrelflight was plucking the ground impatiently as the patrol padded into the clearing. She hurried to Lionpaw's side at once, and Lionpaw shied away. *Don't make a fuss,* he thought.

"He fought like a warrior," Brambleclaw told her.

Squirrelflight blinked at Lionpaw. "Good."

"Brook's got a scratch and Brightheart got her tail bitten," Lionpaw reported. "But WindClan won't be coming onto our territory for a while." He hoped it was true. He was lucky that Heatherpaw hadn't been in the WindClan patrol, but what about next time?

"Your ear looks pretty bad," Squirrelflight fretted.

Lionpaw shrugged. "It's nothing."

"Better get it seen to anyway." Squirrelflight nudged him toward the medicine den where Stormfur was guiding Brightheart and Brook through the bramble entrance. Reluctantly, Lionpaw followed them. He didn't want Leafpool to heal his battle wound *too* well in case it didn't leave a scar that would show how well he had fought.

Fortunately, Leafpool and Jaypaw were already busy with Brook and Brightheart by the time he pushed his way through the brambles.

"I need more cobwebs!" Leafpool called to Jaypaw. Jaypaw spat out the poultice he had been licking into Brightheart's tail and dashed to the back of the den. He returned with a mouthful of cobweb, which Leafpool pressed against Brook's wound. A sodden red wad already lay on the cave floor.

"It will stop bleeding, won't it?" Stormfur watched her anxiously.

"Yes," Leafpool assured him. She pressed both paws on the wound. "Can you hold it like this?"

Stormfur nodded and placed his paws over Leafpool's. She drew hers away and turned to inspect Brightheart's tail.

"Oak leaf. Good choice," she mewed to Jaypaw. "That'll

stop any infection. It'll be healed in a few days." She glanced back at Stormfur, who was staring at his paws as he held the cobweb to Brook's side. "Any news of Hollypaw?"

"We didn't get a chance to ask," Brook admitted.

Leafpool sighed. "I suppose not," she meowed. "I was just hoping they might have given something away."

"WindClan hasn't got her," Lionpaw announced.

Leafpool pricked her ears. "How do you know?"

Lionpaw stared at the ground. "Well, surely, they would have told us if they had?" He glanced up at Leafpool. "Why else would they have her?"

"Then where is she?" Leafpool's mew sounded desperate.

Lionpaw touched Jaypaw's shoulder with his tail. "Can't you ask StarClan?"

Jaypaw's fur pricked, almost as if he were annoyed. "No."

Leafpool snorted and padded to the back of the cave.

Lionpaw frowned. What was going on? "Why haven't you asked them?" he pressed. "She's our sister."

"I haven't had a chance yet." Jaypaw lapped up another tongueful of oak leaf and began licking it onto Brightheart's tail.

Lionpaw stared at his brother, his pelt itching with frustration. "Have *you* had a chance?" he mewed, turning to Leafpool.

Leafpool, cobweb dangling from her jaw, padded to Brook's side. She dropped the pale web at Stormfur's paws. "It's not always possible to speak with StarClan," she explained. "If our warrior ancestors have something they want to share, then they'll find a way."

Was that the best they could do? Sit and wait? Lionpaw flexed his claws.

"Let me get something for your ear." Leafpool padded back to her store of herbs.

"I could try and ask StarClan tonight," Jaypaw whispered to him. Lionpaw felt even more puzzled. What was going on with these two? Didn't Jaypaw want Leafpool to hear?

"This should help." Leafpool brought back a poultice wrapped in a leaf. "Can you manage to rub this on yourself? Jaypaw and I need to check the rest of the patrol." She padded out of the den, followed by Jaypaw.

"Do you want some help?" Brightheart was already pawing open the leaf and rubbing her pad in the poultice. "I'm sure Hollypaw will turn up," she comforted, wiping the ointment onto Lionpaw's ear.

Lionpaw winced as it stung. "Jaypaw will find out where she is," he mewed hopefully. Weariness swept over him again. His night in the tunnels and then the battle had sapped his last pawful of energy. He ducked away from Brightheart's paw. "I think that'll be enough."

"Yes." Brightheart wiped her paw on her chest and turned to Stormfur. "How's the bleeding?"

"I think it's stopped."

Lionpaw padded out of the den, his paws heavy as clay. He couldn't wait to curl up in his nest and close his eyes. Worry pricked his drowsy thoughts. A warrior should always be battle ready. What if he'd been too tired to fight today?

"Lionpaw!" Ashfur was bounding toward him.

Lionpaw's heart sank, but he twitched his whiskers and tried to look as bright as he could. "Do you want me to go hunting?" he offered.

"No." Ashfur stopped beside him. "You look worn out. Get some sleep. You obviously need to catch up."

Lionpaw stiffened. There was a hint of warning in his mentor's mew. Did Ashfur suspect there was more to his exhaustion than an early morning run?

Lionpaw's heart thumped in his chest. "I promise I'll always be ready to fight!" he mewed. "I'm going to become the best warrior ThunderClan has ever known! Really I am!"

Ashfur's whiskers twitched. "I'm sure you will."

Lionpaw smelled mouse, warm and delicious. He blinked open his eyes. A piece of fresh-kill was lying on the moss beside his nest.

Honeypaw was standing beside it. "I thought you'd be hungry."

Lionpaw stretched his paws till they trembled. "Is it late?"

"The sunset patrol has just got back," Honeypaw reported. "They brought this." She dabbed her paw at the mouse.

"Have the kits and elders eaten?" Lionpaw asked.

"Of course." Honeypaw sat down. "Hazelpaw says you really taught Breezepaw a lesson." Her eyes sparkled. "She says he ended up in the stream."

Lionpaw got to his paws. "Yeah." His heart warmed at the memory. "I don't think any WindClan apprentices will be hunting in our territory for a while." A chill ran down his spine. What if it had been Heatherpaw hunting with Harepaw instead of Breezepaw?

"Lionpaw?" Honeypaw was staring at him. "Are you okay?"

Lionpaw shivered. "Just tired," he mewed, faking a yawn.

"Okay." Honeypaw shrugged. "We're at the halfrock if you want to join us." She padded out of the den.

Lionpaw gulped down the mouse and padded into the clearing to join his denmates. He chatted with them, acutely aware of Hollypaw's absence, his paws itching for the other apprentices to go to their nests. He glanced at the moon, slowly crossing the sky, misted by thin clouds. Heatherpaw would be waiting for him.

Berrypaw and Hazelpaw were the last to head for the den, their gray-and-white pelts glowing in the darkness. As soon as they disappeared, Lionpaw padded quickly to the dirtplace tunnel. Glancing over his shoulder to make sure the clearing was still empty, he slipped out of the camp.

His ear was stinging from the cold night air by the time he reached the tunnels. He padded inside, the usual eerie sense of foreboding clutching his belly. But this time it was worse. There was something he had to do, something really difficult, but he couldn't see any other way. However much it hurt . . . Pushing his dark thoughts away, he followed the twisting passageway to the cave. Heatherpaw was already there. She hurried to greet him, rubbing her nose along his cheek. She smelled warm and sleepy, as though she had just woken up.

"Your poor ear!" she gasped when she saw the blood-encrusted wound.

"It's fine," Lionpaw mewed.

"Is that your only wound?" Her eyes glittered with worry in the half-light. "Breezepaw said he'd shredded you!"

Lionpaw stepped back. She should be worried about her Clanmates, not him. He felt more certain than ever that he was about to do the right thing.

Heatherpaw tipped her head to one side. "What?" Could she sense the guilt pricking in his pelt?

Lionpaw gazed at her. "We can't meet anymore."

Heatherpaw's eyes widened. "What do you mean?"

"We just can't."

"But we're having fun. Why do we have to stop? We're not hurting anyone." She sounded desperate, her voice coming out as a squeak.

"I think you're great, Heatherpaw," Lionpaw mewed. He stared at his paws. Why did she have to make this harder? "But you need to find someone in your own Clan. I need to be the best warrior I can be, and I can't do that if I'm here every night."

Heatherpaw flinched as though he'd raked his claws across her nose. "It doesn't have to be *every* night." Her mew was little more than a whisper.

It doesn't matter how often we meet! I shouldn't be here at all! "I was looking out for you in the battle today," Lionpaw told her. "What if you'd been in that patrol?"

"You could have fought Breezepaw or Harepaw or—"

"Battles aren't that simple, and you know it!" *She must understand!* "I can't pick and choose. I have to defend my Clan. I can't be worrying about you all the time." He watched her gaze cloud with grief and his heart twisted with pain.

"That's it, then?" she mewed.

"Yes." He wasn't going to show how close he was to changing his mind, to agreeing to see her once a moon, or maybe twice, or three times. . . . This was what he had to do.

Anger flared in her eyes. "Fine!" she snapped. "I understand now." She turned away and padded toward the tunnel. Before she disappeared into the shadows she glanced over her shoulder, her eyes brimming with pain. "I just hope being a warrior is worth it!"

CHAPTER 16

Hollypaw wriggled against Willowpaw, trying to get comfortable. There was hardly enough moss in this nest for one cat, never mind two. And how could Willowpaw sleep so soundly with the water constantly washing against the rocks?

Rain sprayed the lake, dripping from the overhang, puddling on the floor. Through the entrance to the cave, Hollypaw could see the rocky causeway, slick in the darkness. She strained to see the ThunderClan shore far beyond it, but the air was murky and she could only just make out the shape of the distant forest against the cloudy predawn sky.

She had been in the RiverClan camp for two days. Leopardstar still insisted it was not safe for her to travel home, but every cat—Hollypaw included—knew she was being kept on the island to stop her from reporting RiverClan's weakness to her Clanmates. She rolled over, her belly growling with hunger.

"Can't you keep still?" Willowpaw sighed sleepily.

"Sorry." Hollypaw's heart ached. She was so far from home.

Willowpaw must have heard the sadness in her friend's mew. She sat up and stretched, her eyes glowing sympathetically in the half-light. "You'll be able to go back soon," she promised.

"How soon?"

"The dams should be finished in a quarter moon," Willowpaw mewed. "And we'll be able to move back to our old camp. I'm sure Leopardstar will organize an escort for you then."

A quarter moon! She couldn't stay here that long! "But what about my Clan?"

"I know they'll be worried," Willowpaw commiserated. "But think how pleased they'll be when you get back."

And angry. Hollypaw's heart sank as she imagined Brambleclaw's pelt pricking with annoyance; Squirrelflight's gaze, sharp with disapproval.

"You won't say anything, will you?" Willowpaw's eyes grew round. "You won't tell them about the island and the Twolegs?"

"No, not if you don't want me to." Hollypaw could guess why Willowpaw was so frightened about the other Clans knowing how much RiverClan had suffered. It would take at least a moon for them to recover even if they did manage to rescue their old camp.

"Promise?"

"I promise."

"Everything will be back to normal soon," Willowpaw sighed.

"Yes." Hollypaw felt the word catch in her throat. *Everything will be back to normal.* She was no longer so sure that an end to RiverClan's trouble would stop the hostility that had flared between the Clans. It was almost as if the long peace between the Clans had left the younger cats itching for battle and set the older warriors dreaming of past glories. She thought of the WindClan patrol she had faced with the RiverClan cats. They had bristled with so much aggression. They hadn't wanted to hear RiverClan's explanation. Could this hunger for battle simply vanish like mist in the sunshine?

The sky was lightening behind the clouds. Across the causeway, the cats were stirring on the island. Hollypaw could see pelts moving among the trees, pelts already as familiar as those of her own Clan. Graymist was leading Sneezekit and Mallowkit down to the shore to drink. Mosspelt was heading over the tree-bridge with Beechfur and Pebblepaw. Such a small dawn patrol! Hollypaw knew that most of the warriors' effort was being channeled into recovering the old island camp.

Mistyfoot padded from the trees and crossed the causeway, a slender fish drooping in her jaws. She dropped it in the puddle at the front of the overhang.

Mothwing lifted her head at the splash and stretched in her nest. "Thanks, Mistyfoot," she yawned.

Hollypaw knew it was unusual for the Clan deputy to deliver food to the medicine den. She was painfully aware that Mistyfoot had come to check whether Hollypaw had escaped in the night. But she was grateful that Mistyfoot had chosen such a tactful way to do it.

"It's not much," Mistyfoot meowed. "But it should see you through the day."

Hollypaw's belly growled. *The whole day!* Food was so scarce here that some of the warriors went to bed hungry; she was lucky to be fed at all. But thankful as she was that RiverClan were prepared to feed their unwelcome guest, she couldn't get used to the strange tang of fish and she longed for the musky flavor of forest prey.

"Intruder!" Mosspelt yowled from the tree-bridge.

Graymist instantly began herding her kits back to the island clearing. Hollypaw stiffened, scenting the air.

ThunderClan!

Hope fluttered like a bird in her chest. She strained to see through the drizzle. The dawn patrol were circling a cat on the far shore. *Squirrelflight!* She recognized her mother's pelt and felt the same surge of excitement she used to feel when, as a kit, Squirrelflight returned to the nursery after a spell in the warriors' den.

"You'd better come with me," Mistyfoot growled. She turned and padded back along the causeway. Hollypaw leaped after her, forcing herself not to race past the RiverClan deputy. Her paws fizzing, she trotted onto the island and followed Mistyfoot to the clearing.

Pebblepaw bounded from the undergrowth. "She's come to get Hollypaw!"

Behind him, the ferns rustled and Squirrelflight padded calmly into the clearing, flanked by Mosspelt and Beechfur. Hollypaw tensed. Squirrelflight was alone. Would Leopardstar let them leave together? She glanced nervously toward the Great Oak and saw Leopardstar squeeze out from her makeshift den among the roots. The RiverClan leader was staring at Squirrelflight; Hollypaw could see uncertainty in her eyes and her golden pelt pricked along her spine.

"Leopardstar." Squirrelflight halted in front of the River-Clan leader and dipped her head. "I have come to fetch one of our apprentices."

Hollypaw wanted to race forward and brush muzzles with her mother, but Squirrelflight hadn't even looked at her yet. She was staring steadily at Leopardstar. "I believe she strayed into your territory."

"Strayed!" Leopardstar widened her eyes in disbelief. "She came to spy!"

Hollypaw's ears burned. "I only wanted to help!" The words burst out before she could stop them.

Squirrelflight swung her head around and glared at her. Hollypaw shrank back.

Around the clearing, the RiverClan cats were watching, muscles tense, tails twitching.

"She is only an apprentice, Leopardstar," Squirrelflight meowed. "She lacks the good judgment that I hope will come with experience. I promise she'll be punished for breaking the warrior code, but ThunderClan can't allow her to remain here." Her mew was firm, the politeness only thinly masking an unspoken threat. Would ThunderClan really fight to bring her home? Hollypaw flexed her claws nervously. She couldn't believe she might end up causing a battle after all this.

Leopardstar's shoulders stiffened as she met Squirrel-flight's gaze.

Will she let me go? Hollypaw's heart was racing.

Leopardstar turned to look at her. "Can I *trust* you to show better judgment in future?"

She's asking me to keep my mouth shut. "Yes!" Hollypaw nodded. "I made a mistake coming here, but I won't let any cat suffer because of it."

Leopardstar blinked slowly. "Then you may go home."

"Thank you." Hollypaw breathed a sigh of relief.

Around the clearing, uneasy mews rippled among the RiverClan cats.

"Thank you, Leopardstar," Squirrelflight meowed. "I apologize on behalf of ThunderClan." Hollypaw winced with shame. The tip of her mother's tail was twitching. Squirrelflight was furious. Hollypaw padded to her mother's side, staring at her paws. How embarrassing to be fetched home like a naughty kit.

Squirrelflight dipped her head and turned toward the ferns.

"Wait!" Leopardstar flicked her tail. "Mosspelt and Beechfur will accompany you to the border."

Squirrelflight glanced back, eyes narrowed, and nodded curtly.

Paws suddenly pattered over the clearing. Willowpaw was hurrying toward them. "Good-bye." She brushed Hollypaw's cheek with her muzzle. "Promise not to say anything," she whispered.

"I promise," Hollypaw breathed.

Willowpaw stepped back, glancing awkwardly at her

Clanmates, who were staring at her. Graymist was curling her lip, and Heavystep, a stocky tabby elder, flattened his ears in disapproval. Mosspelt led the way into the undergrowth. Squirrelflight shooed Hollypaw ahead as Beechfur fell in behind them. They padded to the edge of the island and crossed the tree-bridge.

Hollypaw wanted to tell her mother how happy she was to see her, but it didn't feel right to say that in front of their RiverClan escorts. She held her tongue until they reached the WindClan border. Squirrelflight hardly looked at her, checking only that she made it down from the tree-bridge without tripping and steering her away from the waves that gently lapped the shore.

"I'm really sorry!" The words exploded from Hollypaw as soon as the RiverClan cats had turned back.

Squirrelflight's eyes clouded. "Don't ever do that again!" she hissed.

"I won't," Hollypaw promised meekly.

Squirrelflight led the way along the shore, keeping within two tail-lengths of the water. "I *do* understand," she meowed.

Hollypaw pricked her ears.

"I know what it's like to have friends in other Clans." Squirrelflight kept her gaze fixed firmly ahead. "To feel that there's something stronger than your Clan calling you away from home."

She must be talking about the Great Journey.

"But"—Squirrelflight glanced at her—"trying to help RiverClan was a foolish idea. Thinking you could sort out the

Clans' problems on your own was very arrogant."

Arrogant! Hollypaw felt stung. She hadn't meant to be like that.

"Firestar told you ThunderClan wasn't going to interfere. He's older and wiser than you are. You should have obeyed him. You broke the warrior code in disobeying him. You put your Clan at risk."

Hollypaw searched for words to defend herself, but suddenly she couldn't. There was no way she could make her Clanmates understand that she'd only wanted to stop a battle.

"We had to drive a WindClan patrol off our territory while you were gone," Squirrelflight added.

Hollypaw blinked. "Did they try and invade?"

"Not yet." Squirrelflight glanced up at the moor. "But they chased a squirrel onto our land and claimed it as their prey."

"On our side of the border?" Hollypaw could hardly believe her ears.

"Your brother helped fight them off."

Hollypaw's pelt bristled with alarm. "Is he okay?"

"Just a scratch on his ear." Squirrelflight's whiskers twitched. "I think he's proud of it."

"I wish I'd been there."

"You *should* have been there," Squirrelflight meowed. "Your Clan needs you more than ever."

Hollypaw remembered how close she'd come to fighting WindClan with the RiverClan patrol. Guilt gnawed at her belly. She should have been facing them with her own Clanmates.

"There's the smell of battle in the air," Squirrelflight went on.

"But RiverClan isn't planning to invade WindClan territory!" She couldn't explain about the trouble in their camp because she had promised Willowpaw and Leopardstar, but she had to try to keep the Clans from fighting.

"What RiverClan decide to do or *not* to do is none of our business," Squirrelflight meowed. "Our concern is defending our own borders."

How can you be so nearsighted? Hollypaw bit back the words.

Squirrelflight paused and gazed at her. "I know you think you were doing the right thing, but you are only an apprentice. How can you possibly understand? Your duty is to listen and learn and leave the decision-making to the warriors."

Hollypaw's paws itched with resentment. Why did being an apprentice mean that her opinion didn't count? She lowered her eyes to hide her anger.

Squirrelflight clearly took this as a sign of obedience. "Good." She began to hurry along the shore. The border was in sight and Hollypaw felt relieved to see it.

A thought suddenly flashed in her mind. She was surprised she hadn't thought of it before. "How did you know I was with RiverClan?"

"Jaypaw had a dream," Squirrelflight replied flatly. She didn't seem surprised by her son's uncanny abilities; Jaypaw was a medicine cat apprentice, after all. Hollypaw felt proud of her brother, but unease still pricked her paws. What must it feel like to have that sort of power? If he knew where she had been, did that mean he knew about the RiverClan camp? She wouldn't breathe a word about it to Firestar, but would Jaypaw do the same?

The camp fell silent as Hollypaw followed Squirrelflight into the clearing.

Hollypaw heard Brightheart whispering to Sorreltail. "She's back!"

Brook stopped washing and looked up. "Glad to see you're safe."

Stormfur nodded at her but said nothing. Dustpelt and Thornclaw only glanced at her before returning to their hushed conversation. Hollypaw knew she was in big trouble.

"Hollypaw!" Lionpaw raced from the apprentice den. He looked bright-eyed, as though he'd been asleep for ages. He weaved around her, purring. "You smell like fish!"

Jaypaw padded out of the medicine den and blinked, his blue eyes staring directly at her. Yet again Hollypaw had the unnerving sense that he could see her, even though she knew he couldn't.

"You need to see Firestar," Squirrelflight informed her.

Hollypaw's fur tingled as her mother watched her climb the tumble of rocks to Highledge. Heart pounding, she stepped into Firestar's cave. Brackenfur was waiting beside the ThunderClan leader. "Welcome back." His mew was grim.

Firestar narrowed his eyes. "You've caused a lot of worry and effort at a time when the Clan can least afford it," he meowed.

"I was only trying to—"

Firestar cut her off. "We don't want to hear excuses. You broke the warrior code. I told you plainly that we were not going to interfere with RiverClan but you went there anyway. You abandoned your Clan when it needs its warriors and apprentices more than ever."

"But I've found something out. You mustn't fight WindClan!"

"Why not?"

Hollypaw scraped her claws over the rocky floor. "I can't tell you."

"Can't?"

"I've made a promise." Hollypaw's tail twitched unhappily. "You have to trust me. There's no need to fight."

Firestar whisked his tail over the ground. "Do you really expect me to make decisions for the Clan based on *that*?"

Hollypaw opened her mouth, but what could she say?

"You will be confined to camp for a day," Firestar went on. "It should be longer, but we can't spare you right now. Patrols have been stepped up since the incident with WindClan, and you are expected to play your part in them. But you will be responsible for looking after the elders for the next moon. It'll be up to you to make sure they are fed and their bedding is kept clean, and don't think about asking your denmates for help. This will be your responsibility alone."

Hollypaw dipped her head. The promise she'd made to Leopardstar stuck in her throat, but she was determined to honor it. She wasn't going to have every cat who knew her accuse her of being disloyal. At least RiverClan didn't treat her like a stupid kit—they even thought she might have been a spy. "Is that it?" she muttered.

Firestar flicked his tail. "You may as well start now. Mousefur and Longtail will be grateful for fresh bedding."

"Okay." Hollypaw turned and padded out of the den. Why couldn't Firestar have more faith in her? Had *he* been to RiverClan? The Clan leaders only looked as far as the end of their whiskers. *Well, let them!* She'd just get on with her duties and keep her mouth shut. Angrily, she skidded down the rocky slope and stomped to Leafpool's den.

She poked her head through the brambles. "Can I have some fresh bedding for the elders' den?"

Leafpool was unwrapping the cobwebs from Cinderpaw's leg.

"Hollypaw!" Cinderpaw mewed. "Jaypaw's dream was right!"

"Of course it was right!" Jaypaw was sorting herbs at the back of the den. He turned to face Hollypaw. "I suppose Firestar's put you on nettles and water for a moon?"

"Not quite." Hollypaw's whiskers twitched. It was good to hear Jaypaw's grouchy mew again. "Thanks for sending Squirrelflight to find me."

"No problem." Jaypaw shrugged and then went back to his sorting.

Leafpool was staring at her with troubled eyes. "I'm glad you're safe," she meowed.

"I'm sorry I worried everyone," Hollypaw replied.

"Don't do it again." Leafpool's mew was suddenly fierce.

Hollypaw bristled. *You sound like my mother!* She'd had enough of being told off. "Moss?" she asked again.

Leafpool flicked her tail to the pile at the side of the cave. "Help yourself."

Hollypaw took the biggest clump she could carry and padded to the elders' den. There were worse punishments, she supposed.

"Is it true?" Mousefur shifted out of the way as Hollypaw began sifting through the old bedding. "Were you with RiverClan?"

"Yes."

"Did they treat you well?" Longtail leaned forward, nose twitching. "It smells like they fed you."

"Yes."

Mousefur wrinkled her muzzle. "I've never liked the taste of fish. Too watery."

Hollypaw plucked a wad of dried moss and flung it toward the entrance.

Mousefur narrowed her eyes. "You're very quiet for an apprentice who's just had a big adventure."

"What's the point in talking?" Hollypaw flung another clump of moss. "No one wants to listen to an apprentice."

"Was Firestar tough on you?" Longtail mewed sympathetically.

"No."

Mousefur flicked her tail. "It's no use sulking," she snapped. "You broke the warrior code. Did you think everyone would welcome you back like a hero?"

"No!" Hollypaw glared at her. "But at least I was trying to help. Everyone else just wants to fight!"

"We must defend our borders," Longtail pointed out.

"We wouldn't have to defend our borders if we talked to one another!"

"Talk?" Longtail's eyes widened with surprise. "We're warriors! We fight with tooth and claw, not words!"

"Wait a moment." Mousefur leaned toward Hollypaw. "Why do you think talking will help? WindClan has made it clear that they want to steal our prey. They crossed our border once. They're trying to steal our territory."

"Why do you think they want to steal our territory?" Hollypaw challenged.

"Because RiverClan is planning to steal theirs!" Longtail meowed.

Hollypaw swished her tail. "Are you sure?"

"Of course! They've lost their land!" Longtail argued. "They have to go somewhere."

They haven't lost their land! Hollypaw wished she hadn't promised RiverClan she'd keep quiet. "Everyone is jumping to conclusions!" she snapped. "We don't know anything for sure. WindClan doesn't know anything for sure. We're all just guessing! We might end up fighting over nothing!"

Mousefur frowned. "And you think talking might stop the battle?" Her mew was thoughtful.

Hollypaw felt hope flicker beneath her pelt. Was someone listening to her at last? She gazed expectantly at Mousefur. "Can you get Firestar to think about it again?"

Mousefur didn't reply directly. "You'd better fetch some more moss." She began to spread out the pile Hollypaw had brought. "We're going to need more than this."

Hollypaw closed her eyes as the sweet flavor of mouse spread over her tongue. She crunched through a bone. Something worth chewing, at last. She lay beside the halfrock with Poppypaw and Honeypaw, newleaf sunshine warming her pelt. For the first time in days, she pushed away her worries about the coming battle and enjoyed the familiar scents of home.

"So what are they like?" Poppypaw lay beside her, idly hooking a freshly killed sparrow from one paw to another. "RiverClan, I mean?"

"The elders are grumpy, the warriors are bossy, and the kits are a nuisance," Hollypaw replied with her mouth full. "Pretty much the same as us."

Poppypaw purred. "Don't let Brackenfur hear you saying that," she warned. "You're in enough trouble as it is."

"Look!" Honeypaw sat up and stared at the medicine den. Leafpool was leading Cinderpaw slowly out into the clearing.

Cinderpaw was limping, hardly touching the ground with her injured leg, but the rushes and cobwebs were gone. Her leg looked thin, the fur pressed flat against the skin from being bound up so long, but her eyes were bright with excitement.

"Hollypaw!" Leafpool called across the clearing.

Hollypaw leaped to her paws, gulping down a last mouthful of mouse, and hurried to greet Cinderpaw. She flicked her tail over her friend's ears. "You're better!"

"Not completely," Leafpool warned. The medicine cat's eyes glittered with worry. "But she's fidgeting around in the den so much, I thought she'd better get some fresh air."

"Can we go out into the forest?" Cinderpaw mewed.

"No!" Leafpool bristled. She stared at Hollypaw. "I thought you could help Cinderpaw get some *gentle* exercise." She emphasized *gentle* as though she were teaching Hollypaw a new word.

"Of course!" Hollypaw kneaded the ground.

"Stay in the clearing," Leafpool ordered. She glanced at Cinderpaw. "And be careful!"

"She's acting like a badger with sore stripes!" Hollypaw whispered as Leafpool padded back to the medicine den.

"I know," Cinderpaw purred. "She worries too much. She thinks if I breathe too hard I'm going to be crippled for life."

Hollypaw sniffed Cinderpaw's leg. It smelled strongly of comfrey. "How does it feel?"

"Stiff and sort of delicate," Cinderpaw mewed. "But it doesn't hurt anymore. I just have to be careful."

"Can you put weight on it?"

Cinderpaw slowly pressed her pad down onto the ground. She winced and then her face relaxed. "Not bad." Gingerly she padded forward, then walked more easily to the middle of the clearing. Stretching out her forelegs she pressed her chest toward the ground. "It's great to be outside again."

Hollypaw hurried to the honeysuckle bush where she had left a pile of moss after cleaning out the elders' den. She tore a small clump away with her teeth and rolled it into a ball.

"Can you still catch?" She tossed the ball across the clearing. Her heart lurched. What if Cinderpaw stretched up to catch it? Could her hind leg take the strain?

Cinderpaw let the ball land in front of her and hooked it up with a claw. "Not if you throw as badly as that," she retorted. She tossed the moss ball back to Hollypaw.

Hollypaw leaped and batted it back. This time Cinderpaw lifted a forepaw and stretched up on three legs to catch the ball between her teeth.

"Nice one!" Hollypaw raced back to her friend.

"I've been practicing in the den with Jaypaw," Cinderpaw mewed, dropping the ball at her paws.

"He's been playing with you?" Hollypaw was surprised. Jaypaw always seemed so serious when he was in the medicine den.

"Sometimes," Cinderpaw told her. "But only to keep me quiet." She looked at the ground. "Actually, I don't think he likes having me around."

"Nonsense!" Hollypaw mewed. "How can a medicine cat resent his patients?" She butted Cinderpaw on the shoulder. But she could guess just how grouchy Jaypaw had been with Cinderpaw. If only he could hurry up and learn a bit of kindness from Leafpool!

"Can we play?" Foxkit and Icekit came hurtling from the nursery.

Foxkit swiped the moss ball away from Cinderpaw. His fluffy pelt glowed like autumn leaves in the afternoon sunshine.

"Hey!" Icekit skidded past him, knocking the moss ball away. Foxkit lunged after her. "I got it first!" He tumbled her to the ground.

Hollypaw darted behind the squirming bundle of orange-and-white fluff and picked up the moss ball. "Now neither of you has it." She flung it over the two kits, and Cinderpaw reached up with a forepaw and snagged it with a claw.

"That's the trouble with being no bigger than a hedgehog," Cinderpaw teased. "You can only catch worms!" She flicked the ball back over the kits' heads for Hollypaw to catch.

Icekit and Foxkit leaped into the air, reaching for the ball as it flew over their heads.

"You'll have to jump higher than that!" Hollypaw called.

"Not if you can't throw it!" Foxkit dashed at Hollypaw and leaped onto her back. He scrabbled at her fur, making her stagger sideways.

Icekit grabbed the moss ball from her paws. "Trying to steal our prey!" she hissed.

Foxkit dug his claws into Hollypaw's pelt. "Thief!"

"She must be a WindClan warrior!" Icekit cried, dropping the moss ball and throwing herself at Hollypaw. "Attack!"

"Help!" Hollypaw pretended to yelp in terror as she tussled with the two kits but, though she was playing, an icy chill shivered deep in her belly. Even the kits were ready to fight WindClan. The coming battle was waiting like a fox in the shadows.

CHAPTER 17

Jaypaw plucked at the moss in the bottom of his nest, softening it before he curled up for a good night's sleep. Cinderpaw was already snoring, worn out by her game with Hollypaw. She would be moving back to the apprentices' den before long, and the medicine den would be quiet again. *Good.* Outside, the thorn barrier rustled. The last patrol was returning, their unhurried paw steps a signal that everything was fine.

Jaypaw heard water sloshing. Leafpool was soaking a wad of moss in the pool to leave beside Cinderpaw's nest in case the apprentice woke thirsty in the night. "I think we should take a look at the catmint by the old Twoleg nest tomorrow," she meowed. "I want to see if there's much new growth."

"Are we going to pick any?"

"Not yet." Leafpool's paws scuffed across the ground as she carried the dripping moss to Cinderpaw's nest. "But I want to know whether there'll be a good harvest this year."

"There's been enough rain." Jaypaw tucked his nose between his paws and closed his eyes. "Good night."

"Sleep well." Leafpool's nest crunched as she climbed into it and started washing. The gentle lapping of her tongue began to lull Jaypaw to sleep.

"Leafpool?"

Firestar's mew woke him with a start. The ThunderClan leader was pushing his way through the bramble entrance. Jaypaw lifted his head, instantly alert and trying to sense what pulsed beneath their visitor's pelt.

Unease.

Leafpool jumped out of her nest. "What is it?"

"This concerns both of you," Firestar meowed.

Jaypaw got up too, not bothering to pretend he hadn't been listening.

"Is something wrong?" Leafpool whispered anxiously.

Firestar shifted his paws. "I want you both to travel to the WindClan camp tomorrow."

"The WindClan camp?" Leafpool echoed. "Do you want us to speak to Barkface?"

"No." Firestar was choosing his words carefully. "Onestar."

"Why us?"

"Only you can make the journey. If I send warriors, they'll be seen as a threat."

"What do you want us to say to him?" Leafpool sounded puzzled.

"I need you to find out what's going on in WindClan."

A spying mission! Jaypaw felt a surge of excitement. *He wants us to find out their weaknesses.* But something wasn't right. He could detect no scheming in Firestar's mind. Only honest anxiety.

"I've just been speaking with Mousefur," Firestar

explained. "She seems to think Hollypaw is right and that all this talk of battle has grown out of gossip and guesswork. I need you to find out whether RiverClan has actually invaded WindClan territory."

Jaypaw blinked. "What difference does that make?"

"If there's going to be a battle with WindClan, I want it to be for a good reason," Firestar replied.

Leafpool swished her tail over the ground. "But if they cross our border, isn't that reason enough?"

"Yes," growled Firestar, "but we might be able to stop them from crossing the border from now on."

"They've already done it once and gotten away with it," Jaypaw pointed out. He ignored Leafpool's hiss of warning; apprentices weren't meant to speak to the Clan leader in that way.

"That could have just been a mistake." Jaypaw felt Firestar's amber gaze warm his pelt. "Their apprentices would not be the first to stray onto another Clan's territory."

He means Hollypaw!

Firestar went on. "It makes sense for WindClan to invade us if RiverClan has taken their territory. But what if Onestar leads an attack just because he's afraid that RiverClan might take his territory? Blood would be shed for no reason."

"I don't understand what you think *we* can do." Leafpool plucked at the ground. "If we find out that RiverClan hasn't invaded, do you want us to ask Onestar not to fight? Won't that make us look weak?"

Firestar stiffened. "You must make it clear that we are ready to fight if we have to," he meowed. "I'd just rather fight a battle driven by real need, not empty fears."

"But still, you want us to persuade Onestar not to attack us unless he has no other option?" Leafpool pressed. "Won't we look like cowards?"

Anger flashed from Firestar's pelt. "We're not cowards," he snapped, "but why should we fight pointless battles to prove it?"

Dawn was bright but cold. A pale sun peeped over the forest at the top of the hollow but Jaypaw could smell rain on the wind. He waited at the camp entrance while Firestar gave his final orders to their escort. Brambleclaw and Dusltpelt were going to accompany them to the WindClan border and wait for their return.

Leafpool pressed against him. Jaypaw could still sense doubt darkening his mentor's thoughts. "Are you ready?" she asked.

"Yes." Jaypaw's tail twitched with excitement. There was more to being a medicine cat than picking herbs and looking after sick cats after all. The future of the Clan could depend on what he and Leafpool found out.

There will be three, kin of your kin, who hold the power of the stars in their paws.

"Come on, then." Brambleclaw padded through the thorn tunnel. Leafpool headed after him and Jaypaw followed, leaving Dustpelt to fall in behind. He could feel the warrior's dark pelt bristling with uncertainty. Dustpelt thought that Firestar was being hasty, that it was too soon to let WindClan know they would rather avoid a battle. Brambleclaw's thoughts were harder to read, his mind clouded by doubt one moment, brightened by hope the next.

The patrol padded wordlessly over the ridge and down into the open moorland, which stretched into WindClan territory. Dustpelt was the first to voice his disquiet as they reached the border. "Are we just going to sit and wait for a WindClan patrol to ask us if we need help?" His mew was scathing.

"Yes," Brambleclaw growled.

Dustpelt paced up and down, re-marking the bushes, irritation flashing from him so fiercely that it made Jaypaw's fur stand on end. How humiliating to wait for permission from WindClan to go any farther.

"Perhaps Jaypaw and I should go on by ourselves," Leafpool suggested. "That's what we'd do if we needed to speak with Barkface."

Jaypaw nodded. They were medicine cats. They might as well take advantage of their special freedom to travel.

"No." Brambleclaw's mew was firm. "You're not going to speak with Barkface, and it's too soon after our run-in with that WindClan patrol for you to walk into their territory without them knowing. My duty is to make sure you're safe." His fur brushed the grass as he sat down. "We'll wait."

Jaypaw sniffed the air. The sun was warming the earth and he could smell heather budding and young rabbits. Suddenly, he stiffened: A musky tang edged the wind. "WindClan cats are coming." He recognized the scents of Harepaw and Tornear. There were two more cats with them. Their scents were familiar but he couldn't yet name them.

"It's Nightcloud."

Jaypaw felt tension spiking from Leafpool as she identified the WindClan she-cat. He knew there was some connection between his mentor and Nightcloud, who was the mate of Crowfeather. He had felt it thicken the air between them before, but he had no idea what it could be. As he probed Leafpool's mind, his paws pricked with surprise. Was that *jealousy*?

"Tornear, Harepaw, and Owlwhisker are with her," Dustpelt murmured. "Not bad, though I would have preferred it if Tornear had stayed in his nest." Dustpelt's pelt tickled Jaypaw's flank as the warrior fluffed out his fur defensively.

"Relax," Brambleclaw ordered. "They mustn't think we're showing any sign of aggression."

"Because we're begging a favor," Dustpelt muttered under his breath.

"Silence!" Brambleclaw hissed. Then he raised his voice. "Tornear!"

Hostility slammed against Jaypaw like a wave as the WindClan cats spotted the ThunderClan patrol. The air seemed to crackle around him and he tensed, suddenly afraid.

"What do you want?" Tornear's mew was accusing.

Fur brushed heather as the WindClan patrol approached. Jaypaw sensed Brambleclaw squaring himself to meet the

WindClan cats. "Leafpool and Jaypaw wish to speak with Onestar." Brambleclaw's mew was calm, neither hostile nor yielding.

Surprise pulsed from Tornear's pelt. "What for?"

"They wish to speak with *Onestar*," Brambleclaw repeated.

Jaypaw felt suspicion wake in the WindClan cats' minds. He guessed they were looking at one another, wondering how to respond. Could they turn away medicine cats?

"*Just* Leafpool and Jaypaw?" Owlwhisker growled.

"We will wait here for them," Brambleclaw assured him.

Silence hung in the air, like a hawk stalling before a dive.

"Then Owlwhisker and Harepaw will wait with you," Tornear meowed slowly.

He's going to let us cross the border! Jaypaw dug his claws into the grass, eager to get going.

"Can I trust you to see them safely to the camp and back?" Brambleclaw asked.

Tornear snorted. "Of course you can!"

"Leafpool," Brambleclaw meowed, "if you're not back by sunhigh, we'll fetch a patrol and come looking for you." His mew was thick with warning aimed at the WindClan cats.

"She'll be back," Tornear growled.

Jaypaw heard Leafpool's fur brush the heather as she crossed the border. He padded quickly after her and pressed against her. It was exciting to be traveling to the WindClan camp, but he suddenly felt vulnerable. An icy chill swept his fur as clouds blocked out the sun.

"Keep your chin high," Leafpool whispered. She let her

pelt brush his all the way to the camp, guiding him over the unfamiliar ground. Jaypaw only stumbled once when Leafpool didn't warn him in time about a trailing branch of gorse.

Soon he smelled brambles and a stronger scent of WindClan. He sensed space beneath him as the ground dipped away in front of them. They had reached the camp.

"Stay close," Tornear warned.

Jaypaw walked step-by-step with Leafpool as the WindClan warrior led them into a swath of bramble, through a twisting, turning tunnel that led down into a hollow. He could hear Nightcloud's breath behind him as she brought up the rear. Then wind stroked his whiskers; they were out of the tunnel. For a moment he felt overwhelmed by the jumble of scents that filled his nose and mouth: warriors, apprentices, kits, nursing queens, herbs, rabbit. . . .

They must be in the center of the camp. A fresh wind tugged Jaypaw's fur. Watchful gazes stabbed his pelt.

"It's that blind cat from ThunderClan."

"What are they doing here?"

"Shall I fetch Barkface?"

The WindClan cats were emerging from their dens. Jaypaw could feel curiosity, hostility, and even fear throbbing in the air.

Tornear was whispering to a young tom. Jaypaw strained to hear but before he could make out the words, the tom hared out of the camp.

"Onestar is out hunting," Tornear announced. "You'll have

to wait." He raised his voice to address his curious Clanmates. "They've come to see Onestar!"

"Onestar?"

Alarm and suspicion rippled around the clearing. Jaypaw pricked his ears. This was not a Clan determined to expand their territory. They were frightened and confused. His belly tightened. Frightened cats were unpredictable. "Should we speak to Barkface instead and leave?" he murmured to Leafpool.

But Leafpool didn't seem to hear. Her attention was flitting around the camp, as though she were searching for something or someone. Suddenly, an intense emotion sparked from her, almost making Jaypaw flinch. Excitement? Grief? Anger? He couldn't tell.

"You look well, Crowfeather." Leafpool's calm mew didn't betray the storm raging in her mind.

Jealousy spiked behind Jaypaw. Nightcloud's pelt was bristling.

"What are you doing here, Leafpool?" Crowfeather's mew was curt and quiet. *What is he feeling?* Jaypaw studied the warrior's mind but found it barbed with wariness.

"Firestar sent us to speak with Onestar," Leafpool explained.

"He's not here."

"We know." Leafpool sat down.

Jaypaw felt the first drop of rain dab his nose.

The brambles rustled and a few moments later paws pounded into the clearing. Onestar. Jaypaw recognized

Whitetail and Weaselfur with him.

"What's this about?" the WindClan leader demanded.

"Firestar sent us," Leafpool meowed.

"Why?" Onestar paced warily around them. "Are you in trouble?"

"No."

"Then why come here?" Onestar halted so close to them that Jaypaw could smell the rabbit blood on his breath. "Does Firestar still think there's some kind of special relationship between our Clans? Because there isn't!"

"Firestar understands that."

Jaypaw was impressed with how calm Leafpool sounded, even though he could feel her trembling against him.

"Firestar doesn't want to shed blood over our shared border," she went on.

"Why did he attack our apprentices, then?" Onestar's tail swished through the air.

"WindClan warriors unsheathed their claws first," Leafpool meowed. "We were only defending the border they crossed."

"It was our prey!" Tornear hissed.

Yowls of agreement rose around the clearing.

"Not once it'd crossed the border," Jaypaw hissed.

Leafpool's tail brushed his mouth. She shifted, her pads squelching against the slippery earth. The rain was beginning to fall steadily. "We didn't come here to argue!"

"Then why did you come?" Onestar growled.

"To talk."

Tornear tore at the ground. "Was Firestar too mouse-hearted to come himself?"

"Firestar didn't want to provoke you by sending a warrior patrol," Leafpool explained. "He wants to soothe the situation, not inflame it."

Crowfeather was circling them. "Then he shouldn't have sent anyone!"

Anger surged through Leafpool; Jaypaw felt it hot against his pelt. "Not every cat hides from his responsibilities!" she hissed.

Crowfeather halted. "Are you saying that's what I would do?" His whiskers brushed Jaypaw's face as the WindClan warrior leaned in toward Leafpool.

"Get out of the way!" Onestar hissed, nudging Crowfeather aside. "What do you want to talk about?"

"Firestar wants to know if RiverClan has invaded your territory." Leafpool was growing impatient. "Is that why you've been hunting so close to our border? Are you being forced into ThunderClan territory or do you simply want to take our land because you are foolish enough to believe you can?"

Jaypaw was shocked by her fierceness. He felt Onestar freeze; Leafpool had surprised the WindClan leader too. Angry whispers darted between the watching cats. The air seemed to crackle like greenleaf lightning as the rising wind drove the rain harder into the camp. Jaypaw tensed, waiting for Onestar's answer.

"RiverClan has not invaded our lands," Onestar began slowly. "But that doesn't mean they won't. Does Firestar expect us to wait until they do? Does he think we should sit around like fat voles waiting to be pounced on?"

"But you are not voles," Leafpool snapped. "Why not defend your RiverClan border instead of threatening ours?"

"We will defend what borders we have to," Onestar retorted. "And take what territory we need."

"You don't even know that RiverClan is going to invade," Leafpool pressed. "Why threaten us?"

Tornear growled. "You sound like a blackbird singing the same song over and over again!"

"Barkface could speak to Mothwing at the next Moonpool gathering," Leafpool suggested, her mew suddenly coaxing. "He can find out exactly what RiverClan intends. It may turn out you have nothing to be afraid of."

"We aren't afraid!" Crowfeather hissed.

"Then why won't you listen to reason?" Leafpool pressed. "You are honorable warriors. Why let yourselves be driven by suspicion instead of truth?"

"Listen to her!" Weaselfur sneered. "Trying to steal time for her Clan with clever words."

"WindClan fights with claws not words," Tornear warned.

Jaypaw bristled. "It's like trying to show worms to moles!" he hissed. "They're too blind to see beyond their own noses."

"*We're* too blind?" Weaselfur mocked.

"Wait!" Onestar ordered. "Perhaps she's right. Perhaps we should give RiverClan a chance to explain what's going on before we do anything."

"A chance to invade, more like," Tornear growled.

"You saw how desperate RiverClan looked at the Gathering," Crowfeather argued. "And every patrol we see looks hungrier than the last. We can't trust them!"

"But they haven't invaded yet," Onestar pointed out.

"They crossed the border," Tornear reminded him.

"Only once."

Jaypaw sensed the WindClan leader's mind slow. He was thinking.

"We can't let them drive us into unnecessary bloodshed," Onestar murmured.

Suddenly, a panicked yowl split the air beyond the camp wall. The dripping brambles shook and a WindClan queen skidded into the clearing. "My kits are gone!" she screeched.

"Sedgekit?"

"Thistlekit?"

Alarmed mews filled the camp.

"Sedgekit, Thistlekit, *and* Swallowkit!" panted the queen. "All of them! Disappeared!"

"When did you last see them?" Onestar demanded.

The queen was fighting for breath. "I left them in the nursery and went to stretch my legs. They weren't there when I came back, so I went looking for them. They've wandered out before, but not far. But this time there's no sign of them. Their trail heads toward the RiverClan border and then just disappears. A hawk's carried them off, I know it!"

"Calm down, Gorsetail." Onestar was bristling but his mew was steady. "You can't be sure. No hawk's ever taken more than a single kit before. We must send out a search party."

Suddenly, paws pounded through the entrance tunnel.

"Onestar!" Ashfoot pelted into the clearing. Jaypaw scented Breezepaw and Heatherpaw behind the WindClan deputy. "We've just seen a RiverClan patrol heading back into their territory."

"They've been on our land!" Breezepaw spat.

"And there was rabbit blood where they'd been," Heatherpaw added.

Terror flared from Gorsetail. "Are you sure it was *rabbit* blood?"

"What?" Confusion clouded Heatherpaw's mind.

"My kits have disappeared!" Gorsetail wailed.

"You think the RiverClan patrol might have taken them?" Heatherpaw sounded horrified. Her thoughts began whirling like leaves caught in a wind. Jaypaw tried to read them but they were moving too fast. He only knew that at their center something dark hovered, a sense of blackness that made his blood turn to ice. She knew more than she was letting on.

"You must leave." Onestar had turned back toward Leafpool.

"You're not going to attack RiverClan, are you?" Leafpool gasped.

"We'll do what we must to get our kits back!" Onestar hissed.

"But you don't know they've taken them," Jaypaw objected. "A moment ago you thought it was a hawk."

"That was before RiverClan crossed the border."

"But they may have had good reason!"

Ashfoot growled. "To steal our kits!"

"But why—"

Onestar cut Leafpool off with a snarl. "Go home!" Jaypaw flinched as the WindClan leader leaned in close. "You can tell Firestar that it's too late. You've wasted your time trying to protect RiverClan. We'll attack at once!"

CHAPTER 18

Lionpaw shivered. The rain had reached right to his skin. He dropped his vole on the fresh-kill pile and shook the water from his pelt.

"Good hunting," Ashfur congratulated him. "You've improved a lot these past days. It seems like your mind is on your training again."

Lionpaw blinked at his mentor. It *had* been a good hunting patrol. He, Ashfur, Stormfur, and Brook had caught nearly enough to feed the whole Clan and it was great to feel energetic again, a little faster, a little sharper than his Clanmates, as though StarClan guided his paws. But his heart still ached when he thought of Heatherpaw. He missed being a DarkClan warrior.

Stormfur tossed a wet blackbird onto the pile. "Something's wrong." The gray warrior glanced anxiously around the clearing. Beside him, Brook narrowed her eyes.

Cinderpaw was tugging twigs toward the thorn barrier where Cloudtail was stuffing them into gaps. Poppypaw and Mousepaw were hurriedly patching the nursery with fresh brambles. Their rain-soaked pelts were spiked, their tails bushed out. Thornclaw and Spiderleg were circling the edge of the camp, staring up through the rain at the walls.

Thornclaw flicked his tail toward a rift in the cliff face where the rocks jutted out. "We should reinforce the top there. It's too easy for cats to climb down."

Lionpaw's belly tightened. He scanned the clearing. Had Jaypaw returned safely from his mission? He felt relief wash his pelt as he saw Jaypaw emerge from the dirtplace tunnel.

Leafpool was calling to him from the medicine den entrance. "We need more dock."

"I'll find some," Jaypaw answered at once.

"Not by yourself," Leafpool meowed.

Jaypaw nodded. "I'll take Hollypaw with me."

Lionpaw's paws throbbed with unease. His brother normally bristled with rage at any suggestion that he couldn't manage by himself. Now he accepted it without a murmur.

"Don't go far from camp," Leafpool warned.

"Lionpaw! Have you heard?" Honeypaw was charging toward him, her eyes stretched wide. "There's going to be a battle!"

Lionpaw hurried to meet her. "When?"

"WindClan is going to attack RiverClan right now," Honeypaw panted.

Lionpaw flattened his ears. "Has RiverClan invaded WindClan territory?"

Honeypaw shook her head. "RiverClan stole three Wind-Clan kits," she mewed. "WindClan are going to get them back. We have to be ready to fight!"

Lionpaw tensed. There weren't many kits in WindClan right now. Could they be the same three who had followed Heatherpaw? "Are you sure RiverClan took them?"

"RiverClan was hunting in WindClan territory when the kits went missing," Honeypaw told him.

"But it doesn't make sense." Lionpaw's mind was whirling.

"Who cares if it makes sense?" Honeypaw trotted around him. "There's going to be a huge battle anyway. Leafpool said so."

Sorreltail was heading toward them, eyes clouded with worry. "You're jumping ahead of yourself, Honeypaw," she meowed.

"We have to be ready," Honeypaw argued. "Who knows what WindClan will do next?"

Lionpaw backed away from the two cats, his heart pounding. Had RiverClan really stolen the kits? There was another way off the moor, one their Clanmates didn't know about. *What if the kits had found the tunnels?*

He jumped as a voice sounded behind him. "You should eat," Spiderleg was stretching, flexing his muscles. "You must be ready for battle at any moment."

"But WindClan is fighting RiverClan, not us!"

"Anything could happen," Spiderleg growled. "RiverClan might chase WindClan off the moor. They might decide to accuse us of taking the kits instead. Leafpool told Firestar that WindClan is desperate enough to do anything."

Lionpaw froze. *I must find the kits! I must stop this!* But what about his Clan? He ought to be thinking about defending them. He should be helping fortify the camp like Cloudtail and Cinderpaw, or joining a patrol to check the border. He couldn't go off and search for kits. What if WindClan attacked while he was gone?

This battle will be a chance to prove yourself a true warrior! Tigerstar's voice murmured in his ear. *The kits mean nothing! Think of your Clan.*

But I am thinking of my Clan! Lionpaw shook his head, clearing Tigerstar's voice from his mind. Cats would be injured. Some might die! He shuddered as he thought of Heatherpaw caught in the midst of the fighting. If the kits were only lost in the tunnels, the battle would be over nothing.

"Lionpaw!" Brambleclaw was padding toward him. "Get something to eat and help with the preparations. Firestar's organizing extra patrols and the barrier needs to be strengthened."

Lionpaw blinked at the ThunderClan deputy. His belly was churning. "I'm not hungry."

Brambleclaw shifted his paws. "Are you scared?"

Lionpaw opened his mouth, searching for the words to explain.

"It's natural." Brambleclaw's mew softened. "I used to worry about seeing my Clanmates wounded. But defending the Clan is part of the warrior code; it's what we've all trained for. I know it's tough but we're doing the right thing in the eyes of StarClan." He ran his tail along Lionpaw's flank. "You have the makings of a great warrior, Lionpaw, and I'm proud of you. Just remember what you've been taught and stay sharp."

"Do we really need to fight?"

"If your leader tells you to, then yes," Brambleclaw murmured. "Firestar won't lead any cat into battle unless he believes it's the right thing to do."

But Firestar doesn't know everything. Lionpaw suddenly felt weary. If only he didn't know about the tunnels. Then he could just do as he was ordered without question. Miserably, he nodded at Brambleclaw. "Okay." He padded to the fresh-kill pile, sick at the sight of the prey piled there as though it were any ordinary day.

"Why can't we fight?" Icekit's small mew wailed across the clearing.

"I don't want to wait here until WindClan come and shred us!" Foxkit hissed.

"You'd only get in the way," Ferncloud told them sternly. She swept her tail over them, shooing them back toward the nursery. "The best way you can help is to hide inside your den till the danger is passed. Your time for fighting will come, but not this moon."

Lionpaw watched Ferncloud nudge them through the nursery entrance. It wasn't just Foxkit and Icekit who were in danger. He couldn't possibly put his Clanmates at risk, not when there was something he could do about it. Narrowing his eyes against the rain, he veered away from the fresh-kill pile and headed past the medicine den. Slipping in among the dripping brambles he pushed his way through to the camp wall. He reached up to the first ledge and scrambled onto it. Ledge by ledge, he clawed his way to the top of the hollow, panting with the effort as he hauled himself over the top.

Crouching in the rain-soaked grass, he caught his breath and peeped over at the busy camp below. No one had seen him leave. His Clanmates were still busy pressing twigs into the thorn barrier, gathering in groups to plan patrols, their wet pelts bristling with excitement. He crept into the trees and began to run down the slope, heading toward the tunnel entrance.

Suddenly, voices sounded from behind a clump of ferns. Lionpaw squeezed between the dripping stems and peered out.

"Try to pick the juiciest leaves," Jaypaw was advising.

Hollypaw sat beside him, stripping leaves from a small plant and piling them on the wet earth.

Jaypaw lifted his nose and sniffed. "Lionpaw?"

Lionpaw straightened and pushed his way out, shaking the drops from his pelt.

"What are you doing here?" Hollypaw's green eyes flashed with surprise. "Do we have to go back to camp?"

Lionpaw shook his head. "I think I know where the kits are," he blurted out.

Paw steps pounded on the forest floor nearby. Lionpaw ducked back into the ferns, crouching down among the stems. Hollypaw and Jaypaw stared after him in surprise, then glanced at each other as Thornclaw and Whitewing raced out of the trees.

"You two had better hurry," Thornclaw meowed.

Lionpaw ducked down farther as Hollypaw glanced at the

ferns where he was hiding, her eyes glittering with suspicion. Would she give him away?

Whitewing flicked her tail. "Is everything okay?"

"Yes." Jaypaw's answer was firm. "We've just got a few more leaves to pick and then we'll go back to camp."

"Good." Thornclaw nodded. "We're heading up to the ridge to see if there's any sign of WindClan. We may be able to see if they've begun their attack on RiverClan from up there."

Suddenly, Whitewing sniffed the air. "It smells like Lionpaw's been here."

"Yes." Jaypaw plucked another dock leaf from the soggy plant in front of him. "He came to tell us to hurry up."

"Has he gone back to camp?" Thornclaw asked.

"I suppose so," Jaypaw replied.

"Don't be long." Whitewing padded to the fern where Lionpaw was crouching. He held his breath, praying that his golden fur wouldn't show through the green leaves.

"Come on!" Thornclaw bounded up the slope toward the ridge. Whitewing turned and pelted after him.

"Why in StarClan did you hide?" Hollypaw demanded as Lionpaw slid out of the ferns.

"They mustn't know what I'm up to," Lionpaw whispered.

Jaypaw's tail was twitching. "What *are* you up to?"

"What's this about the kits?" Hollypaw narrowed her eyes.

Lionpaw took a deep breath. "There are tunnels under our territory."

"Tunnels?" Jaypaw's fur stood on end.

"Yes. They lead onto the moor, to WindClan territory. You can travel right through if you want. The kits followed Heatherpaw to the tunnel entrance once. I think that's where they might be."

Hollypaw was staring at him in horror. "You've been meeting Heatherpaw! You told me you'd stopped seeing her!"

Lionpaw stepped backward. His sister was digging her claws into the earth as though she were trying to stop herself raking his pelt.

"You lied to me and you lied to your Clanmates!" she spat. "I always thought that you were the most loyal of us. And now you've betrayed your Clan!"

"I haven't betrayed them!" Lionpaw mewed. "I've stopped meeting Heatherpaw now. We were just playing, but then I realized that—"

"That an enemy Clan knows a secret way into our territory!" Hollypaw snapped. "Were you ever going to tell anyone, or were you just going to sit and watch while your little friend led her Clanmates to our camp?"

Lionpaw glared at his sister. "I would never let that happen!"

"Calm down." Jaypaw weaved between them. "It's done now." He swung his head toward his sister. "Lionpaw's not the only cat who's made mistakes this moon. You're still in trouble for trying to help Willowpaw."

"That was different," Hollypaw growled. But she shifted her paws as she spoke.

"There's no time to argue," Jaypaw mewed. "Are you sure

that the kits are in these tunnels, Lionpaw?"

"Not definite, but it seems the most likely place they'd be." He glanced anxiously at Hollypaw. "Will you help me find them?"

Hollypaw's tail quivered. "Okay," she mewed. "I don't want WindClan attacking RiverClan. Not when they're so close to solving their problem."

Lionpaw blinked. "What do you mean?"

The fur on Hollypaw's spine rippled. "I promised not to tell."

"Promised who?" Jaypaw demanded.

"Willowpaw and Leopardstar."

"But we're kin," Jaypaw pressed. "We have to stop keeping secrets from one another. That's not how it's meant to be."

Hollypaw's eyes glittered with uncertainty. "Okay." She took a deep breath. "RiverClan's camp was being threatened by Twoleg kits. They're making the stream around it deeper and wider to keep the Twolegs away. I saw it myself. They're so close to making it work. They should be back in their old camp by the next Gathering." Her paws were trembling. "I promised not to tell, but it doesn't seem right. Everything's gone wrong."

"No, it hasn't." Lionpaw lifted his chin. "We're going to stop the battle."

"But how?" Hollypaw mewed.

"By finding the kits."

Jaypaw padded to Lionpaw's side. "Where are these tunnels? How do we get in?"

"Follow me." Lionpaw headed into the trees. He broke

into a run, checking over his shoulder that Hollypaw and Jaypaw were keeping up. They weaved after him, skidding to a halt on the slippery leaves beside him as he reached the bottom of the slope where the tunnel opened into the forest.

"Where is it?" Hollypaw squinted over the swath of brambles.

Lionpaw flicked his tail toward the rabbit hole Heatherpaw had first disappeared into. "There."

"That?" Hollypaw mewed in surprise. "No wonder no one's ever noticed it before."

Jaypaw was sniffing the air as though searching for something. His tail was quivering.

Lionpaw frowned. "Have you been here before?"

"I don't think so." Jaypaw's ears twitched.

Why did he seem so afraid? There was no time to worry. Lionpaw squeezed under the brambles. "Follow me." He pushed his way through; it was easier now after all his visits, although one or two fresh branches had grown since he was last here, and he ducked as they snatched at his ears. Jaypaw stayed close behind him, his nose brushing Lionpaw's tail.

"The entrance is here." Lionpaw scrambled out of the bushes and guided Jaypaw to the hole in the side of the hill. He stopped beside it and sniffed the familiar scent of musty air flowing from the tunnel.

Hollypaw scrabbled out of the brambles after them and stared doubtfully at the hole. Rain dripped from her fur and each ear was tipped with a quivering drop of water. "We go in here?"

Lionpaw nodded.

"What about the rain?" Jaypaw sounded wary.

"It won't be raining inside the tunnel." Lionpaw was puzzled; surely he'd be glad to get out of the downpour?

Jaypaw flattened his ears and sniffed at the entrance. "Have you been here before in the rain?" he asked suspiciously.

"No." Lionpaw was getting impatient now. There wasn't time for this. "We must find the kits before the battle starts." He squeezed into the entrance and started to pad quickly along the familiar tunnel.

"Wait!" Hollypaw called from behind. "It's too dark to see where I'm going."

Lionpaw waited while Jaypaw and Hollypaw caught up with him. They were both moving cautiously, their paw steps pattering unevenly on the rocky floor. Surely Jaypaw should be able to travel through the tunnels more easily than the rest of them? He was used to darkness. "There's a cave ahead," Lionpaw reassured them. "There's a gap in the roof so it'll be lighter there." He moved on, slower this time. He could hear Jaypaw sniffing the air, and Hollypaw's fur brushing the walls.

"Do these tunnels really lead all the way to WindClan territory?" Hollypaw's mew echoed eerily in the darkness. "Have you been that far?"

"No, only as far as the cave," Lionpaw answered. Then he froze. He could smell familiar scents up ahead. *WindClan!* Had Heatherpaw already led a patrol into the tunnels?

Jaypaw's breath stirred his ear fur. "You know there are WindClan cats ahead."

"Yes," Lionpaw sighed.

"Perhaps we should go back," Hollypaw whispered. "We don't want WindClan to realize we know about this place. It would ruin our advantage."

"They probably know already." Lionpaw's heart felt as heavy as stone. Heatherpaw had betrayed their secret—he wouldn't be surprised if she'd betrayed him as well. They hadn't exactly been friendly the last time they met. He padded toward the dim light and stepped into the cave.

In the gloom, he could just make out Heatherpaw on the other side of the river.

Breezepaw was pacing the edge of the cave behind her, sniffing at each tunnel in turn. "I've lost their scent."

"Lionpaw!" Heatherpaw sounded surprised.

Breezepaw spun, hissing, to face Lionpaw.

Heatherpaw's gaze darted anxiously toward her Clanmate as she went on, "H-how did you know about this place?"

Lionpaw understood at once. She was pretending she had never met him here before. It was a sensible plan, but it felt wrong to act like strangers after they'd shared so much time here. "I found it a few days ago by accident," he lied. Hollypaw and Jaypaw were creeping out of the tunnel behind him. "I was chasing a rabbit and it led me down a hole and I ended up here." He flashed a warning glance at Hollypaw.

Breezepaw's pelt bristled. "These tunnels lead into ThunderClan territory as well?"

"I didn't realize," Heatherpaw mewed, wide-eyed. "I've only been as far as this cave before."

"What are you three doing here?" Breezepaw demanded.

Hollypaw padded in front of Lionpaw, lifting her chin. "When we heard that the kits were missing, Lionpaw guessed they might be here."

"How did you know there was another entrance in WindClan territory?" Breezepaw flexed his claws.

"It was just a guess." Lionpaw shrugged. "There are so many tunnels. They might lead to ShadowClan territory as far as I know."

Breezepaw stared at him. The damp, stuffy air was thick with mistrust. "Is there any scent of the kits in your tunnel?"

"No," Hollypaw replied, her voice taut.

"We followed their trail here, but it's disappeared," Heatherpaw explained.

Jaypaw had cautiously crept forward and was sniffing at the river. Its usually sleek surface was rippling as though blown by the wind, and dark water lapped over the edges, forming pools in the dimpled rock on either side. "Is the water always this high?" he asked.

"Only after it's been raining," Heatherpaw answered.

"Does it get higher?"

Heatherpaw tipped her head on one side, puzzled. "I don't think so."

Lionpaw felt hot with embarrassment. Why did Jaypaw keep fussing about the rain? He wanted to find the kits and get out of here.

Breezepaw paced around his Clanmate. "These intruders might as well go home," he mewed. "*We're* looking for the kits. There's no need for them to help." He glared at Lionpaw. "Why are you bothered about WindClan kits anyway?"

Hollypaw flicked her tail. "There's going to be a battle over them, or haven't you heard?"

"Can we stop chatting and get on with the search?" Heatherpaw snapped.

Breezepaw shot her an angry look. "What about them?"

"We may as well let them come with us," Heatherpaw mewed. "How are we going to carry three kits by ourselves?" Before he could answer, she headed for the tunnel nearest her. "We have to find those kits before any of our Clanmates gets hurt."

"I agree!" Hollypaw leaped the wide river and glanced back at Jaypaw. "The water is about two foxtails wide," she told him.

Jaypaw crouched, preparing to jump. Lionpaw could see his paws trembling. *Let him make it!* He tensed, ready to dive into the rushing river if he had to, but Jaypaw sprang high over the river, clearing it with a tail-length to spare.

As Lionpaw jumped after him, Heatherpaw ducked out of the tunnel she had been sniffing. "They haven't been this way."

Lionpaw crept into another dark opening, tasting the air. No scent.

"This way!" Jaypaw was crouching in front of a narrow entrance, his whiskers twitching.

Hollypaw pushed past him and peered at the ground. "He's right! There's a paw print."

Lionpaw squeezed past her to look. Sure enough, there on the silty ground was a tiny fresh print. "They went this way." He glanced up and met Heatherpaw's gaze. Fear glittered in her hazy blue eyes.

"Oh, Lionpaw," she whispered. "What have we done?"

CHAPTER 19

"I'll go first."

Jaypaw hardly realized he had said the words out loud until he heard Breezepaw snort scornfully.

"You're blind!"

"And you can see perfectly in the dark, I suppose!" Hollypaw snapped.

Jaypaw sensed Breezepaw bristle, but the WindClan cat didn't argue. He was glad, because he was on the verge of turning tail and fleeing back along the tunnel to the forest, where rain pattered on leaves and earth and didn't collect in cold stone tunnels to sweep away everything inside them. . . . All he could think of ever since he set foot in the first tunnel was racing for his life, terrified, with Fallen Leaves. Images filled his mind: the dark tunnel, the roaring of the water, the shock as the wave hit him and swept him up like a leaf caught in a storm, gasping for air and finding only water to breathe. *Don't think about it!* At least this time there would be no glimmers of light to distract him; instead he could focus on his instincts.

Lionpaw stepped out of the way to let Jaypaw pass. As

Jaypaw brushed past him, he felt relief flooding from his brother's pelt. *He thinks I'll do better in the dark than he will. I hope he's right.* Cold air blasted over him, making his whiskers tremble. But the breeze carried something else, whispers he felt rather than heard, flooding from deep inside the tunnel like the pulsing of blood in his veins. He padded into the tunnel, feeling the darkness swallow him up. This wasn't darkness he was used to. Blind in the forest, he could feel the warmth of the sun on his pelt, smell the fresh tangs that flavored the air, hear the wind that rustled the leaves. This darkness was suffocating, musty, and cold, pressing against his fur and filling his nose and mouth. Nothing but blackness, thick as fur, soft as water, drawing him in.

The rock beneath his paws was covered in fine silt, the walls so narrow they grazed his pelt as he crept slowly forward.

"Can't you go any faster?" Breezepaw's mew was as jagged as the walls.

"Shh!" He tried to block out the fear pulsing from the other cats, and padded on, feeling the path slope downward, the tunnel widen, cold air jab his pelt as they passed under a slit in the roof. Was this really the right way? The draft flowing through the tunnel like water carried no kit scent, only forest air seeping through fissures in the roof.

Suddenly, a pelt brushed his flank.

Jaypaw bristled. "*I'm* leading, Breezepaw!" He barged the cat away.

"What are you talking about? I'm back here!" Breezepaw snapped from behind.

Hollypaw's nose brushed his tail-tip. "There's no one near you, Jaypaw."

Surprised, Jaypaw tasted the air. A new scent bathed his tongue. Not a Clan scent, but still faintly familiar. He tasted the air again, his pelt pricking with unease as the other cat pressed against him, matching him step for step.

"I will walk with you, my friend, as you once walked with me," the voice whispered in his ear.

Fallen Leaves! Jaypaw's heart lurched. The memory of a great, black wave engulfing him made him stop dead. He fought the urge to turn and run, to pelt back to the cave and the forest and the safety of the open sky.

"I could not leave you here to walk alone, when you walked with me like a brother."

Jaypaw blinked, trying to see. "Am I dreaming?"

"No," Fallen Leaves whispered. "I have come to help. I know where the kits are."

"Why have we stopped?" Breezepaw mewed crossly from behind.

Hollypaw's nose flicked Jaypaw's tail. "Are you okay?"

"Fine," he told her, then he lowered his mew to less than a whisper, breathing the words so that only Fallen Leaves could hear. "Have you seen them?"

"I know where they are." Fallen Leaves pressed his pelt to Jaypaw's, urging him forward. "But we must hurry."

Jaypaw resisted. "Why should I trust you? You couldn't even get yourself out of these tunnels!"

"I have walked them ever since," Fallen Leaves murmured

sadly, "and I know them better than the moors above us."

Jaypaw steadied his breath. "You've really seen the kits?"

"They are alive, but they are cold. We must hurry."

Instinct alone might not be enough down here. Touching his tail to Fallen Leaves's flank, Jaypaw let the tom guide him forward into a tunnel that branched to one side. The passage sloped steeply down; Jaypaw's pads slipped on the floor. The rock was slick with rain.

"Are you sure you know where you're going?" Breezepaw called.

"Can you still smell them?" Lionpaw asked anxiously.

"They went this way," Jaypaw replied.

Fallen Leaves swerved again, nudging him toward another tunnel. "Duck!" he warned. Jaypaw dipped his head just in time, squeezing through a shallow gap.

"Keep down!" he warned his Clanmates as he wriggled beneath the pressing rock. The gap grew lower and lower until he was scrabbling on his belly.

"This feels like a dead end!" Hollypaw panted as she squeezed after him.

"It opens up in a moment," Fallen Leaves promised in Jaypaw's ear.

Jaypaw smelled the sweet scent of heather and felt rain on his face. There must be an opening in the roof ahead. He slithered out of the gap, relieved to feel space around him.

"Which way now?" Heatherpaw's fur brushed the rock as she squirmed out after him.

"There are three tunnels," Lionpaw told him.

Jaypaw tasted the air, but there was no scent of the kits.

"This way," Fallen Leaves whispered. Jaypaw felt his whiskers brush rock on either side as he let Fallen Leaves guide him into another tunnel.

"How do you know we're going the right way?" Breezepaw's mew was sharp, but Jaypaw could sense the panic throbbing beneath his pelt. It came from every cat, filling the darkness with a suffocating dread that Jaypaw tried to block from his mind.

"I can smell them," he lied. He mustn't let their fear overwhelm him. *Listen to Fallen Leaves!*

The tunnel twisted and veered upward, then widened. Air filtered through a gap overhead. The patter of paw steps slowed behind him.

"I knew it was a dead end," Heatherpaw sighed, stopping.

Jaypaw halted. A boulder was blocking the tunnel ahead. He sensed its unyielding bulk.

"We'll never get past that," Breezepaw mewed.

Rain pounded overhead, dripping through a gap into the tunnel and echoing off the rocks as Jaypaw sniffed the wet stone. He ran his nose along the boulder, following its smooth contours until his whiskers touched the tunnel wall. A tiny gap opened between boulder and wall, too small to squeeze through.

"Now what?" Breezepaw snapped. "Do you think you can lead us back?" He didn't sound convinced. "Or did you just bring us here to show us this boulder? Let me guess, it's a special StarClan rock and it's going to tell us where the kits are."

"Shut up!" Heatherpaw hissed at her Clanmate.

"Why?" Breezepaw snarled. "We're lost underground! Do you want me to thank him?"

"Shh!" Hollypaw mewed suddenly.

"I'll say what I like!" Breezepaw retorted. "Just because he's your brother—"

"I can hear something!" Hollypaw hissed.

"What is it?" Lionpaw's pelt was tingling with excitement.

Jaypaw strained to hear.

A tiny squeaking sound, just louder than the rain, echoed ahead of him.

The kits?

"Anyone there?" he called.

The squeak turned into an excited mewling.

They were behind the boulder!

Jaypaw felt Fallen Leaves breathe in his ear. "I told you I'd help you find them."

"I think I can climb over it!" Lionpaw mewed. Jaypaw heard claws scrabbling against stone as his brother clambered over the boulder. Shallow water splashed faintly when he jumped down the other side.

"They're here!" His joyful mew echoed around the tunnel. More claws scraped against rock as Hollypaw, Heatherpaw, and Breezepaw scrambled over to join him.

"Thank StarClan we found you!" Heatherpaw purred.

Paws splashed and a frightened mew answered her. "We couldn't climb back over!"

"We thought we were stuck forever!"

"We'll take you home," Breezepaw reassured them.

"Go on, Swallowkit," Heatherpaw urged. Tiny claws scraped stone and a soggy bundle of fur slid clumsily down onto the ground beside Jaypaw.

"Are you okay?" he asked. The rain was pounding harder. They had to get out quick.

"I'm fine but—"

Breezepaw's mew interrupted her. "Your turn, Sedgekit."

Fur brushed rock and another kit thudded lightly on the floor. Jaypaw reached out his nose to the newest arrival. "Are you hurt?"

"No."

Jaypaw swept the two kits together with his tail, pressing against their sodden pelts to warm them.

Breezepaw landed beside him. Jaypaw stiffened. He was holding the third kit in his jaws. She was barely breathing and when Breezepaw laid her on the ground, she didn't move.

"Thistlekit went to sleep and now she won't wake up!" Swallowkit wailed.

Jaypaw pushed the trembling kits against Breezepaw and crouched beside the limp, wet body at his feet. She was cold, shivering with small convulsions. Jaypaw began to massage her body with his paws, trying to rub some warmth into her pelt.

Heatherpaw slithered back over the boulder. "Is she okay?"

"Help Breezepaw warm the other two!" Jaypaw ordered.

"We're hungry!" Sedgekit's mew was muffled by Heatherpaw's fur.

"It serves you right for wandering off!" Heatherpaw

scolded. She sounded cross but Jaypaw could feel her fearful gaze jabbing his pelt as he worked on Thistlekit. Rain dripped down harder through the gap in the roof. The silt had turned to slimy mud around his paws. He rubbed Thistlekit more urgently. He had to get them out of here.

Lionpaw and Hollypaw leaped down from the boulder.

"Do you know the way out?" Swallowkit asked, trembling.

"Of course we do," Breezepaw declared. "We found our way in, didn't we? Getting out will be even easier."

He doesn't believe that.

"We'll get out," Jaypaw mewed softly. He waited for Fallen Leaves to whisper encouragement but he only felt the quiver of the young tom's tail against his flank.

Thistlekit began to cough and fidget beneath his paws. Warmth was seeping back into her body. She struggled to her paws. "You found us!" she gasped.

Hollypaw folded herself around the shivering kit. "Did you think we'd leave you in this horrible place?"

Surprise pulsed from the kit. "You're from ThunderClan."

"We've been helping your Clanmates to find you," Hollypaw explained.

"You've caused a lot of trouble," Breezepaw growled.

Lionpaw's tail swished over the floor. "We can worry about that once we're out."

A noise like rushing air suddenly filled the tunnels.

"The rain's getting harder," Hollypaw mewed.

"That's not rain," Lionpaw murmured. "It's coming from inside the tunnels."

"Inside?" Sedgekit squeaked.

"What is it?" Breezepaw demanded.

Jaypaw felt sick. He knew what it meant. "The river is overflowing."

Lionpaw darted to Jaypaw's side, pelt bristling with alarm. "How do you know?"

Jaypaw closed his eyes. "I've heard it before. The tunnels are going to flood."

Energy exploded from Lionpaw. "We've got to get out of here!" Swallowkit squealed as he snatched her up in his jaws.

"Breezepaw, Heatherpaw, take the other two," he hissed out of the corner of his mouth.

"I'll lead," Jaypaw mewed. He had brought them here. He had to get them out. He pelted back along the tunnel. Fur brushed stone and claws skittered after him.

Fallen Leaves fell in beside him and matched the rhythm of his stride.

"You've got to get us back to the cave!" Jaypaw hissed.

"I will," Fallen Leaves promised. The young tom's paws made no sound on the tunnel floor as they raced onward, but his pelt was hot with fear and his mind flashed with memories that echoed in Jaypaw's mind: paws churning through muddy water, struggling against currents too strong to fight, gasping for air and finding only water, disbelief as the world closed in and life ebbed from his body. *He's remembering how we drowned!*

Jaypaw pushed on harder, ducking just in time to squirm under the low roof. He wriggled forward, the rock scraping his spine, his claws splintering against the stone. Struggling out the other side he paused, waiting until he heard the others emerge. The kits squealed with fear and pain as they were dragged over the rough stone.

"Nearly there!" Jaypaw encouraged. The tunnel was sloping upward now. Water washed his paws. One more twist, another turn. He could smell the scent of fresh air. He burst into the cave, hope springing in his belly.

We've made it! He could feel Fallen Leaves trembling with relief beside him.

Ahead, the river was roaring.

Lionpaw shot out behind him. "Take Swallowkit!" He thrust the kit at Jaypaw.

Jaypaw snatched her in his teeth.

"What's he doing?" Hollypaw exploded from the tunnel with Heatherpaw and Breezepaw.

Jaypaw heard water splash as Lionpaw plunged into the river.

"Lionpaw!" he yowled, dropping Swallowkit. He strained to hear over the roaring of the water. "Can you see him?" he begged Hollypaw.

"He's swimming!"

"He's crazy!" Breezepaw gasped.

"I'm okay!" Lionpaw coughed as he struggled, splashing, from the far side of the river.

"How are we going to get the kits across?" Heatherpaw called.

"There's no point!" Lionpaw yowled back. "The tunnel's

blocked!" Panic edged his mew. "The rain has washed soil into the entrance. There's too much mud to dig through."

"What about our tunnel?" Heatherpaw called.

Breezepaw bounded away as Lionpaw splashed back across the river.

"Blocked, too! Boulders have fallen from the roof!" Breezepaw called from the WindClan tunnel. "It's like a waterfall in here. We'd never get the kits up it!"

"We have to try!" Heatherpaw screeched.

"I don't think there's enough space at the top to get through," Breezepaw argued. Fear made him angry. "If a kit got swept down over the rocks, it might die!"

"We have to do something," Hollypaw yowled.

Jaypaw pressed against Fallen Leaves, trying to read his thoughts, but the young tom's flank seemed to be fading, and Jaypaw's shoulder passed with a shiver through the soft fur. "Fallen Leaves?" he hissed.

"I'm sorry!" Guilt and grief hung like mist in the air. Jaypaw suddenly felt cold where the tom's warm body had been. Panic gripped him and time seemed to slow. For a heartbeat Jaypaw glimpsed a pair of amber eyes.

"Wait!" he called. "Come with us!"

Fallen Leaves blinked, his gaze filled with sorrow. "It's not my time to leave," he mewed faintly and then he was gone.

Not again!

"Are we going to die?" Sedgekit's terrified mew rose above the torrent.

Jaypaw's mind whirled as he tried to work out some way to

escape. Water sprayed his face as the river frothed and bub-
bled against the cave walls. Lionpaw pressed him back with
the others until they were huddled on a narrow strip of earth,
water snapping at their paws.

Help us!

Blood roared in Jaypaw's ears.

Could StarClan hear him down here?

Suddenly, a silvery light glowed at the edge of his vision,
like moonlight creeping across a night-black forest. Jaypaw
looked up and saw a smooth ledge near the top of the cave. A
cat was sitting there. It was the cat from his dream, with
twisted claws, balding pelt, sightless bulging eyes. The cat
who had sent Fallen Leaves into the tunnels to die.

The cat looked straight at Jaypaw.

Anger rose in Jaypaw's chest. *Have you come to watch us die too?*

A shadow moved beneath the cat's paws. He was rolling
something toward the lip of the ledge. Something long and
slender and smooth. Jaypaw's fur stood on end. *The stick from
the lake!*

Its markings were clear in the moonlight and, as Jaypaw
stared in confusion, the cat lifted his paw and held a trembling claw over a row of scratches. Five long and three short.
Jaypaw gasped. *Those scratches weren't there before!* He had counted
the marks so many times he knew them by heart.

Five warriors and three kits! He means us!

Jaypaw stared, panic-stricken, into the old cat's eyes. *Are we
going to die?*

The cat bent his head to look at the stick before slowly

lowering his claw and running it through the scratches. With a rush of hope, Jaypaw understood.

We're going to survive!

The cat nodded.

A paw clapped him sharply on the ear. "Stop staring at nothing and help us think!" Breezepaw snarled.

The vision disappeared and Jaypaw was in darkness once more. He turned to the others, his pelt bristling with excitement. "There's a way out of here!" he mewed. "I know it!"

"What is it, then?" Lionpaw demanded.

"I'm not sure," Jaypaw admitted. "Let me think for a moment."

"Thinking won't move boulders!" Heatherpaw screeched. "We're trapped!"

"We could wait till the cave floods and swim up to the hole in the roof," Hollypaw suggested.

"It's too small to escape through," Breezepaw growled.

"And the kits might drown!" Heatherpaw pointed out.

Jaypaw shook his head. There was something at the edge of his thoughts. An idea he could sense but not reach. *The stick!* It had been here in the cave. But he'd found it by the lake. How did it get out?

Water splashed at his paws. He recoiled, then froze. He pictured the river reaching up to the stick, lifting it, washing it away. Of course! The river must flow out into the lake.

"We'll have to swim!" he cried.

"Swim where?" Lionpaw spluttered.

"The river runs into the lake. It'll carry us there!"

"But it disappears underground!" Breezepaw hissed.

"It comes out in the lake!" Jaypaw insisted.

"We're not RiverClan. We can't swim!" Heatherpaw wailed.

Lionpaw pressed against Jaypaw. "Will this really work?"

"There's no other way."

"If you say we must do it, then we have to trust you," Hollypaw mewed.

"*You* might!" Breezepaw growled.

"If we don't do something, we're all going to drown!" Heatherpaw screeched.

Hollypaw kneaded the ground. "Let's try it!"

Swallowkit squealed in terror. "I'm not going in the water!"

"We'll hold you by your tails," Lionpaw promised. "We won't let go."

"By our tails?" shrieked Thistlekit.

"If we hold you by your scruffs, we'll swallow too much water," Lionpaw mewed. "You'll have to keep your head afloat by paddling with your forepaws like this." Water spattered from his paws as he churned the air, showing the kits how to paddle.

"I'm scared," Heatherpaw whispered.

"It's going to be okay." Lionpaw dropped onto four paws and pressed against the WindClan cat. Jaypaw was close enough to hear him whisper into her ear, "Our time together will be something I remember even when I'm with StarClan."

Heatherpaw trembled. "There will be no borders between us there."

Jaypaw blinked, startled by the emotion flooding between them. Then light flickered in his vision and he saw the old cat again.

Leave now!

He thought of all the cats who had ventured into this place; their fear and hope seemed to whisper in the air around him. The scratches on the stick had marked their fate. Did the new lines really predict the Clan cats would survive? He had to believe that they did.

"We have to go!" he ordered.

"Line up at the edge of the river," Hollypaw instructed. "Lionpaw, you take Sedgekit, I'll take Thistlekit, Breezepaw can take Swallowkit."

"What can I do?" Heatherpaw asked.

"Hold on to my tail," Jaypaw mewed. "We'll help each other."

"Okay," Heatherpaw agreed. He felt her take the tip of his tail lightly in her teeth.

"I'm not going!" Swallowkit's paws splashed through the shallows as she tried to make a run for it. She shrieked as Breezepaw grabbed her and dragged her toward him through the water. "Don't worry, Swallowkit," he soothed. "I won't let go. There's no way I'm going to let you drown."

Swallowkit whimpered but didn't try to escape again.

"Come on," Lionpaw urged.

Jaypaw waded through the shallows. His paws throbbed

with dread as he felt the tug of the river.

"Ready?" Lionpaw mewed.

"Yes!" Hollypaw answered.

Jaypaw tensed. "Jump!"

He hurled himself into the rushing torrent. Heatherpaw tugged on his tail as the water swirled her downstream. The current dragged him under and he was lost in his dream of drowning again, choked by the tumbling water with the bodies of cats all around him and his ears filled with roaring.

CHAPTER 20

Water roared in Hollypaw's ears as the pale light of the cave faded from sight. The river dragged her into the tunnel, the current pulling her under. Her lungs screamed for air. She fought the urge to suck in water and kept her jaws firmly clamped around Thistlekit's tail.

Rock scraped her ears and she felt air on her face as the river swirled her upward. She drew a quick breath before the river dragged her down once more.

A body brushed hers and was swept away. Thistlekit struggled, raking her nose with thorn-sharp claws. She resisted the urge to fight, trusting Jaypaw, letting the flood carry her, feeling stone graze her flanks as the water tossed her against the sides of the tunnel.

The roaring grew louder till she thought her ears would burst.

Then peace.

The current let her go and the noise died away. She strained to see through the darkness. Was that light? Bright dots sparkled in the distance. Was StarClan waiting to welcome her?

Her head swam and blackness pressed in on the edges of her consciousness. She fought her way upward, frantically seeking the surface, praying that she wouldn't find rock above her. With a final desperate effort she pushed up and up until she thought the whole world must be water.

Suddenly, she burst through the surface of the lake, startled by the chill of the wind as it swept her face and filled her nose and ears. They had made it! She gasped and spluttered, drawing in lungful after lungful of cold, wonderful air. Blinking water from her eyes, she saw that the dots were stars, glimmering through wind-torn clouds. The rainstorm was moving away.

Thistlekit thrashed in the water beside her, fighting to keep her head above water. Hollypaw grasped the kit with her forepaws, let go of her tail and grabbed her scruff, paddling with her hind legs to keep both their heads out of the water. She forced herself to relax, letting the water support her and working her paws in a steady rhythm that held them afloat. Thistlekit coughed and wheezed, trembling against her chest.

Hollypaw scanned the dark surface of the lake for the others. Joy sparked in her belly when she saw Lionpaw's golden head bobbing a few tail-lengths away. Sedgekit was clinging to his back, eyes shining in the moonlight. Bubbles exploded near him, and Breezepaw burst to the surface with Swallowkit.

Jaypaw? Heatherpaw? Panic started to grip Hollypaw. Had they made it? She heard splashing behind her and she twisted around, dragging Thistlekit so fast he squealed with surprise.

Jaypaw and Heatherpaw were flailing beside each other, their paws spraying water as they fought to stay afloat.

"Jaypaw!" she called.

"We're okay!" Heatherpaw coughed.

Hollypaw swam toward them, kicking out with her hind legs, surprised to find herself swimming like a RiverClan cat. "The shore's over there!" She could see it not far off and, reaching Jaypaw, she nudged him toward it.

Heatherpaw was splashing toward Lionpaw. Why wasn't the WindClan apprentice trying to help her own Clanmate? Then she realized that Lionpaw was thrashing in the water, ducking his face under. As he came up for a breath, she saw his eyes were wild with panic.

"Sedgekit's gone!" he yowled.

Heatherpaw dived beneath the surface. Hollypaw held her breath, treading water as Lionpaw ducked under again. Had the current dragged the kit back down into the black, bottomless water?

Suddenly, Heatherpaw bobbed up, Sedgekit between her jaws. The kit's paws flapped wildly. He was alive!

Lionpaw broke the surface, his eyes lighting as he saw Sedgekit. He swam to Heatherpaw's side and grasped the kit's tail between his teeth, and together they headed for the shore. Hollypaw swam beside Jaypaw, casting an eye back to make sure Breezepaw was still managing. The black Wind-Clan apprentice was pounding through the water with Swallowkit's scruff in his jaws and his eyes fixed on the shore.

Hollypaw's muscles burned with exhaustion, but she

didn't dare stop moving. With Thistlekit's fur blocking her mouth, every breath was a struggle, but she kept her gaze pinned on the shoreline and pushed on. At last, she felt pebbles graze her hind paws and, reaching down, touched the bottom with a forepaw. *Thank you, StarClan!*

Wading from the water, she dropped Thistlekit in the shallows and stood panting for a moment, struggling to get her breath back. Heatherpaw and Lionpaw already lay farther up the shore, their flanks heaving while Sedgekit crouched beside them, vomiting water onto the pebbles.

Pebbles clacked behind her as Jaypaw followed her out of the lake.

"How did you know it would carry us into the lake?" Hollypaw gasped.

"It . . . it made sense," Jaypaw mewed between coughs. He splashed onto the beach, and Thistlekit stumbled after him.

Breezepaw was struggling out of the shallows a few foxtails along the shore. Swallowkit dangled from his jaws, her paws flailing as she fought to be put down.

"We're all safe!" Hollypaw breathed. She padded to Lionpaw and Heatherpaw, her trembling paws slipping on the wet pebbles. "Are you two okay?"

Lionpaw lifted his head. "Only *half*-drowned."

A purr burst from Heatherpaw. She flicked Lionpaw with her dripping tail and got to her paws. "We'd better get the kits back to camp."

Hollypaw glanced up the beach. Brambles and ferns crowded the shoreline, the forest dark behind them. This was

ThunderClan territory. "Let's take them to Leafpool," she suggested. "It's nearer and we need to make sure they're okay." Sedgekit was still coughing up water. Thistlekit had collapsed beside him, and though her eyes were open, her breathing was rapid.

"Hollypaw's right." Jaypaw joined them. "They need treatment for shock."

Swallowkit hurried toward them, Breezepaw at her side. "That was the horriblest thing I ever did!" She shook the water from her fur.

"You wait till you taste Leafpool's medicine," Jaypaw warned.

Breezepaw's eyes glittered with suspicion. "Leafpool?"

"The ThunderClan camp's closest," Heatherpaw told him. "We should get them treated."

Breezepaw stared at Swallowkit. There was blood on her fur where the rocks had scoured her pelt. "Okay," he agreed.

Jaypaw pricked his ears. "Listen."

Threatening yowls rang through the night air. Hollypaw stiffened as she recognized her father's voice, countered by the menacing growls of WindClan cats.

"It's coming from the forest border," Jaypaw mewed.

Had their disappearance made things even worse? "There's going to be a battle if we don't get back soon!" Hollypaw gasped.

Lionpaw leaped to his paws. "We can show them the kits. If they know they're safe, there doesn't need to be a fight."

"Are we going to the battle?" Swallowkit's eyes grew wide as an owl's.

"I can help fight!" Sedgekit mewed.

"There won't be a battle if we get there quickly," Hollypaw mewed. Sedgekit had no idea that he'd helped cause this mess, or that he'd be fighting some of the cats who'd just saved him. "Do you think you can make it?"

"Of course we can!" Thistlekit flicked her tail.

Jaypaw sniffed each kit in turn. "They need herbs," he mewed doubtfully. Then he lifted his chin. "But it can wait a while."

"Walking will warm them up," Heatherpaw pointed out.

Hollypaw led the way up the beach. She scrambled up the bank and pushed aside a swath of ferns, holding back the fronds to let the others pass. Heatherpaw nudged Swallowkit up the slope while Breezepaw followed Thistlekit, pressing his muzzle against her flank to stop her stumbling. Lionpaw grabbed Sedgekit by the scruff and swung him up the steep bank, letting him drop beside Hollypaw. She pressed the ferns back as the kit padded past. He was staring up at the branches, eyes wide as though he'd never walked beneath trees before.

"What's Jaypaw doing?" Lionpaw was staring at his brother on the shore.

Hollypaw narrowed her eyes. Jaypaw was crouched beside a stick.

"You stay with the others," she told Lionpaw. "We'll catch up with you."

She darted back onto the beach. "Are you okay?" she called to Jaypaw.

He didn't seem to hear her. He was staring at the stick, eyes closed like he was asleep. She padded closer, feeling as if she were intruding.

"All safe, just as you promised," Jaypaw was murmuring, his muzzle pressed against the smooth, pale wood. "Thank you."

"We have to go!" Hollypaw urged.

Jaypaw didn't stir. "Go carefully, Fallen Leaves," he whispered. "I hope you find your own way out one day."

"Come on, Jaypaw!" They must hurry. The yowls from the border were growing fiercer.

Jaypaw lifted his head. "I'm coming." He left the stick and padded to her side.

"What were you doing?"

"It's not important," Jaypaw replied, turning his sightless eyes on her. Hollypaw knew him well enough to guess that it was. Sometimes she wished she understood Jaypaw better. Lionpaw was easy. His friendship with Heatherpaw had broken the warrior code, but there was no mystery in his liking the pretty WindClan cat. But Jaypaw seemed to be guided by invisible paws, as though he walked in a secret world she could never be part of.

They caught up with the others. Hollypaw's chest ached and her paws felt raw after the journey through the tunnels. How soft the forest floor felt on her pads after so much rough stone. Breezepaw pushed the pace harder and the kits had to scurry to keep up. Thistlekit tripped over a root. Lionpaw instantly scooped her up and she didn't complain, hanging limp from his jaws, her eyes glazed with exhaustion.

Sedgekit was panting hard.

"I can carry you," Hollypaw offered. The kit shook his head, too breathless to speak.

Suddenly, Swallowkit squealed. A bramble had snagged her fur. Jaypaw plucked it free with his teeth. Hollypaw's chest tightened. It was cruel to make the kits travel so quickly through the forest. But they had to stop the battle.

"We're nearly there," she mewed.

The ground sloped down and Breezepaw broke into a run. Sedgekit and Swallowkit skittered after him.

An angry yowl echoed from the forest ahead. "I told you, we don't have your kits!"

It was Firestar.

"Then where are they?" Onestar spat back. "RiverClan swears they don't have them either. But they must be somewhere and we mean to find them."

"Put one paw across the border and we'll shred you!"

Hollypaw strained to see her Clanmates. Through the trees, she could make out Brambleclaw squaring up to Ashfoot on the WindClan side of the gully. Firestar stood shoulder to shoulder with his deputy. Thornclaw, Whitewing, Spiderleg, and Berrypaw were bristling behind them as the WindClan cats faced them, fur on end, lips drawn back in threatening snarls. Crowfeather was tearing at the ground beside Onestar and Ashfoot, claws unsheathed, while Owlwhisker and Tornear paced up and down behind them.

Heart pounding, Hollypaw swerved past the kits and chased after Breezepaw. Brambles sprang back in his wake, lashing her muzzle. She burst from the undergrowth just in time to see Breezepaw leap across the gully.

"Stop! We found the kits," he yowled.

"There's no need to fight!" Hollypaw stared anxiously over her shoulder, willing the others to hurry.

"Where are they?" Onestar demanded.

"They're coming," Hollypaw promised.

The warriors stared in astonishment as the undergrowth shivered and Heatherpaw nosed Sedgekit and Swallowkit out into the open. The kits stumbled to a halt and stood blinking in the moonlight. Lionpaw padded out of the brambles, Jaypaw following, and placed Thistlekit gently beside them.

"Where in StarClan did you find them?" Onestar's eyes stretched wide.

Lionpaw's fur was prickling along his spine. He glanced at Heatherpaw and stepped forward. "They found their way into—"

Hollypaw cut him off. "They were down on the shore," she mewed. "They'd made themselves a camp to shelter from the rain."

What was the point in giving away Lionpaw's secret? The tunnels between the two Clans were blocked now. Any tactical advantage was lost and it would only get Lionpaw into trouble. She glanced at the others, silently praying that they would agree.

Heatherpaw nodded. "They were just inside the Thunder-Clan border, right down on the beach." Her gaze fixed on Breezepaw. "Lionpaw, Hollypaw, and Jaypaw saw us looking for them and called us over when they picked up their scent."

"What scent?" Onestar meowed. "We didn't find one."

Breezepaw blinked. "The rain must have washed it away," he mewed.

Onestar beckoned the kits toward him with his tail. "Come here!"

Gingerly, Sedgekit, Thistlekit, and Swallowkit approached the border, ears flattened and tails down, and stopped at the edge of the gully.

"Why did you leave camp without permission?" Onestar growled across the gap.

Sedgekit lifted his chin. "We were exploring."

"Exploring?" Onestar echoed. "We've almost fought battles with RiverClan and ThunderClan looking for you."

Swallowkit hung her head. "We're sorry."

"We didn't think," Thistlekit added.

"It seemed like fun to build our own camp on the beach." Sedgekit's gaze darted toward Hollypaw with a mischievous twinkle in his eyes. He had no idea how important it was that the tunnels remain a secret.

Lionpaw padded to the scent-line. "You said *almost* fought RiverClan?" he mewed to Onestar.

Hollypaw's pelt rippled with hope. "There hasn't been a battle yet?"

"We gave RiverClan till dawn to return the kits." Onestar gave an exasperated sigh. "But now it looks like we need to apologize for falsely accusing them."

"Apologize?" Tornear lashed his tail. "Don't forget they crossed our border!"

"They were chased by a dog," Onestar reminded him.

"That's what they said last time," Crowfeather growled.

"I smelled the dog scent myself," Onestar snapped. "We have to trust what our eyes and ears tell us."

Crowfeather bristled. "But they still might invade."

Onestar narrowed his eyes. "Or they might return to their old camp as they've promised. We'll find out at the next Gathering. Until then we patrol our borders as usual. And if we see that dog, we'll teach it to stay on its own land."

Hollypaw felt weak with relief. The threat of battle was over. The WindClan kits were safe. She noticed Firestar staring at her.

"It looks like you were right, Hollypaw," he meowed.

She dipped her head. "It was never about being right," she mewed.

Brambleclaw ran his tail along her flank. "You look exhausted. We should get you all home."

"Yes," Onestar agreed. He hopped across the border and lifted the kits, one by one, over the gully. "I'm sorry that our kits caused so much trouble."

"We have kits of our own," Firestar replied, a hint of warmth in his voice. "So we know what it's like."

Tornear snorted and grabbed Thistlekit by the scruff. He turned sharply and padded away through the trees. Owlwhisker picked up Swallowkit while Crowfeather lifted Sedgekit.

"Thanks for bringing us back!" Sedgekit squeaked as he was carried away.

Brambleclaw glanced at Jaypaw, who was hanging back beside the undergrowth. "Are you okay?"

"I'm fine," Jaypaw assured him. He began to wash his tail.

Hollypaw blinked. Didn't he care they had stopped a battle? It was as though his quest had ended the moment they'd left the lake.

"I'd better go too." Breezepaw nodded curtly at Hollypaw and Lionpaw. "Are you coming?" He stared at Heatherpaw, who was lingering on the ThunderClan side of the border.

"In a moment."

Breezepaw snorted and hurried after his Clanmates.

Heatherpaw padded to Lionpaw and entwined her tail briefly with his. "Thanks for helping."

Firestar narrowed his eyes and Hollypaw stiffened. She stared at her brother, claws itching as she waited for his reply. One battle had been averted, but was another one still looming?

"We would have done the same for any cat," Lionpaw mewed flatly.

Pain flashed in Heatherpaw's eyes. "You're going to be a great warrior, Lionpaw."

Lionpaw watched as she leaped the gully and disappeared into the shadows. Then he blinked at Firestar, his eyes expressionless. "Are we going home now?"

Firestar nodded and began to lead his Clanmates away.

Hollypaw dug her claws into the soft, wet earth. Lionpaw had learned his lesson. The warrior code was more important than any friendship. It guided their paws in everything and it stopped more battles than it started. Jaypaw could get away with testing the code's limits—he had his own mysterious relationship with StarClan—but she and Lionpaw were warriors. Without the code, they were nothing.

I'm not a medicine cat anymore. I can't be friends with Willowpaw, not like we used to be. Obeying the warrior code is all that matters; if we do that, the Clans will be safe.

Muscles aching and paws weary, she followed her Clanmates into the forest. She could sleep soundly tonight.

CHAPTER 21

Lionpaw's muscles still hurt from the race through the tunnels and the long swim to the shore, but he couldn't rest in the den any longer. He had slept till midday and Ashfur had refused to take him training until he'd had another good night's sleep. But Lionpaw's heart ached to the point of making him fidget and shuffle his paws in the dried-up moss in his nest. Finally, he gave up trying to get comfortable and pushed his way through the barrier of thorns, into the forest.

"You need to stretch your legs?" Brook's mew surprised him. Lionpaw had been lost in thought as he padded out of the camp entrance. The evening sun was glittering through the trees as it sank toward the horizon.

"I'm bored with resting," Lionpaw told her.

"You look better," she commented. "Last night you looked like you'd been as far as the mountains and back."

Lionpaw looked at his paws. "The kits were hard to find."

"But you found them," Brook reminded him.

"Yes," Lionpaw murmured. He began to pad up the slope, treeward.

"I'll watch for you!" Brook called after him.

"I won't be long," Lionpaw promised.

He headed for the tunnel entrance, weaving slowly through the trees. As he saw the brambles that guarded the tunnel entrance, the pang in his belly grew stronger. He wriggled beneath the prickly branches and climbed the slope, pausing in front of the small burrow where Heatherpaw had once called to him. He imagined her now, her blue eyes shining with excitement.

He would never see her again in that way. As a friend. As a fellow member of DarkClan with their own hidden territory. He couldn't have all that and still be a loyal ThunderClan warrior.

He closed his eyes, imagining he could still smell her scent drifting from the tunnel entrance. He knew that was impossible. A mudslide blocked the way now. It marked the end of the most precious friendship he'd ever known.

"Good-bye, Heatherpaw," he whispered into the tunnel, hoping the wind would carry his words through the darkness, picturing her waiting at the other end. . . .

There will be no borders between us in StarClan. He remembered the moment they'd shared in the tunnels when he'd thought they might die. The intensity of it still throbbed in his paws. How could he turn his back on their friendship?

He had to.

So must she.

A half-moon hung in the sky as Lionpaw headed home through the shadowy forest. The wind brushed the treetops, and the ferns crackled as they slowly began to unfurl bright new leaves.

Fur brushed his flank.

Lionpaw jumped, tail bristling.

"We're proud of you." Tigerstar's mew drifted on the evening air. Lionpaw turned his head and saw the dark warrior's shimmering outline and his amber eyes glowing in the twilight.

A second pelt brushed his other flank. Hawkfrost.

"You made the right decision," the tabby warrior told him. He nudged Lionpaw with his shoulder, and Lionpaw shivered at his ghostly touch.

"I've lost my best friend," he murmured. "I never thought I would feel so empty."

"Friendship is worthless," Tigerstar growled. "You have learned an important lesson, one that I could never have taught you. But I will teach you much more. There'll come a day when you'll be so powerful, you'll have no need of friends. And when that day comes, I promise you will never regret that you chose to be a warrior."

Every hair on Lionpaw's pelt prickled with excitement. At last the moment he longed for had come—the chance to go to the mountains! Four ThunderClan cats wouldn't be enough to deal with the invaders, not if they were as strong as Stormfur and Talon said. Surely StarClan had arranged this, so that he could go to visit the Tribe and find out about them, and show them how real warriors lived.

His claws scratched the earth floor of the hollow as the walls loomed overhead, closing him in. He had never felt so confined before. The weight of stone seemed to press on his fur. He wanted to race up the sheerest cliff and run through the forest, across the hills, all the way to the mountains, with the wind in his fur.

"Calm down," Jaypaw mewed. "They're hardly going to take apprentices along!"

Lionpaw rolled his eyes. "Jaypaw, I wish you wouldn't *do* that."

"You mean *you* want to go to the mountains?" Hollypaw asked.

"They'll need more cats," Lionpaw pointed out, ready to defend himself. "Four's not enough. But Jaypaw's probably right," he added, his excitement fading as he realized that what the Tribe needed was help from experienced warriors. "They won't take apprentices."

"Hollypaw wants to go, and so do I," Jaypaw announced unexpectedly. "Brambleclaw and Squirrelflight are going, so why shouldn't we see if we can go too? Even if they say no, they can't claw us just for asking."

"You really want to go?" Lionpaw meowed to Hollypaw.

She bounced to her paws, her tail fluffed out and her whiskers quivering. "I want to find out how the Tribe cats live. I've never met cats who are different from us. We could learn a lot."

Jaypaw murmured agreement, though he said nothing about his own reasons for wanting to go. But that was Jaypaw, Lionpaw reflected; he always buried his thoughts deeper than hidden prey.

"I want to know what else there is beside the forest, too," he confessed. "I know this is ThunderClan's home, but there are loads of other territories out there. What are they like?"

"Well, then, we should—" Hollypaw began, breaking off as Firestar rose to his paws from where he was sitting by the fresh-kill pile.

"We need to discuss this," he meowed, "but my den is too small for all the cats who are going. Let's go into the forest." Glancing at the other cats who stood listening, he added, "Graystripe, Sandstorm, Leafpool, you come too."

Lionpaw watched as the cats headed toward the thorn tunnel. The rest of the Clan seemed reluctant to go back to their dens or return to their duties. They huddled together, their eyes doubtful.

"There's no way we should risk our own warriors to help the Tribe," Spiderleg complained, loud enough for the departing cats to hear him. "Haven't we got enough problems of our own?"

Firestar's ears flicked as if he had heard what the young warrior said, but he didn't stop to reply before vanishing down the tunnel.

"Things are pretty peaceful right now," Whitewing pointed out.

"Whitewing's right." Ashfur rose from where he was sitting between Cloudtail and Brightheart. "We can easily spare a few warriors. Brambleclaw's doing the right thing by helping the Tribe. Remember what they did for us when we made the Great Journey. We would have died in the snow if they hadn't found us."

"Well, I think that's all nonsense!" Mousefur stalked up to Ashfur, her skinny brown tail lashing. "If the Tribe can't defend their own borders, that's their problem, not ours."

Longtail padded up beside her, and touched her shoulder briefly with his tail-tip. "I'd love to go back to the mountains." His voice was wistful. "I know I couldn't see where the Tribe lived, but I could feel the wide open spaces and the wind in my fur, and all the scents the wind carried from far away."

"I'd like to go back, too!" Birchfall's eyes glowed with memories. "The Great Journey was fun! I had three good friends in ShadowClan: Toadkit, Applekit, and Marshkit. I wonder how they are now."

"Who cares?" Berrynose flicked his tail; Lionpaw thought he could see jealousy in the cream warrior's eyes. "Shadow-Clan cats can't be your friends anymore. Have you forgotten how you nearly got your fur clawed off on the border?"

And whose fault was that? Lionpaw asked silently, while Birchfall looked downcast, his tail drooping.

"Anyway," Berrynose went on, "I don't see what's so great about the mountains. It sounds bare and cold up there, with no prey."

"You know nothing about it," Dustpelt rasped, narrowing his eyes. "You weren't there."

As Berrynose rudely turned his back on the senior warrior, Lionpaw beckoned with his tail for his littermates to follow him out of earshot of the group.

"That does it!" he exclaimed. "If Birchfall could travel through the mountains and survive when he was just a kit, why shouldn't apprentices go? You'd be okay too," he added to Jaypaw. "Longtail coped, after all."

He saw Jaypaw's neck fur begin to fluff up, but Lionpaw was too excited to fret about offending his brother. If he wanted to be prickly when some cat mentioned his blindness, that was his problem.

"We've got to go and find Firestar and ask him right now," he meowed. "Before Brambleclaw and the others leave." He glanced around to see if any cat was paying attention to them. By now the group of cats was beginning to break up. Cloudtail called Brightheart and Dustpelt to go out on a hunting patrol, while the elders returned to their den. Two or three of the other warriors padded over to the fresh-kill pile and picked out prey. Outside the nursery, Daisy and Millie stretched out in the sunshine and began sharing tongues, with Daisy's kits skipping around them.

"Quick, while our mentors aren't looking!" Hollypaw urged, angling her ears to where Ashfur and Brackenfur were talking together in the middle of the clearing.

Lionpaw dived after her as she bounded across the clearing and thrust her way through the thorn tunnel. When all three apprentices were out in the forest, she turned to Jaypaw.

"Come on, you're best at scenting. Which way did Firestar go?"

The scent trail left by the Clan leader and the other cats had begun to fade, but Lionpaw could still distinguish it among the competing scents of the forest, especially the unfamiliar scent of the Tribe cats.

"You know," he mewed to Hollypaw, as they followed Jaypaw through the trees, "I've just realized how Brook smells like a ThunderClan cat now. Do you think she'll be able to settle in when she goes back to her Tribemates?"

Hollypaw flashed him a brief glance. "That's for Stoneteller to say. He seems to speak for the Tribe."

"Stoneteller speaks too much by the sound of it," Jaypaw mewed. "I'm glad Firestar isn't like that."

He led through the forest until Lionpaw could hear the soft splash of waves on the lakeshore. The scent of cats was very strong here; Jaypaw crept quietly up to the top of a gentle rise and parted a clump of bracken carefully with one paw. Without speaking, he signaled with his tail for his brother and sister to join him.

Beyond the bracken, the ground fell away into a sunlit clearing with a soft covering of moss and leafmold. On the opposite side the lake was just visible between the trees. A breeze rustled through the leaves, blowing toward the three apprentices, so the group of warriors would be unlikely to pick up their scents

Firestar was sitting in the middle of the clearing with his paws tucked under him. "Squirrelflight, you'll need to find a temporary mentor for Foxpaw," he was saying.

Squirrelflight dipped her head in agreement. "I'd like to ask Sorreltail, if that's okay with you. She's never had an apprentice, so it would be good experience for her as well."

"Sorreltail would be *great*," Leafpool added warmly.

"Fine, I'll have a word with her when we get back to camp." Firestar turned to Brambleclaw. "I'm not sure that four extra cats are going to be enough to help the Tribe. But I daren't weaken ThunderClan by sending more warriors with you."

Hollypaw nudged Lionpaw. "Maybe that's a chance for us," she whispered.

"I already thought of that," Brambleclaw replied to Firestar. "I'd like to take cats from all four Clans with us. The ones who went with us on the first journey, to find Midnight by the sun-drown-water."

Lionpaw pushed Jaypaw and beckoned Hollypaw with a flick of his ears to creep along the top of the rise as far as a holly bush, where they could hide and still see and hear everything that was going on. Firestar began to speak again as they settled among the debris under the branches, their pelts brushing.

"That makes sense," Firestar meowed in reply to Brambleclaw. "The cats who've known the Tribe longest should be the ones most willing to go."

"It would be good to see Crowfeather and Tawnypelt again," Talon murmured.

"This isn't part of the warrior code," Firestar went on. "I can't ask any cat to go unless they already want to—and of course I can't speak for cats in other Clans. But I believe that helping the Tribe is the right thing to do."

Lionpaw was puzzled. "If it's the right thing, why isn't it in the warrior code?"

"It *is* in the code," Hollypaw insisted. "The warrior code says that we're allowed to help other Clans in trouble. Firestar's obviously thinking of the Tribe as another Clan."

"That's decided, then," Firestar meowed. "Squirrelflight, you'll go to WindClan to ask Crowfeather, and Brambleclaw can go to ShadowClan to ask Tawnypelt."

"There's no need to go to RiverClan." Lionpaw's pelt prickled with sympathy at the sorrow in Stormfur's eyes. "Feathertail was the chosen cat, and she died in the mountains. I went with her, so I shall stand for RiverClan now."

The cats in the clearing were silent for a moment. Squirrelflight rested her tail comfortingly on Stormfur's shoulder.

"The Tribe will always honor Feathertail's memory," Night mewed softly.

Jaypaw fidgeted, but he didn't explain what was bothering him. *Maybe there's a sharp bit of twig sticking into him*, Lionpaw thought.

"This is a good plan." Talon broke the silence at last. "Stoneteller knows the five of you better than any other Clan cats, so he's more likely to trust you."

"What?" Brook's ears flattened and she turned her head to stare at her brother. "Stoneteller did send you to fetch us, didn't he?"

Night and Talon looked at their paws; Talon's tail twitched uncomfortably. "Not exactly," he mumbled, then added, "but I'm sure he'll be glad when he knows you've come to help."

"Great." Stormfur's voice was bitter. "I get to be told I'm dead all over again."

Brook pressed her muzzle to her mate's. "Please, Stormfur, we have to do this. Stoneteller won't be the Healer forever, but the Tribe deserves to last beyond his lifespan."

"From what Talon and Night say, we don't have much

time," Firestar meowed. "Brambleclaw, you can leave for ShadowClan right away."

"And you three can come out now." Squirrelflight rose to her paws and stared straight at the holly bush.

"Fox dung," Hollypaw muttered. "We'll end up searching the elders for ticks instead of going to the mountains."

"Come on," Squirrelflight repeated. "If you don't want to be seen, Lionpaw, don't leave your tail sticking out."

His fur hot with embarrassment, Lionpaw emerged from the bush and padded down the slope toward his mother. "Mouse-brain!" Hollypaw hissed as she followed him with Jaypaw.

"You shouldn't have been spying," Squirrelflight mewed severely when the three apprentices were standing in front of her. "Cats who listen uninvited might hear things they don't want to."

"But we had to listen!" Lionpaw burst out. "We want to go with you!"

Squirrelflight's green eyes stretched wide in astonishment, while Brambleclaw's neck fur was fluffing up ominously. But to Lionpaw's relief Firestar blinked in amusement.

"Don't be angry with them," he told Squirrelflight. "They remind me of a certain ginger apprentice who insisted on going on a journey when she hadn't been invited."

Squirrelflight huffed, fluttering her whiskers, and gave a single lash of her tail.

"Why do you want to go?" Firestar prompted.

Lionpaw was opening his jaws to reply when Hollypaw

gave him a nudge. "We want to help the Tribe cats, too," she announced. "Lionpaw and I are good fighters, and Jaypaw . . . well, Jaypaw can help heal cats who are injured."

"Thanks a bunch," Jaypaw muttered.

"Jaypaw can do more than that," Leafpool meowed calmly. Jaypaw jumped as if he was surprised to find the medicine cat on his side.

"For what it's worth," Leafpool went on, "I think they should be allowed to go. When we lived in the forest, all the apprentices made the journey to Mothermouth, to visit the Moonstone, before they became warriors. We seem to have left that tradition behind, but I think there's value in apprentices making a long journey, to see what lies beyond their territories."

Warmth spread through Lionpaw from whiskers to tail-tip to hear Leafpool putting words to the longing in his own mind. "*Please* can we go?" he begged.

"I agree with Leafpool," Sandstorm mewed. "There's nothing to be lost in meeting other cats and seeing how they live." Her gaze held Firestar's for a moment as if she and the Clan leader were sharing memories.

"Brambleclaw, what do you think?" Firestar asked. "They'll be an extra responsibility, and it could be very tough for them. A long, hard journey, and fighting at the end of it."

"I'm sure my kits can manage it." There was a glow of approval in Brambleclaw's amber eyes as his gaze swept over the three apprentices. "I'd be proud to take them to meet the Tribe of Rushing Water."

"Even if we're not sure of our reception?" Stormfur reminded him softly.

No cat answered him. Instead, Brambleclaw rose to his paws. "Are you ready?" he asked Lionpaw.

"For what?" Lionpaw meowed, his paws tingling with a mixture of excitement and nervousness.

"We must go to ShadowClan and see if Tawnypelt will come with us," his father replied.

"Great!" Lionpaw couldn't stop himself from bouncing eagerly, then froze, disgusted that he was behaving like a stupid kit and not the warrior he longed to be. "I'm looking forward to seeing Tawnypelt's kits. They're my kin," he added, trying to sound more dignified.

"Hollypaw, you can come with me to WindClan, and find out if Crowfeather will come with us," Squirrelflight meowed.

"What about me?" Jaypaw asked.

"Come back to the clearing with me," Leafpool told him. "We'll need to prepare traveling herbs."

"If the other cats agree to go with them," Firestar mewed, "bring them back to the hollow. You can leave in the morning."

"Fine. Let's go, Hollypaw." Squirrelflight waved her tail and set off through the trees toward the WindClan border. Hollypaw darted after her, almost stumbling over her paws in her haste.

"All set, Lionpaw?" Brambleclaw asked.

Lionpaw nodded; his chest felt tight at the thought of

crossing the border into another Clan's territory.

"Good luck, all of you!" Firestar called.

Lionpaw waited until Hollypaw's black pelt had vanished among the rustling bracken, then turned and plunged into the undergrowth, following his father.